The Tragedy of Woman

RAY DACOLIAS

Contents

A Child Is Born

She was born needing someone who would one day rescue her from those inherited traits that make us all fail. He had to be a savior who would deliver her from those terrible things that will not let us live fully, happily, and contentedly.

One day the savior would come.

Everyone pronounced her name O-scene, even though the proper spelling of her name was O-s-c-i-n-e, but it was the modern age of inventive spelling and word pronouncement, and no one seemed to mind. She was fortunate enough to have parents to raise her, but unfortunate to have parents who did not understand the character and psychology of chronic illness nor its gnawing effect on their growing child; consequently, her medical condition became something for her parents to live with and manage, much as a man with a bullet wound to his side might choose only to put his finger into the gaping hole as he stumbles through the bitter darkness past towering white hospitals.

When Oscine was two years old, her tiny, wasted body was so perforated with the yellow scourge of disease that her parents wondered if an institution for the physically disabled might be a better place for her.

"For goodness' sake, Henry," Alison Exene exclaimed one day, after cleaning up another gigantic mess of stinking waste her romping daughter had deposited onto the fading wooden floors. "That child," she whined, "fills up her shoes with this misery every day, and then she tears out her hair and rubs it in the foul dung," and she began to weep as she said it, as if the speaking of this unpleasant business was worse than the thinking of it.

"Dr. Morrissey says the child must grow out of it," Henry retorted, accidentally listening to his wife as he moved from one safe place, the garage, to another safe place, the backyard. His wife, following the normal routine of things, would thus begin to whittle away at the provisional army that guarded her husband's sanity until he emotionally cracked under the weight of her verbal barrage, at which time he would undo his black leather belt and unleash the fury of his suffering male psyche onto his bowlegged, helpless daughter, slaughtering her legs until there were a thick lather of red welts and thick streams of freely flowing blood upon them. This course of action, though not explicit in his wife's demands, was nevertheless implicit, and although Alison feigned resignation at the brutal beatings, secretly she dined on them, as does the vulture on his butchered cuisine.

"Peace at last," Alison often whispered after such an incident as she gazed at her daughter's prostrate form; and then, after observing the bloodstained floor, she would sometimes say, "Oh, look at what you did, you naughty girl," and then slap the girl's wounds with a wet rag. "You made another mess; if it isn't a mess you deliberately made, it's one you made after your father punished you—oh, you're such a terrible brat!" And sometimes, at the thought of what her daughter had forced her to do, she would commence beating the frightened child;

and Oscine would simply lie there, looking up at her mother, her small stomach and chest rising and falling, and her green eyes, like pure, uncut emeralds, full of fear as she stared like a wounded fawn at her tormentor.

Oscine would take the beatings without an utterance, for the pain was now secondary to her mortal failings.

By the age of five, Oscine, her poor body abused from without and from within, had rendered certain things unto her inner self—in particular, solace and harmony—so that she might survive this turmoil from which she could not escape. In effect, she had become her own agent of salvation, as those things normally looked to by children for safety and survival—Mother and Father—were ungentle monsters to her. She found a respite from the horrors inside her room by talking happily to herself and consoling her own emotional wounds, and by sailing her own ship—one built by her own mind in between the moments of the omnipresent chaos of disorder she could not decipher.

A great part of her youth was spent in her home, as opposed to being in the outside world, where she might spill the contents of her bowels in the most conspicuous of places; and so it was better for her parents to isolate her in her room of solitude, where she talked to those imaginary characters who would listen to her desperate desires for attention.

"Well, Mr. Handsome Man," Oscine would say, "are you my friend? Oh, you are so good," and she would hug herself, to fill the horrible black void of no human love. "I love you so much, I love you more than anybody else!" and she would weep, fervently. "One day, I know you will come for me and save me, won't you, Mr. Handsome Man—because I will love you so very much that you will need me." Her beautiful, fragile mind seemed to burst from her ardent ache to love and be loved, a deep, penetrating ache that made her feel too old, too soon.

Her poor heart was feasting on itself.

Her family never touched her, praised her or complimented her; it was as if she were an inanimate object. They just couldn't bring themselves to physically hold her, for it just never seemed right to them to hold something in affection that had caused them so much grief and sorrow; to them, to hold her and cuddle her and smile at her and love her and praise her would be encouraging her bad and outrageous physical actions, which they considered as acts of the highest order of terrorism; yes, they considered her a tiny messenger from a terrorist cell—not to assault them physically, but emotionally: a small, innocent-looking soldier bent on devouring their sanity through incessant acts of aggression; yes, to them she was a foreign, invading army marching against them by day and plotting against them by night, and every morning they woke up, they secretly wished she was dead, dead and buried and long gone out of their lives so they might not be crushed by her medical bills and the restraints she kept on them, which did not allow them to go anywhere as a family lest she soil herself and their wonderful image.

There was an inward flow, like a soft, warm current of bubbling water that fed Oscine's fondest hopes and desires into her hungry mind, but it seemed to lose its potency every day and instead gained a single drop of a hot malignancy that sought to spread its nefarious wings and poison her Good wellspring; she died every night, knowing that something essential was missing from her life, dying every night because she could not understand why her parents seemed never to say a kind word to her, dying because she felt no love from them, slowly dying because she was treated as a nuisance and an outsider, a mere tenant.

But she had to have relationships, she had to have communication, she had to have emotional ties and bonds with living things, and her parents—perhaps out of pity, perhaps out of selfishness; it really depended upon their mood and the weather and the economy of the household—indulged her with diverse animals to keep her company in her room. Oscine, by age seven, had three hamsters with distinct limps; two lizards, each of whom had a leg missing; two Western Pond Turtles with broken shells; twenty tropical fish in her large aquarium that she planned on returning to the sea; a purple finch with a broken wing, which sometimes lived in a golden cage that hung from the ceiling right over her bed, but mostly ran about the room freely. And she was certain to keep the place extraordinarily clean, a strange phenomenon that commenced when she began to finally wipe up after her own waste messes. When her parents sent her into her room, they felt satisfied that she had everything she needed during the winter months, and quite easily forgot about her for days. "She is with her own kind," the mother would say; "let her be their Keeper."

And so, when the spring warmth came and the snow melted and the sleepy foliage and fauna began to wake up, Oscine was allowed to leave her inner sanctum and spend her free moments exploring the delicate ecosystem of her curious backyard.

And it was a grand and expansive backyard, too, much too big for the family to properly tend to, too big for their small family—five acres of green pasture and rich, fertile soil, all surrounded by a tall wooden fence the father had built so his dysfunctional daughter could be lost in utter anonymity. It was here that she began to know herself, and by age ten she had created a garden paradise that was the wonder of the neighborhood.

There was a specific routine she now kept that was never verbally agreed to by her parents, but their lack of disapproval against it was sufficient for her to pursue it, to wit: whatever she did that gained them peace and quiet from her irksome presence they allowed her to do, no matter how perilous or absurd the project or ridiculous the event was. She was a legal entanglement to them until she was eighteen, at which time they would disengage her from their consciousness and turn her clean and clear away from them as she drifted out into the cruel world.

She was confined to her room from the last warm vapors of autumn until the last vestiges of winter that bow before the coming tide of spring, and then she was unleashed, like a wild horse that had been harnessed to a giant boulder, into a magical world without boundaries.

Where before there was only pale and fleshless life and inanimate grey rock and dull brown dirt in the backyard, she brought her wakeful and restorative vision to bear; everywhere there were curvaceous flumes and small tributaries that poured their precious cargo of crystal cool water to small mounds of dazzling roses and golden daisies and white snapdragons and pink foxgloves; and the silvery liquid poured into the symmetrically shaped octagon vegetable garden, with its cucumber and tomato and pumpkin and carrot, and to the fruit garden, with its ruby-red strawberries and sweet cantaloupe and green-and-white-striped watermelon. The entire area was attired in this carefully crafted wonderland of dazzling plant life, up to and around the animal sanctuary that adorned the point furthest from the house.

It was near the wire cages and wooden crates and carefully constructed tunnels and dirt igloos where Oscine spent most of her day; it was here, amongst the varied animal and insect life, that she gave the fullest measure of her childish energies and skills and love to those artless creatures who neither grumbled nor quaked, neither accused nor attacked, but responded only in kind to her loving and gentle nature.

Oscine, being a naive child, did not know much about the world, and being a very young girl, did not know much about herself, but this much she did know, and it was that she loathed the suffering of any living organism; it did not matter the age of the creature or the appearance of the struggling insect or the apparent danger of the slithering animal, for she felt an urging to bring solace to them all.

All who had been scorned or cast out or dragged into the dark pit were welcome in this humble mansion of soil and plants. Even those not blessed with thought have a keen sense about a human being who welcomes them without reservation or fear or conditions; and so they came, these animals, one and all, drifting in from the right, falling in from the left, digging up from underneath, falling down from the sky, burrowing in from the north, limping in from the south, all of them drawn here by a gently reassuring spirit of love to rest and heal.

Why, at any given time during the hot summer months, there were stray dogs and stray cats and escaped birds and soft, furry brown and white rabbits and Red Squirrels and often Deer Mice and sometimes a Common Porcupine and once even two shot but boldly moving Virginia Opossum. For each creature she had built a small wooden or wire cage to protect them from outside predators, and once the creature was healed, she encouraged them to leave, but too often, the creatures decided they enjoyed the tranquility and safety of this blessed fellowship, and so they stayed.

Once, her Mother, not for solicitude but out of perverse curiosity, looked at her daughter in the backyard, and beheld a long, brown, slithering snake crawling toward Oscine. "Henry, come quick," she yelled, not able to take her anxious eyes off the rustling green grass as her husband ran to the kitchen window, "look," she whispered, excitedly, and the two of them stared in a state of hopeful bliss.

"The end of our medical bills," he whispered, electrified by the prospect of the death of the blonde-haired nuisance, but his glowing countenance soon fell when, to his horror, his own flesh-and-blood daughter simply turned round and casually picked up the snake and held it on high and swayed it back and forth the same way a little girl moves a cute kitten this way and that. He cursed, nodding his head.

"That girl is a freak," the Mother grieved. "She must die soon or we will have to start selling our stocks."

"And that won't be happening," the Father theorized; "our nest egg is our future, no one individual is more…"

Without even turning to face him, without even a tremor from her dominant body language, she shut him down as easily as if she had just flipped off a switch, her voice drenched in a hard rancor, "I don't want to hear your babbling on what I already know, I want to hear how we are going to survive the little dollar burner out there." After looking at him, she turned to stare at the child she had given birth to. "Look, look now, would you just look…" and her mouth was paralyzed by awe as she witnessed several black-feathered and orange-breasted, black-hooded Baltimore Oriole birds alighting atop Oscine. "Freak, freak, what a ridiculous freak…"

It happened one day late in the fall, when the heat is no longer master of the land and the cold has begun to announce its royal presence, that a renowned horticulturist, visiting a neighbor, happened to glance over the fence and observe, incredulous, the garden of Oscine. He stared for the longest time and checked his special glasses and then, once satisfied, went out to his car and came back with a big blue book filled with fine pictures and words on the lives and habits of flowers, and he quickly searched through the glossy pages until he found the right one and then planted on his wrinkled but wise face a distinct and disturbing frown; with that done, he uttered, rather without thought of where he was or who he was addressing, "Say, you there, young lady, yes, you, are these your flowers, hmm?"

Oscine, unaccustomed to hearing her identity spoken in kind human terms in her private utopia, jumped up and turned round to behold the bespectacled, balding man smiling at her and shyly holding up his right hand as if to wave away any apprehension that might emanate from her childish mind. "Oh my, forgive me, oh please, I did not mean to startle you, young lady, but as I was admiring your magnificent garden, I was consumed by curiosity, and compelled to address you on the peculiar matter of—yes," and he looked up and then down, as if to retrieve his drifting thoughts, "on the matter of *Calochortus amabilis.*" He hesitated as the girl seemed plagued by ignorance. "Why, of course, you are a child, yes, indeed, and more simplification is necessary; it is of the Liliaceae family—I mean," and he shook his head, as if to shake loose any entanglements holding back his lucid translation into child verse, "a lily, the lily family."

Oscine smiled, pointing to the yellow lily, and when she saw the man smile and nod his head, she invited him to hop the fence and inspect the flower, which he did, forthwith.

Of course, he fell, nearly headfirst into the soft mounds of dirt, but managed to survive and then walked over to the girl, energetically shook her hand, introduced himself, and then turned his impatience to the flower. "Its common name is Yellow Globe Lilly, or the Golden Fairy Lantern," and he turned to his small host. "I prefer the latter name; which do you prefer, missy?"

She put her index finger to her small chin and cocked her head. "I think I like the Golden Fairy Lantern, because it reminds me of fairies." She nodded, smiling, but then became serious when she said, "But I have to keep him away from Mr. Cat," she whispered, nodding to a pure white feline in the distance, and then to a special covering she had constructed, "or he gets a tummy ache."

"Good for you! Precisely right!" he replied, acknowledging the feline, and then continued on, "And isn't that the effect flowers have on our psyche, but wonder and fantasy?" And then he bent down, and adjusting his black horn-rimmed glasses, further inspected the flower, whispering of his astonishment and incredulity. "Just incredible, incredible, indeed! Yes, a rare phenomenon that such a plant as this could flower now, not that it couldn't be planted here, but to flourish here now—extraordinary!" He stood up and walked around the place and crawled about the garden and inspected every flower, muttering praises all the while, and when he did stand, he was all atwitter at the discoveries he had made. "Never have I seen such healthy plants in such a soil at such a time, and for them to be growing as long as they have—I can tell, of course, by their singular roots and stems and stalks—is truly inspiring! What is your secret, young mistress? What fine solutions do you pour onto these eager wildflowers?" And upon hearing the methods by which Oscine planted the flowers and tended to them, and inspecting her composting pile, mulch, and variety of natural, biological controls for pests, and an irrigation system replete with furrows, basins, and emitter lines, he sat down, speechless. "Well, I suppose it is just that you care so very much for them, and that you planted them in such a fashion as to expect nothing from them but to grow, and they expected nothing from you but love, and there we have it, the magic combination. Miraculous! Most flower enthusiasts would never have planted," and he began to point amongst the flowers, "Desert Marigold...*Baileya multiradiata*...and Golden Eardrops...*Dicentra chrysantha*...and Scarlet Bouvardia—*Bouvardia ternifolia*—here, and then expected them to bloom now, but you did not tell these flowers what they could not do, nor did you read some old stuffy textbook," and he leaned over to her, his hands cupped to his brown-mustached mouth, "many written by yours truly," he nodded. He sat amongst the flower beds for the longest time and discussed the techniques Oscine used to bring her plants to a robust life, and then he turned his gaze to the animals. "And, might I say, a curious collection of birds and whatnot, I do say," and he stood up and walked over to the cages and crates and began to inspect them. "Dr. McGillicutty might like to examine this diverse collection of species; yes, I do believe he would, seeing as how so many would seem to be natural antagonists to each other but are merely lounging about the place and curled up near each other like a family of blue jays in a nest. Yes," he abruptly cried, "may I bring him to this wonderland, young missy?" She assented, much to his delight.

Professor McGillicutty came the next day by the same amusing route as the Professor of Ornithology, stumbling over the creaking, wooden fence of the neighbor, and he, too, once in the folds of Oscine's garden paradise, was in utter amazement at the fantastic sights therein. He marveled at animals that should have been on their way to other habitats so late in autumn, and he was perplexed by animals that should have been hostile to other animals they were living with but who were now resting soulfully next to each other.

And then, while the two professors were discussing the singular instances of wildlife resisting their inborn instincts, they noticed that Oscine was looking on high, specifically at a flock of Snow Geese that were flying in their proper V formation in the azure sky. Professor McGillicutty stood, awe-struck. "Why, indeed, they are circling, circling," he restated, as if to reassure himself of this weird vision; "geese simply do not circle at this time of the year, they fly south, as is their custom; now, why would they be circling..."

Oscine pointed. "They are waiting for you to leave, sirs," she said; "they will not land if strangers are here."

"Land, land," the Professor of Ornithology exclaimed, "how do you know such a thing?"

"Because," Oscine pointed again to the end of the aero-dynamically correct pattern, "they have landed before, I mean the ones who need me, see?"

The two professors stood in awe as they stared at one strug-gling goose, which had fallen slightly behind the others, and the Professor of Ornithology said, "And you say that fellow wants to land here to recuperate?" And when he restated his question so she could understand it, he received an affirmative response. "So, if we go back over the fence, they will land?" And once more receiving a nod from Oscine, he and the other professor quickly ascended the fence, like clumsy acrobats, and crashed over onto the other bushy side.

And then the miracle occurred.

Oscine was sitting in the bosom of innocence and peace when one of the white-feathered geese finally dove straight down and nearly landed with a thud onto a high mound of dirt; another bird came swooping down and landed next to it and tended to his fallen comrade. Oscine approached them and began to stroke the creatures just as surely as if they were her own pets. The two professors stood bent over, peering through the knotholes in the picket fence, flabbergasted. "We must fly to the University and document this phenomenon," the Professor of Ornithology whispered, and the two men hurried back to their beloved playground, and having attained the blessings of their Grade Chair and the Dean, they came back in a week with the proper equipment in the proper black bags, but this time they pursued the proper route and knocked on the door of the seemingly proper Exene family home.

Once introductions were made and the professors were seated inside the lovely home and the Mother and Father were pricked wide awake by the kind of curiosity that greed created, the two professors confessed with complete contrition to their stealthy actions in the backyard of their hosts, and then they came straight to the point and with great force argued that the little custodian in the backyard possessed remarkable talents hitherto unknown in the precise annals of science, and that they desired to document her abilities forthwith. The Exenes could smell the musty scent of money just as if freshly minted greenbacks were wrapped around their snooty noses; after some lengthy discussions, the Exenes secured a good sum of money to allow the University full access to their home. They signed the papers of consent and smiled.

Thus began the association between the local University and Oscine, wherein scholars and students and newspapermen and newspaperwomen came to observe the little girl with the extraordinary skills; but in a year the economy began to teeter and the years where the universities were flush with cash began to wane, and soon, the grant that had generated income for the Exenes dried up, and so the Mother and Father forbade anyone to visit their mystical backyard without monetary rewards for them.

By age twelve, though her body was ravaged by disease, Oscine's person had maintained a certain lithe beauty that seemed to come from her solicitous and genuine tending of the Earth and its children, an airy, classic array of features that, so arranged, would later attract many male suitors; primarily, it was her creamy white skin and slender figure, her finely aligned thin, pink lips, her straight-edged nose, the fierce twinkle of jade green in her luminous eyes, her fair, golden-blonde hair, and the sweet, gentle face that projected joy, love, innocence and vulnerability that drew men toward her.

The birth of her two younger brothers removed the burden of her being a disappointment to her parents, but now with two more possible successors to the Exene high standards, she was pushed even further back into the black hole of emotional oblivion.

As her parents diminished Oscine's role as a human being, she magnified those qualities in herself that she needed most to survive in her special world, but this did not mean she focused on herself, but on others. She began to visit the local homeless shelters and retirement homes to bring solace to the sick and dying and emotionally distressed; she raised money for impoverished children in faraway lands through funding drives in her neighborhood and at school; and she started a petition drive to have traffic lights put in at a dangerous street corner, a campaign that she easily won.

Her sixth grade teacher did not look upset or aghast when her student often came in very tardy, for Oscine was a girl who, being utterly trustworthy and loyal, operated on her own unique plateau. And as she had consistently high grades and an undying devotion to lost causes around the school and community and was a good Samaritan to anyone who needed a kind word, she was left alone by staff and administration.

One day, after Oscine had once again returned from a trip to the bathroom, she noticed that one of the boys in the classroom,

Lester—whose mother had successfully committed a criminal act without prosecution, by gorging herself on massive doses of cocaine and alcohol while Lester was in her womb—had once more collapsed into a fit of black rage and absolute obstinacy. Oscine took him by the hand, led him outside and, talking to him in a soothing, calming manner, subdued his angry spirit.

A Nightingale, with brown feathers and a whitish, tan breast, sat singing in an elm tree amongst the orange and yellow leaves.

Oscine, feeling a subtle fluxion in the air—as if the sound waves from the bird were like soothing heat waves pouring over her face—reached up her hand and then waved to the creature, beckoning it to her; and lo, the bird obediently fluttered down toward Oscine's right shoulder, resting on her spring dress, and singing a beautiful melody.

Her classmates, watching intently, rushed outside into the fresh morning air and gathered around her in awe.

"All things made joyous by those pure and kind things," Oscine sang. And she lifted up her arms toward the clear, cerulean October sky, where a brilliant rainbow cloud hovered high above them. She bent her head and looked at her classmates and teacher, and then said, smiling, "The world wants to be in harmony; you just have to Love."

Her stature as a bringer of miracles began that day, and her hallowed image of a saint began to grow prodigiously.

Her reputation around her neighborhood had grown to one who was also a caretaker of lost and abandoned animals; neighbors brought her their sick cats and injured dogs and other people brought her homeless cats and homeless dogs, and Oscine never rejected these animals or the good intentions of her neighbors and always cared for them just as if they were her very own brothers and sisters.

Soon, though, as the backyard carnival was no longer securing monetary benefits for the family, Mother and Father hatched a plan one summer night as they stood at the window observing their daughter ministering to her collection of misfits in the silvery moonshine. "Soon," the Mother cooed, gleefully, "they will all be martyrs in the fiery red glare," and she let her hand fall onto her husband's hand not in love but to seal the nefarious deal.

By the morning, the deed was done.

Oscine had heard the wailing and crying of her blessed children in her dreams but she could not penetrate the nebulous haze around her eyes to see where they were or why they were in trouble, so she had only shouted to them to be strong and her love would protect them; she had not felt right about this response, but still, she could not move, and her eyes were veiled, so she did what she could do.

She was finally awakened by the wailing of the fire engines and the screaming of the neighbors and the hollering of the firemen, and when she had arisen and run to the back door she beheld the blazing inferno that was her garden paradise; and her Mother and Father did not hold her back nor even attempt to as she ran by them and sought to penetrate the thick row of firemen who were overseeing the quenching of the conflagration.

The struggling and weeping girl was placed back next to her parents and was chastised by them for her emotional outbursts and was told to abate her foolish display of tears for stupid animals and inanimate objects. But Oscine was not quite able to think clearly and decisively on the issue of the fire until her Mother said, rather easily, "You just can't beat the smell of roasted animal flesh," and then inhaling the pungent aroma, said with abandon, "and with a sprig of peppermint and orange blossom." It was then that the steel curtain of authority surrounding her parents began to break in large sections and evince tiny holes that allowed their daughter to peer through.

Oscine looked up to her Mother just as if she were looking at a stranger.

When it was all said and done, the chief of the firemen came up to the parents and offered his condolences and said that as bad as it had been, it might have been worse if the Exenes had not recently applied the natural flame retardant lubricant all over the house and dug natural firebreaks in the backyard. Oscine looked at the chief and then looked to the smug looks on the faces of her Mother and Father, and then looked to the smoking field of dead animals and plants, and then back to her parents, and noticed something odd, that somehow, between the look at her parents and the look to the charred remains of her field of love, the countenance of her Mother and Father had changed. She studied their earnest faces and examined their lack of concern and tidy shreds of arrogance and glittering patches of power and tiny buds of glee, and she nodded her head and then decided that she was no longer a part of them; she took several steps back from them and nodded again to be sure, in the same way a woman nods her head to be sure that she is dissolving her love bond from a man she has decided is no longer worthy of her.

Later that night, after the policemen were gone and the firemen had evacuated the backyard and her parents and brothers were in bed, Oscine crept out into the still-smoldering fields and lay down in her white nightgown in the warm black ash and sobbed over the deaths of her beloved friends and children; she was not mature enough to erect an indestructible vow in her mind, but she was old enough to pledge to herself that she must find a savior who would one day come and take her away from all of this dread and sorrow.

By her junior year in high school, Oscine had secured the profile of a girl without sin, a perfect creature who solicited nothing in return for her good deeds.

She listened to everyone's woes, helped those students in pain, never complained about her own troubles, and spent most of her day dedicated to those causes that benefited individuals who were in need of solace and succor; and although disease continued to plague her delicate body, her svelte form and lustrous beauty still won the hearts of many young and handsome boys.

When she entered her house, a place the neighbors thought a model family resided, her status remained as a nonentity, for the turmoil and horrific bouts of her disease as a child had spilled forever into her parents' bitter memory of her. Here, she was like an employee, neither loved nor scorned, but an integral part of the mechanism that contributed to the overall functioning of a typical home.

Her father no longer loved his wife, and subsequently, his wife, anxious for other mischief, had taken to managing her daughter's career as revered person in the community.

"Where were you, Oscine?" asked her Mother one night, as the family ate their quiet supper at the glass dinner table.

"At the Veterans' Home," Oscine responded, obediently.

"Don't play games, young lady, you know I meant after that..."

"Danny." To lie meant that the vicious clamps of control would tighten even more for Oscine, for her Mother somehow always found out the truth about her daughter's whereabouts.

Her Mother asked Oscine for the butter, and watching her daughter lean over to grab it, she reached out and viciously slapped her face. "Thank you," her Mother said, taking the porcelain tray with the hard cube of white death. She felt an intensely electrifying sense of power in her ability to physically punish and humiliate a girl who was seen by the general populace as a beloved saint.

Oscine's fair complexion upon her slender face spun a vulgar crimson. The rest of the family continued to devour their food as if nothing extraordinary had occurred; and indeed, the boys, knowing nothing else, and the father, himself physically abused as a child, too thought this was the way of the world.

Her Father proceeded to take off his black leather belt and lay it on the table, and once the meal was done, he said, his face flaccid, his tone restful, "You lie to Mother, you lie to me."

Oscine obediently stood up and turned round to take the searing cracks of the belt upon her bottom, a place her Father had chosen so no bruise marks would show.

"Leaving," the eldest boy, age fourteen, said.

"Me, too," the other youth, age fifteen, said.

The slam of the belt onto Oscine's dress caused the air to fairly crackle and pop. "Be back before light," the father said, smiling, looking proudly at his boys.

"It's Friday," the boys said, laughing, and departed.

The room lit up with the boom of leather pressing hard through a thin dress and mangling the bare, tender skin. To see Oscine's face was to see someone who might merely have been lost in pensive thoughts.

That night Mother performed her regularly scheduled bed check on her daughter, only to find, to her great displeasure, an empty room, and upon further inspection of the house, no sign of Oscine.

The Father, accompanied by the righteous wrath of outrage, cried, "That girl should be wearing armor when she gets back," and he opened the door of the house to see his daughter standing in a field adjacent to their home. "Get back in here," he shouted in a hoarse whisper.

"Touch me again and I will become a prostitute in town," Oscine cried, fearlessly. It was a virgin's bluff, but she was sincere in her anger, and it sold well.

Her Father, vexed and yet secretly glad to cease the nasty operation of whipping his daughter, stared with those familiar black eyes that are worn by ignorant, hateful, vengeful men who know their mission to punish the innocent at will has been forever circumvented.

Oscine laid waste onto the ground, and her parents, anxiously looking round at the neighbors' houses, motioned her in with conciliatory gestures and words. Yes, the physical beatings were over but the emotional beatings stayed.

Outside her home, Oscine had built an image of perfection, and inside her home, an image of a stowaway, ensconced in her room, talking to herself, dreaming of a man who would one day rescue her; few friends came her way, as she was so busy pleasing everyone but herself.

She was fast becoming an American Woman.

Oscine Grows Up

At the point of moving out of her house and into the free world of sin and misery, and love and joy, Oscine was released from the natural ties that bound her to her parents and brothers, removed now from the massive bulwark that had hung over her head, which daily crushed her will and desire to live.

She had a vision one hot night while she slumbered in her college dorm.

She had lain in a field of dense weeds since birth and had managed to sometimes rise up to see in the distance the tips of the spinning faces of yellow daisies and amber-colored wheat stalks moving in the gentle breezes, but never had she risen too high, for taut bronze chains held her fast to the rocky surface below her; it was only when she had managed to will herself to want to leave her birth home and venture out amongst a world not literally narrated by her parents for her sole benefit and designed for her narrow pathways to travel that she could see clearly now; and at that precise moment she smelled the sultry cargo of fire sweeping toward her, and she yanked at the chains but could not move; and then at once willing herself to flee and forget all that had kept her enslaved, she felt the metal links split and she stood up as the waves of yellow and red flames swept over the crackling grass and flowers; and then she rose up into the embracing sky and looked down and saw the screaming fire sweep over the spot where she had been enchained; and then she beheld the Earth as if it were bleeding, its ruby-red-colored blood seeping up from where she had lain and the Earth groaning where she had lived; and behold, as she rose higher and higher in the clear cerulean sky, she saw the burnt remains of the brightly colored faces of the flowers fall as small beads to the planet and form images and letters just as if it she were watching a whirling kaleidoscope; and soon, as she proceeded higher and higher above the carnage and assumed a safe place to discern what arcane vision formed beneath her, she saw a fearful engraving upon the scorched, black land, and it quivered and quaked with its villainy, and blew its violent storms of fire at her, but nay, she was too high to be reached; and she clasped her bosom as her eyes swept over the malevolent anthem that mocked itself against her and the murderous letters that sought to bring her back down; and the more she beheld the fantastic vision, the more she felt herself begin to fall into a gaping black mouth that exhaled a stench-filled venom that dazed her and inhaled a mighty wind to suck her back down and devour her; all beneath her the Earth was spinning and spewing dust and debris and belching smoke and fire and singing her death song and shooting up red sparks to engulf her and bring her back down, down, down into the filthy hole from whence she was born; and the land cracked and split open and the molten flesh of the Earth spat up at her as she fell faster and faster into the dark, fiery-red pit; she was blinded now by this piercing soul of wickedness whose very hot embers now scorched her flaxen hair, and she felt as if one dead; and then she closed her eyes and raised her head to the Celestial Heavens and her mind caressed the love and joy and happiness in her heart and she shut out the noisy discord below and listened to the ethereal music above and let it enwrap around her and lo, she felt as if gossamer wings were attaching themselves to her, and she could feel them fluttering in the violent streams about her; and so she willed to beating these feathery appendages and she felt herself lifting up and up and higher and higher and higher until she ascended to the isle of white clouds and lay on their soft beds; and as she wept pious tears of freedom and joy and love, they seeded the clouds, and birthed within them a fearful expansion of righteous judgment, and then these black clouds wept their pain onto the conflagration below and quenched it and seared it as if it were a deadly wound, and the small planet sealed itself up and the boiling lava melted into the Earth and the fire consumed itself and the winds laid down their sword; but lo, she was not yet done; and then she plunged the sharp talon of one of her wings into her heart and forthwith out came a single blood drop and it proceeded to fall; and Oscine watched as the tiny missile plummeted into the atmosphere and then touched the ground and she raised her head as a burst of screams wailed from below and cleft the air, and behold, the small planet began to heave and contract and rise and fall just as if it were gasping for dear life, and soon the entire planet began to tremble and break apart, and then its blood and guts came bubbling and boiling up, and she marveled at it; and as she rested her head on her cloud bed, she observed the small planet abruptly abate its ill humor and rest in an eerie silence, and then it just blew up and out and far apart into the great expanse of space. Oscine lifted up her silken wings and dropped down through the cumulus clouds and glided down the columns of warm air and hovered at the precise spot where she had lain for so long, and then extended her wings and began to turn her body in a swirling circle, faster and faster and faster, sweeping in all of the scattered debris and dust and gas, and all the while her mind and heart and soul were assigning tasks to every atom and molecule, that they might assemble themselves in the proper sequences; and when she was done, yea, there was a naked planet beneath her feet, formed in her own image, and she stood upon it and looked about at the resplendent streams and verdant grasses and golden and purple and white flowers, and she was pleased.

It was only much later that she realized it was she who had caused the flames to come and free her from her prison in her vision, and that her ardent desire for better things would be gained only through her own actions.

At college, Oscine continued to nurture her gentle, kind, warm and loving status, while discovering at the same time that keeping a clean and stylish house amazed and delighted girls as well as boys. She was the sorority mother, and did not sleep much, cleaning her room to immaculate perfection, studying for hours a day, dating many young men at once, and yet still managing to aid those people in emotional and physical pain.

She had an uncommon hunger for men, sifting through them like an impatient miner who searches through tons of dirt for that one special nugget of gold.

Men said she was beautiful, yet her parents had never spoken of her beauty. She felt a powerful urge to please these creatures that made her glow internally, these enthralling, dangerous-looking hunks of muscle and cologne, men who treated her as if she were truly the image she had so carefully crafted.

And she was free to go anywhere, anytime, with anyone, even though her Mother called nearly every day to find out just where Oscine had gone, and with whom and why. Oscine found herself lying to her Mother, and though she felt it a necessity, still she felt guilty.

There is a narrow window of opportunity for women concerning their future career as a wife, a small number of years when they intuitively know that despite what they do nutritionally or physically to themselves, they will still retain a special beauty that attracts the proper male. For most women, by age thirty, the game is waning thin, and the wearing of age begins to evince itself through the drooping of arms and sagging of breasts and spreading of bottom and wrinkled, flaccid skin, and through many areas on their body where thickness and flabbiness and dullness of color are entirely undesirable.

In their twenties, thusly, too many American women, with this organic license deeply imbedded in their feminine psyche, go purely mad, adopting one man after another as lover and friend as they search for that one mate who will bring them happiness, security, love, and babies.

"I just want to be loved," Madelyn, her roommate, said one day. "But I don't think men know how to love or want to; it's so entirely frustrating. It's like their fathers never talked to them about it, perhaps because their fathers never knew either. It's all so hopeless. Why wasn't I told I was born into a world gone mad?"

"I don't want to believe that men have no internal emotional intelligence about women, it's too depressing," Oscine said, lying supine atop the pink covers of her bed. "For goodness' sake," she continued, bent on being candid so as to explore everything, "my parents only live together, they have no marriage."

"Typical," Madelyn, exclaimed. "I don't think Love truly exists."

"What?" Oscine laughed, sitting up.

"No, I really don't; look, I think it's all infatuation and meeting someone else's needs—where is Love in the end? It's a business partnership in the end, I say."

"You say," Oscine said, smiling, running to the bathroom to erupt, and then later returning with a subdued smile.

"How do you manage it?" Madelyn asked, with great sympathy upon her face. "I mean, your illness—it's so unpredictable."

"Oh, it's not so bad, and I have learned to get around it; you can get around anything, you know."

Madelyn laughed, but her visage quickly sobered. "But you get sick so often."

"Oh, I'm all right," she said, and staved off the topic with the wave of her hand. "But about men, you really don't think they're all one-dimensional, egotistical, misogynistic slobs?"

"Yes, unfortunately I do," Madelyn said, nearly weeping, "I'm twenty-two and giving up. I guess I'll just find some man who looks pretty, with lots of money; I'll sell out because the good ones are only in novels—novels written by romantic, foolish men and blind women." She sat down next to Oscine, sobbing gently now. "O, Oscine, maybe it is me, maybe those men I pursue are the wrong ones, the good-looking, shallow types who are self-absorbed—but haven't I tried? Do I have to marry a loser?"

"A loser to whom?" Oscine said, holding her friend's hand.

"That's it, isn't it? The good ones are boring to look at but their hearts are right; but I want the looks and the heart, and with my horrible temper, well—no man will rein me in!"

Oscine walked to the window and turned round. "It's a beautiful day! Let's go out and have fun." Her smile was so pure and honest in its desire for others to be happy that it melted the bitterness in Madelyn's heart.

"Oh, it's dark and gloomy, raining too," she responded, still wanting to be a martyr.

"No," Oscine said, and closing her eyes, she stood very still, and then let the white shades roll up to reveal a bright golden stream of light piercing the heavy darkness.

"Oscine," Madelyn said, bouncing up and embracing her friend, "you're wonderful."

Madelyn, a year later, did marry a man who seemed to be both handsome in physical stature and of heart; it was a December wedding, and Oscine spent the moments before the wedding and after the reception vomiting into any receptacle that would accommodate her rejected meals. Still, she looked deliciously sweet and innocent to the young men who hovered about her like nervous adolescent boys.

At the reception, Madelyn's grandmother choked on a chicken bone, and Oscine performed the proper abdominal thrusts to the elderly woman to dislodge the object, thus saving the old woman's life (so, in the very near future, the old woman could die a miserable, drawn-out, gnawing death after a stroke in which her already worn-out and diseased body wasted away in bits and pieces, but such is life—to be saved from one doom for another).

"My mother says that marriage ruins a good woman and hardens a good man," one of the male ushers said to a male friend, staring at Oscine's stunning beauty, "and that it's best not to marry if you're not seeking a wife; but if you must have a wife, make it an occasional wife because that way it will take longer until hate, like slowly drying oatmeal, sets in."

One man who stood next to him did not hear these words of woe and sorrow, but saw only the wispy, svelte beauty and porcelain-colored skin and the straw-colored hair of the exquisite Oscine.

"Boy," said an elderly usher who had been chewing on the rotting corpse of wisdom for fifty years, "you're looking at a star too far removed from what you perceive as being Heaven."

"No woman is above any man," returned the youth, who felt the conflagration of lust for flesh and treasure in his small heart; and being a handsome man with a pinch of intelligence and a preponderance of charm for those he did not know, he was certain, as are all in his station in life, to gain access to his prey. This was the pivotal moment for him, as it is for all handsome men such as he, which is to say, it is the way in, prepared by a chance genetic makeup.

And for those males born with an incidental composition that renders them freaks to females, in other words, those males who are too kind and sensitive and plain looking, why, they are kept out of the small circle of the mating ritual.

A woman, any living woman, breathing and cognizant, will allow a handsome man, in a safe setting, to approach her, for this very act validates her inner sense of self-esteem in the complex area of self-reflection concerning her own physical appearance. A woman needs to be told she is beautiful, no matter how ugly or pretty she feels, and often.

"Hello," the man, whose name was Heath, breathed in his virile, deep voice, "would you be so kind as to dance with me, lovely lady?"

Oscine, being a woman, and now having been told she was indeed lovely by a comely, masculine man, could not possibly refuse.

Madelyn, watching from the comfort of her Man's big shoulders, thought, "Pair any handsome man and woman, by chance, or better yet, let them choose each other, and the outcome will be the same—unhappiness. So, why not her, now? Is he not just as good as any other? Aren't all men savages? And don't all women become nagging boors a day past bliss? In the end it all caves in on you." Madelyn had a sense about marriage the way veteran soldiers have a sense about an impending ambush.

Tell a woman that a man in whom she is interested is merely flattering her for the sole reason of mating with her, and still she will let him persist in his biologically driven charade. It is his verbal massaging that ignites a small flame at her core being which, despite his palpable chicanery, will grow prodigiously, and unhinge her faculty for reasoning, allowing her to think he will change.

It is possible for a human being to portray oneself as someone else, to project an image minus those traits the human being knows others might deem undesirable, to apply a thick solvent on those normally overt lumps and humps and bruises that have resulted from combatant engagements with others; it is possible and is executed every day in every situation, and thus, it is done with cunning, for no good gardener prunes blind, it is by design, to impress those around him; and for those who engage in romantic interludes, each player plays a part that carves a beautiful image of themselves, but to the degree that the image is false is oft the bringer of great woe.

As it was, Oscine and Heath, after the wedding, concentrated on those activities that fed their fleshly lusts, and they filled their time with fun and loving and games and amusement parks and places to go and tour and sit and places to ride in and swim in and take a boat in and fly to and marvel at; it was the thing that they attended, the people they joined, the event they attended, the activity they engaged in, it was the fun, and short bursts of laughter and more laughter meant greater laughter, sprinkled with little talk and little whispers and little thought that soon bound them together. Oscine reasoned she was happy because she was laughing and free and Heath was so handsome and spirited and unbinding and relaxed and strong and ready to defend her and quick to please her and always there for her when she needed him most; but mostly they bonded by exchanging bodily fluids in every circumstance and situation and location and parlor, exchanging those aromatic chemicals that ignite our passions and bind our flesh to each other; it was through these countless encounters of fleshly unions that they built what they perceived as love and friendship and devotion and loyalty to each other; it was through the feasting on the fleshly part of their mate that they built a singular biome in which lay all their triumphs and time spent together, a delicate ecosystem that would be their foundation upon which their future relationship rested; it was as it always has been in the beginning of any great project, it is the foundation that will determine if they weather the storm or crumble before the mildest rain. It has been the way of the world before them and it is the way of the world now, and will be, until the world is no longer our world.

Oscine and Heath were married one year later at the same church, and once the ceremony was consummated, Oscine stood there in adoration at the family of her husband and the many friends gathered therein—nodded in glee at the absence of her own family and then breathed out the last remnants of a dead life and breathed in the beginning of new one. "I am free," she whispered, and proceeded to dance away the night in the arms of her incredibly handsome and masculine husband.

"How romantic," thought Madelyn, gazing at Oscine and Heath as she danced at their wedding. She was beginning to believe she had reached the point of the next day after bliss with her husband. "It is a year to the day after my marriage for dear Oscine, and perhaps so it will be a year to the day after this day that she will understand that there is no such thing as Love until marriage—if there is to be Love at all." Madelyn also fancied herself a philosopher, to wit: "All women know most men are no good as companions, but they think their husband is different, as if he alone is civilized the way the wife defines it." She laughed then, and looked up at her husband and smiled, thinking, "Men do what they have to do to get what they want, then they do whatever they want and we let them because we fear life without them." She intellectually understood it, but could not emotionally cut herself from this anchor she felt dragging herself into the slimy green sea. "It is the way marriage is; it just isn't any good. It's all a lie to perpetuate the state, so chaos won't rule."

In another year, Madelyn's husband would be flaunting his mistresses in their home, boasting to his friends in front of her about his adulterous affairs, humiliating her, degrading her, whittling her identity as woman to fine dust; and yet, stay she did, desperately hoping her love would change him.

And then one day she was pregnant and later gave birth and the chains round her swollen, tired feet and aching hands tightened. "The children now are my life, now life begins," she insisted to herself; "my joy shall come from them. Nothing else matters." She remembered her female identity at Oscine's wedding. "She no longer exists. My temper is now renting space from his heavy hand. We, all of us, are in various states of happiness until that inevitable horror, marriage, binds us forever to sorrow. But we must endure for the sake of the children. What would the world be like if every Mother ran away from their husbands when they realized he was not their hero?"

Secretly, in her basest thoughts, she enjoyed the control her husband exerted over her, for it gave her great solace that he was the commander who was the point man, a man who had all of the power and took on all of the stresses and responsibilities. She was glad to trail behind him and take orders as long as she did not lead. This imparted security to her. "Safe, safe, at least," she often murmured in between the laundering and changing of the diapers and cooking and running of the errands and mowing of the lawn and raking of the leaves and taking out of the garbage.

In Which Oscine Learns About Her Wifely Duties

Oscine and Heath exposed themselves to as much gaiety and frivolous activities as possible, and consequently, their lives were exciting, though not very fulfilling.

"That isn't marriage," Madelyn said, after listening Oscine talk about her life with Heath, while she was holding the white, plastic walk-about phone in her left hand and holding her baby in her other; "where is the responsibility? You don't even know if he loves you yet."

"Oh, Madelyn," Oscine said, laughing, holding the phone lightly as she lay on her silver satin sheets, "can't you just be happy for me?"

"And what do you talk about all day? You have to have something to talk about—intellectual things, Oscine, not just about the bills and making babies; and you can't spend your entire day worried about the butcher, the baker, the candle-stick maker…"

"Oh, come on, Maddy—nursery rhymes?"

She never hesitated in her return, feeling anxious to relate what she regarded as incontrovertible Fate. "And what about goals—do you have goals with him? I mean, intellectual goals, creative goals, spiritual goals—look, any kind of goal that will keep both of you learning and growing and reading toward something other than the mundane, something that might unite you both as you research it together."

She was disappointed now. "For goodness' sake, Madelyn, you act as if we are sixty years old and the kids are all grown and gone, and we're just two old folks sitting around staring at each other."

"That will be soon enough, mark my words—I don't want to be right, I just know I am."

"Well, it just won't get to that point, I just won't let it…"

"O, it's all an illusion, Oscine, until…" She heard the rude click of the call waiting, and she heard Oscine click the rude formula to hear the interloper.

"Who are you talking to, sweetheart?" Heath asked.

"Oh, just Madelyn," Oscine replied, and in a moment, after both of them had said, "I love you," to each other, she was talking once again to her friend.

"I think it's creepy," Madelyn continued, who was used to coloring most things with the sinister stroke of the master conspiracy theorist, "the way he calls you so much."

"I feel safe when he does," Oscine said, still smiling about a night of passion with her husband. "He even calls me when I am at the store."

"You can't even see the noose tightening," Madelyn whispered, thinking of her own marriage; "you have to experience it first, and then it is too late. That is the tragedy…" but another call from Heath came through, and their conversation ended.

"But why don't you have dinner ready, you got home two hours ago," Oscine asked of Heath one day after she had just come home from her job at the hospital.

Heath laughed. "It's a woman's burden, darling," he replied, never averting his eyes from the television screen, "it's your station in life; you do what you do, and I do what I do. Oh, and don't be a nag. Love you."

"All right," she said, smiling, "love you, too." Yet it was not all right, but she would not speak of it, hoping that in time he would see her increased burden and naturally proffer assistance.

He had instinctively waited until she had begun the irrevocable path toward motherhood to unleash his true identity, which was locked stealthily in his aggressive-male dominant genes.

Oscine gave birth six months hence, and thus it all began for her.

She would get up during the night and check on the baby and she would get up an hour later to check on the baby and she would get up three hours later and check on the baby and she would do this night after dreary night after sleepless night and she would want to ask Heath for some help but she would always think about how hard he worked at his job; so, she would just get up the next night and drag herself to the white crib and hold the baby and feed the baby and rock the baby and talk to the baby and sit there and wonder if this was right and if the role of the man during this crucial time was to sleep soundly and the role of the woman was to suffer; she wanted to read books on the subject but she had no time and so she asked friends at work and friends in the neighborhood and they were split on the dilemma; so, one day she asked Heath if he could maybe get up and help with the baby and he gave her a look that caused her heart to leap and her mind to numb and to think of those scary horror shows she used to watch as a child on dark and rainy nights. She never asked him to help again with the baby during the night.

Sometimes when she was up during the night with the baby she would try and go back to bed but she could not, and she simply lay there exhausted but disturbingly awake; so, she would wander the house and begin to clean those areas that seemed to not sparkle and shine as they needed to; and in the beginning of it all, she seemed to have infinite energy stores to engage in such wanderings, and this became her routine, at least for a little while, she mused.

"Could you help with the baby," Oscine said one day, thinking that she was being reasonable to ask for assistance on a weekend when her husband was rested and relaxed.

"Honey, can't you see I'm busy," Heath shouted, vexed that she would dare interrupt him while he and his father were conversing on the proper method of remodeling cars.

"Oh, it's fine," she said, smiling, and she walked near him so he could see her "it's fine" smile; but her face, having just acquired a ruddy complexion, now glowed crimson, for in her mind she was going mad with burden, and she had thought very much of slapping his handsome countenance so hard that it turned clockwise on his big bull neck. She cried about these thoughts later, thinking herself a vicious and cruel wife and simply not good enough for her husband.

"I am very much a bad person to have such thoughts about such a good man who loves me so much—yes, my husband loves me, and I must show my love for him," she thought, lying in bed that night. "I will show him how much." And at twelve o'clock midnight she got up, determined to win praise from him. "I will clean like never before," she whispered, "and I will not complain about my wifely duties."

Oscine had long ago learned that practically perfect people had practically perfect-looking houses, inside and out, but especially clean houses, aesthetically radiant houses that elicited incredulity and wide eyes and gaping mouths from guests. Oscine brimmed with a special joy when people gushed approval at the marvelous pristine glory and immaculate cleanliness of her fine home; but now, she would clean even the glass picture frames and under the hardwood handrails and around and behind and atop things no one ever even looked at. Yet, in her mind, it was completing a picture of honest cleanliness, and pride swelled in her breasts that morning at precisely five-thirty in the a.m. when her man awoke to see this sweet vision of hospital-standard cleanliness. His tasty breakfast, as usual, was hot and waiting for him.

"Good job, honey," he said, kissing her cheek, "keep it this way."

"Oh yes, I can't imagine it being any other way. It was so filthy; why, you should have seen…"

"Not now, honey, I have to see Dad this morning before work," he mumbled, food bulging out his big mouth, and he kissed her cheek. "Love you."

"And I love you," she said, smiling brightly, her head slightly askew.

Heath's father would often talk about the ways of his world, and he would do so in front of any family member, for he reasoned that his philosophy was truth, and his truth, he reasoned, must never be silent.

"Women have gone past the natural boundaries that Nature has set up for them," the father began, while pouring himself a bottle of red wine, and feeling like a professor again and not a retired educator. "The feminism of this last century has created an artificial lowering of the concrete wall men carefully built, brick by brick, to keep women in. Throughout history, men instinctively understood a woman's purpose—to help man, to raise children, to keep home, to cook while the man went to war or hunted or planted the fields; her physical weakness made her a domestic housemaid, and her emotional demeanor allowed it. When women tried to stray, like in the nineteenth century in this country, men were allowed in some states, by the courts, to whip wayward women; by golly," he cried, jubilantly, "why, men had black leather whips on the walls to remind women who was in charge! What times those, eh?"

"Just because one woman can do what a man can do, they all think they can do it; it's so wrong," Heath said, cutting his thick, tender, bloody steak.

"Now, wait a minute," Oscine said, as she buttered a warm muffin she had baked from scratch. She smiled to evince she understood the men were not serious—at least, not speaking of her and her mother-in-law, who sat next to her. "You fellows don't really..."

"Hey," Heath shouted, bringing his fist down like a sledge-hammer upon the tablecloth Oscine had washed three times to get it exclusively white, "you don't ever interrupt when I am talking to my father."

Oscine smiled and acquiesced, the way a dog smiles and acquiesces with its wagging tail and its bent head after its master has just struck it. "All right, Heath, everything is fine," she cooed, sustaining her "it's fine" smile, and then looked at her mother- and father-in-law to let them know she was a faithful and obedient wife. "I love my husband," she thought. "I love you, Heath," she said, thinking it was like a bandage over the wound she had just opened.

Heath shook his head. "See what I mean?" he declared, in disgust, looking at his father. "Women have to know their place."

"Three steps behind their husband," said the father, loosening his belt.

"This isn't an insult, honey," Heath said, feeling slightly remorseful. "Men have their place in society and women have theirs; it's God's plan. Love you," he finished, touching her hand.

"And I love you," Oscine said, sweetly, "you're so good to me."

"Would you mind leaving the dinner table, sweetheart?" Heath suggested. "And you too, Mom?" After both of the women had obediently departed, he said, almost sneering, "Can you imagine men being ordered about so easily?"

"Proves my point," said his father, rubbing his black-and-white goatee, "it is a woman's nature to be submissive; if you're weak, she will sense it and she either will go out of control or control you."

"That'll be the day," Heath said, looking at the family room, to where the women had retired.

"No problems, then, son?" the father continued, placing his thick fingers upon his son's big shoulders.

"No, and when she even comes close, I shut her down."

"Good boy," the father replied, nodding his head, as he was so very proud. "Oscine is a good woman, as long as she stays in her place."

And so it went on, the invisible fortress around Oscine continued to build, dense red brick by brick, with her doing the heavy lifting, and Heath doing the careful placement.

Diminishing Returns

Males of the animal kingdom have a hardwired plan when it comes to winning the hand of their lady love; some males come together to perform wondrous feats of derring-do or stylish rumbas and sambas or the congas and even the cha-chas, or merely to build sand castles; other males come together to hoot and holler and roar and do just about anything their juvenile brains urge them to squawk about during courtship for their heart's desire; now, it is a fact that this phenomenon has crossed over into the vulgar brain of the human male as he seeks to win the affection of a human female.

In the beginning, when Heath had first beheld Oscine's rare beauty and stroked her fine hair and kissed her fair brow, he had obeyed the natural instincts in his reptilian brain to heighten his level of passion concerning her beauty, as certain male birds do when they address the female bird who sits in a treetop, and just as certain male birds, upon seeing the iridescent, metallic purple-green beauty on high, dance and hum and sing their love song and place gifts before her to separate themselves from other potential suitors, so it had been with Heath; he too had danced and hummed and sung his love song to ensure that his female would choose no other mate.

Once Heath acquired his woman and then realized that she was his and his alone, he soon realized that she no longer had to be wooed, thus he no longer wooed her; and when he realized that her fidelity to the marriage was exceedingly high and beyond question, he no longer gave her gifts; and once she gave birth, he realized that she was now a mother and so the idea of telling her she was beautiful seemed no longer unnecessary, so he did not. But these were little things he sometimes thought about during commercial breaks in sports games or while working on his cars or pushing weights in his garage. And now he also felt an increasing urgency to call her here and call her there and call her in between and everywhere else she might be that he was not; he would call her when she was at work and when she was at the grocery store and when she was at her friend's house and when she was at home and when she was in the car and when she was just about anywhere and awake, and if she was awake, why, he reasoned, then he would call her until she would pick up, all the while speculating that she was doing something no good wife ought to be doing. Indeed, if he had mapped out the times and locations of his daily calls, he could have determined where she was at every hour and every moment of every day of every week and every month, year after year after year; but no, he did not map anything out, he just called and called and called until she answered and then he would just say a few things about whatever happened to slip into the widening crags of his slippery mind, and then he would always finish with a quick "Love you," and hang up, and she would always respond, "Love you, too," and then let the black cell phone linger in her lithe hand for a while, almost as if she were waiting for it to ring again, and then put it back into her white leather purse.

And then he began not to touch her very often.

The Fears of Illness

I n December, when the expenses of her wifely and motherly duties far exceeded her income of minimal health, Oscine collapsed with a high fever, and experienced excessive bouts of emesis over and over again until she was dehydrated and not able to take in food nor water. Her bodily systems screamed for rescue, but for that Friday night, as she alternated between cooking dinner and releasing her past meals into the plastic-lined, clean white trash can, she found no rescue. After eating very little of the Christmas dinner she had prepared, she was smiling and saying everything was fine to her husband, but this did not make the virulent bacterium that had infiltrated her porous body go away. The following two days, Heath and his friends watched the important college and professional football games on the television as Oscine lay upstairs like one dead. She intermittently emptied the contents of her inflamed intestines by mouth, into a round metal pan or the porcelain sink, or by anus, into the immaculately clean, shining white toilet bowl. Even in her viscous stupor she managed to wipe the bowl—knowing it would please her man—each time after she vomited into it.

On Sunday, Heath came in during half-time to check on her as she lay in her glazed condition. She could hear the upstairs cry of the baby and the talk of the other men and their laughter. "Need anything, sweetheart?" he said, begrudgingly, hoping she would issue a response that proffered a fast retreat for him.

She knew this, knew the terror of asking him to take her to the hospital during the important college games—or any college or professional game, actually, any sporting event Heath happened to be watching, and if he happened to be watching it with his family or friends, woe to her if she interrupted them. In the past, when she had reached this level of illness, which was too often for him, he had offered to take her to the hospital, and when she had accepted, she suffered his rude, belittling tirade en route and his riotous wrath back, and his sulking attitude at home for days. She had learned not to ask. "I'm fine," she said, now, lying on the bed, dripping in toxic, yellow sweat, and looking like a beaten rag doll.

He didn't kiss her for fear of contamination, which would ruin his weekend spectacular of alcohol and male friends and good, fat and greasy, sugary foods and a deep saturation of ubiquitous sports. "Love you," he said, in an anesthetized chant, just as if the words he spoke were the same as "what time is it?" or "where is the hammer?"

"I love," she began, but more bile-tasting fluid came rushing up her raw, outraged larynx, and she excused herself to the bathroom once more.

He cursed silently and walked back downstairs.

"That has got to get old, bro," one of Heath's compatriots said, as he sat his corpulent self on the finely combed brown sofa, his hand deep in a red plastic bag of deep-fried potato chips.

"I know," Heath returned, irritated, and then said, smugly, "but she does keep a tight house, she's a tiger in the bedroom, and cooks like a champ."

"Hey, doesn't she want you to take her to the hospital?" another of the male sports clan asked, alarmed.

Heath laughed. "Are you kidding? You keep them in place by not doing irritating things like that, and she knows what will happen because of the last time I took her," and here, he tossed them a hard-cased macho-grenade that exploded with that knowing, cruel look that men of their creed implicitly understand; "I mean, look, man, it's like training a dog; sure, she learns, and like any housebroken pet, she knows her limits."

"Bro!" they yelled, each male taking turns striking Heath's outstretched hand.

Heath, feeling invigorated by this male validation, and in concert with the surroundings, felt it incumbent upon himself to expound further on the matter of taming the gentler, unsuspecting sex. Little did he know that these ignorant, bachelor peasants, in their stunted, still-adolescent minds, accepted any advice from a married man about women as absolute gospel. Of course, he would have been much pleased.

"You have to find a way to shut these women down or they take over," he said, leaning closer to them, alcoholic drink in hand. "Having babies," he said, in earnest, screwing up his face, "knocks the stuffing right out of them." He waved his hand over an imaginary finish line. "You have them beat, then; they become obsessed with that nurturing nonsense, and they are too tired to argue. Hey, watch this," and he sat back, leaning against the grey sofa that Oscine had scrubbed so unmercifully to get it so smooth and clean it looked new every single day. "Sweetheart, could you come down here and fix us a sandwich?"

"Man, oh man, no way, bro!" one of his comrades cried in a hoarse whisper, smiling and giggling. His other friends had to hold their mouths to keep their riotous laughter inside.

The silence Heath heard he interpreted as a challenge to his role as authoritarian and absolute ruler of his domain, and so for his next voice expulsion he constructed a tone smoked with a portent of flavorful retribution. "Honey, you really need to get down here, now; you're keeping my friends waiting."

In her leaden haze, Oscine aroused herself from bed, crawled to the doorway, felt a tingling of regurgitation signaling her, rushed to the sink to empty her contents, splashed her face, put on some red lipstick, forgot what she was doing, and then lay down upon the soft, wet bed and neared sleep. Hearing her master's voice again, she remembered the command, managed once more to get to the door, stood up, and walked down the stairs, smiled sweetly at the guests and then disappeared into the kitchen.

"I do it," Heath said, looking at his astonished friends, "because I can; it lets her know I want it and she'll do it, without argument; I'm telling you, boys," he folded his arms behind his head as he lay back on the sofa, "this is a man's life—nineteenth-century living, the way it should always be. Fellas, I'm breaking her will just as I would a wild mustang."

"Heath, man, she can hear you," whispered John, a twenty-year-old youth who had not yet acquired the art of total domination over a female.

"No," Heath said, confidentially, "not when she is like this—yes, she hears, but no, she doesn't—she doesn't remember."

"Ah," they all said in unison, feeling enlightened.

"But why doesn't she just refuse to do stuff like this?" one of his brood asked innocently.

Heath leaned over with a huge grin on his face, and said, full of himself, "Because it is her nature to serve man."

The brawny youth shook his head in disbelief.

Oscine, executing this ritual without thought, felt the vomit begin to rise, but she was able to suppress its volcanic eruption and thus swallow it back down. She subsequently served these men food and drink, smiling sweetly all the while.

"I love you," Heath said, and he meant it, for when she obeyed absolutely, he was absolutely in love with her.

"I love you," she smiled, and her attempt to kiss him was rebuffed, but she smiled again to demonstrate understanding, and she then walked up the stairs—as if iron balls and iron chains were attached to her legs—as the guests looked on in awe. Once she reached the safety of her own bathroom, she vomited again.

"Man, it's like having a slave," one of the men said in utter adoration.

Heath smiled. "I could make love to her right now if I wanted to and she would not deny me, but I've got my boys with me," he shouted, and once again he exchanged hearty hand slaps with his comrades.

Oscine lay like one near death, still cognizant of others around her; it was a skill, this ability to comprehend clearly what those about her were saying, regardless of her physical state, a talent she had acquired all those suffering years as a youth while she lay in a quiet and desperate oblivion in the midst of her human gargoyle caretakers, a kind of sixth sense that she wore like a protective veil about her fragile form. And now it rendered one lucid and honest truth that bubbled up through the fissures in her awful torment: "I would like to run a sharp pair of scissors across his thick neck, and watch him choke on his mottled black blood." But then she would cry at these sordid thoughts, and so massaged her wounded conscience with those words that had become so ubiquitous they no longer meant anything, "I love you, Heath." But uttering these words did not assuage her guilt, for at times like this she saw him in her mind in postures of pain, and her guilt was magnified. "I'm a bad person," she whispered, "I deserve to suffer; he's such a good man. He cares for me so." This was the most often repeated refrain in her private womb during times when she loathed him, for to think otherwise would have allowed her to see the failure of her marriage, and she would have died of shame for others to think she would divorce a man and have her children grow up without their biological father at their side.

On Monday morning, Heath, ready for work, stuck his head in the doorway of the bathroom, winced at the kneeling, vomiting figure, and said, rather casually, "Well, hope you feel better soon. Love you."

"Heath," Oscine said, wiping vomit spray from her pink gums, "do you think," but her frail voice stopped, as if she was perched on the sloping edge of an abyss and feeling a strong gush of wind.

"I'm late," Heath cried, "you've got to stop getting sick, honey, that's the answer—goodbye. Love you. Have fun with the kid."

"Love you," the dying, raspy voice gagged, like a dying, cool ember far from the rich, red flame.

Two hours later she had just enough strength to pick up the phone and call a neighbor for a ride to the hospital, where she had an IV solution begun and massive antibiotics injected into her dehydrated and infected body. She had only called because in her weakened condition, she could no longer care for the baby.

That night, in front of Heath's parents, Heath raged, albeit in an affectionate tone, about Oscine not asking him to take her to the hospital.

"Oh, you're so busy," Oscine cooed, feeling much better now.

"Oh, honey, I love you," Heath said, hugging her, "but you need to tell me when you really get sick—promise?"

"Promise," she smiled, looking proudly at his parents, wanting to believe in her husband's sincerity.

"For goodness' sake, honey, what if the baby had gotten hurt while you were unable to care for him?"

Oscine's face blushed a deep shade of pink with embarrassment, and then blanched to shock as she lost her breath.

"And about dinner? Oh, I should cook, honey."

She wanted to answer his subtle charge of endangering the welfare of their child, but she could not find the words. "No, it's fine," she finally said, "I'll get to it."

"That's my girl," Heath said, smiling proudly.

And she did get right to it, like a dutiful wife, for she knew no other role than one of pleasing her man regardless of the circumstances.

The Way It Was

Heath was a master of soothing the wounds of women before the wound festered and poisoned the internal psyche of them. His simple ploy was called entertainment.

Heath was always amazed at the ease with which women forgot the emotional torment he had inflicted upon them. "It's as if they're children," he had said to his father long ago, from whom he had gained the revolutionary idea of entertainment as mender of emotional pain.

"They are," his father had replied, in earnest, "childlike, really; make them do an inordinate amount of chores, mistrust them, humiliate them, and then dish them a plateful of good loving or pure, unadulterated fun, and they'll love you more than ever before." His voice had become more sober. "But it is important to begin the cycle soon after you are married, first by putting them in their place through outrageous commands, and then by pacifying them with frivolous fun; why, it's like training a dog, really—you know, son, the rolled-up newspaper or the treat."

"But don't they know we're doing it to them?" Heath had asked that day, before he was married.

"Now, that is the curious part, son, for they do know it; look here, boy, before I met your mother, I would deliberately date women whom I knew didn't care for me, but I was drawn to their beauty, and I also wanted to see if flattery truly worked. Well, child, doggone if it didn't work, and these women knew exactly what I was doing, but they couldn't turn off that mechanism in their female brain that responds to flattery and praise—it's called vanity."

"Vanity," Heath repeated, as if to memorize it.

"Vanity, thy name is woman."

"Yes, sir," he said, mesmerized.

"Courting a woman is a science, son, plain and simple; show me any woman and I can apply sound, scientific principles and—slapdash, she's mine. Of course, it has to be the right kind of flattery and praise or it's like talking Italian to an Eskimo."

"Does every man know these secrets?"

"Some do, most stumble onto them at one time or another; and then there are, of course, the 'nice guys,' those insufferable freaks, really, who think they can treat these fragile women with equality." Both of the men laughed till they were teary eyed. "Thank goodness," the father continued after composing himself, "for those pathetic freaks, because women get to see what a man shouldn't be, and they know intuitively that this version of man is wrong, and then they get very mean and downright nasty and run right into the arms of a real man, like us, who will give them security and guidance through our total domination of them. Don't fool yourself, women not only need men like us, they yearn for us. The honest women will tell you it's true."

"Sounds like they need to be dominated."

"Absolutely. It's a mistake to treat them as if they are sensible like a man. Look, son," he said, putting his arms around his only male child, "women are illogical, irrational creatures with infantile brains; without Man they have no emotional compass; and here is one of the greatest secrets I can tell you about Woman: her greatest strength—her delicate beauty, which so powerfully attracts us—is also her greatest weakness, because, my boy, it takes a truckload of hormones to make such an exquisite loveliness, and that is her ultimate destruction, which makes her, after all, an emotional cripple; son, we give them meaning and direction; and don't fall for that pseudo liberation movement—those women think that because a few female freaks can do manlike things, all women can. One genetic freak doesn't mean we have to throw out the baby with the bath water. Why, they're the exception to the rule, that's all."

"Dear, your football game is on," Heath's mother had said that day as she sat beside her husband while knitting his black woolen sweater.

"See?" Heath's father said, smiling, and he embraced her. "It's all worth it for the hug, isn't it, dear?"

"Yes, dear," she responded.

This was the foundation upon which Heath had successfully built his empire of domination over women, a paradigm generally not disputed by the actions of the women he had met.

Vacation

After Oscine's severe illness, Heath planned a three-day holiday in Las Vegas, where the two of them could be free of all restraints and responsibilities. Oscine fairly glowed during this special time. "Everything is all right again," she kept repeating to herself. She called Madelyn, who was as sober as a hanging judge concerning this whole affair.

"Heath is so wonderful," Oscine said, lying on the soft white sheets on the bed inside her hotel room, "he's so much fun to be with; everything is all right again. We just had a bad period, and we just needed some time to ourselves..."

Madelyn, unable to suppress her outrage, spun an attack formed by the very hot-tempered molecules of enmity toward Heath. "Don't you see, Oscine? It's a game. He'll never change! This is the 'sweetheart phase' where he tries to win you back," and here her voice became mean and hard, "but don't let him fool you, girl. You remember those days lying in the dark, wondering who was taking care of the baby. Being alone in Vegas isn't responsibility. Who can't have fun there?"

"Who are you talking to, honey?" Heath said, coming back unexpectedly from the downstairs lobby.

Oscine, hanging up the phone, and thinking everything was good again, did not hesitate to speak the truth. "Oh… Maddy."

"Madelyn! That whore!" Heath shouted, and then, realizing his mistake after he saw the bewildered look on Oscine's face, let his countenance grow gentle. "Baby, she is full of ideas about the way things should be for her, but not us." He sat next to her, holding her fast, kissing her. "We're fine without her," he whispered. His inoculation against Madelyn continued on, interspersed with passionate lovemaking, and soon Oscine was deep within the high borders of complete loyalty to her man. She wanted to love him and be loved by him and be happy with him. She would exude loyalty to him, she had decided long ago, as long as he did not commit adultery. "All marriages have problems," she told herself, "and we can work our problems out."

Less than two years later, she had another baby, a boy, and now Oscine had twice the burden; nay, her burden increased even more, for Heath had acquired no more share of the responsibilities, and Oscine's bitterness, silent and brooding, grew like a red blaze fanned by a mighty wind.

The Provinces of House, Skin and Communication

The trip to the land where money is funneled down glitzy drainpipes and into the silver-lined coffers of people who use gold bars as paperweights ended after a logical sequence of events for Heath, as it would for him, for his goals there were the Clubs and Shows and Gambling and the occasional acts of sexual commerce with his wife; but for Oscine, she knew the trip must end but she thought that the idea of it, the acts of merriment and utter abandon, would hitch a ride with them and come home with them and plant its joyous self into their home; but once they were inside the four walls of their home again, Heath stepped back into the exact proportions and ratios of his responsibilities and duties as Father and Husband, no more and no less; but Oscine wanted this trip to alter forever the worn fabric of their splintering marriage; she yearned for something magical to repair the damage done, to recover that which was once lost, to have what she had always wanted to have, real love, true love with a man who would talk to her and be with her and listen to her, always. But then she would hear the admonishing voice of Madelyn echoing in her thoughts, "You cannot have what you never had! O, Oscine, what you have in the beginning is what you will have in the end! You cannot make a silk purse out of a sow's ear!" But Oscine had never believed in any of Madelyn's bittersweet symphony, musical musings that formed pessimistic notes and cynical instruments; truly, every word out of Madelyn's mouth was an old tune of *caveat emptor*, a constant vibration of sinister pitches and tones that went straight through her black orchestra to proclaim all things bad in love and marriage. But Madelyn's influential incision into the Younger home was slowly covered over by Heath's dominant will and insistence that she be relegated to the status of persona non grata, until one day the memory of her just seemed to sink into the well of forgetfulness in the mind of Oscine. The last thing Madelyn ever said to her best friend was whispered in a hushed, hurried voice, "Please, please remember, Oscine, that the man you married is the man you married—he will not change because of your good love. He is who he is."

As it was, she had rejoined her regularly scheduled life in its boring progress, and she stepped back in reluctantly and dreamed of Las Vegas and dreamed of abounding joy there and she dreamed of what she had had with Heath there and what she wanted with him here; she dreamed it all every night and every day and she sometimes would talk to Heath about it but he would simply frown and tell her he loved her and walk away.

And then there was the province of the skin, the area of silent communication between husband and wife, for her a gateway into her heart, an organ easily attained by cuddling and caressing and fondling, an organ easily won over by kissing and massaging and stroking; but her fair skin lay like a frozen sheath of discarded flesh, its memory of intimate touch from a male now fading fast, the sensitive atlas of her skin slowly losing its lovely curves and hills and valleys for want of living touch, its memory of uniting with a male fading fast; her female skin, overcoat to her heart, listening for every word from the subtle language of touch, losing its capacity for understanding what once was, was losing its desire to know the thoughts and emotions of a man's skin.

Heath rarely held his wife, rarely kissed his wife, rarely visited or cherished his wife's soft, creamy flesh. She would initiate contact with his skin and he would not reciprocate; she would try and hold his hand, and he would move his own hand away; she would seek to kiss him passionately, and he would turn his head. She would talk to him about her physical and emotional needs, and he happened to say, one day, and rather succinctly and honestly, too, "Look, honey, do you ever remember me telling you about my problems? Do you ever remember me asking you for advice or needing a shoulder to cry on?" And when she suggested that they read books on relationships or seek a marriage counselor, the skin on his face became red with indignant rage, and he screamed, "I don't ever want to hear you say that again, do you hear me! We are not going to talk about our problems with an outsider!"

"Well," she replied meekly, "how do we solve our problems?"

"What problems?" he had cried. "Your problems, not mine; I'm fine, it's you with the problems, your stupid female problems, it's always your problems you want to talk about," and he threw a hammer across the room that smashed through the door leading into the garage. "Go," he screamed, "go and do something useful, like cleaning the house; do something you're good at, clean," he cried, ushering her along toward the kitchen wherein sat the necessary tools for her household chores, and watching her nervously take out the soap and sponge and bleach, he said, his anger somewhat assuaged, "You talk too much about your stupid female problems, honey," and his wrath was shorn from his mind as he watched her clean the white-tiled entryway; and so he approached her bent form and patted her flaxen hair. "There, honey, don't you feel better already?" He cursed under his hot breath when he saw the damage to the door. "Guess I'll have to call Dad," he whined, and he left, leaving her to her task.

And then there was the province of communication: and this was the way it was, and had been from the beginning, her eyes had simply been shielded from seeing it—in fact, had never seen it, never even suspected it, that conversation between a loving husband and wife could become so banal, never thought that a loving couple would need any words other than those cascading magically from the inviolate registry of Love: that their minds and hearts needed to be joined by, encouraged by, mended by words of substance and meaning, and would thrive on an enduring, building, honest dialogue that would heal their past and strengthen their present and guide their future; that her life would be so vacuous, and hurtful, and wanting, without stimulating discourse from the man she was determined to live with unto death, that she would feel so lonely, and listless, without this basic communion, that having her life filled with only physical chores and small talk would make her feel so unhappy.

He simply did not speak to her about issues outside of family matters—the bills, his friends, his life, his interests, his work, the children; and subsequently, she slowly withered away on the social vine, no longer having anyone close to talk to about issues she was interested in; but in the main, she was worrying about the house, the children, the bills, her work, his life, her life, his work, doing errands, his family, his friends, his desires, and more important than anything else, his mighty will be done, and she found the only person she could rely on and dialogue with about her complicated life was herself.

And so she continued to exist and slowly move along in her own ineffable universe, her identity disintegrating every day she did not procure and practice for herself the simply joys of exchanging intimate thoughts with another intimate human being, until it seemed that the woman who woke up every day to serve others, and then went to sleep so she might serve them the next day, seemed to be devoured completely and with utter anonymity.

And then there was the province of the house, where she reigned as Queen; any visitor who came to the house of the Youngers was witness to a remarkable phenomenon rarely seen in any culture, a domicile that seemed to have a built-in, automated cleaning system twenty-four hours a day—day in, day out, rain or shine, holiday or workday, during good times and bad—an automated system with two whirring arms and two strong legs and a rugged determination to best every bit of dust and dirt.

Oscine was a whirligig of energy, resolved to wipe up every errant drop and spill from her boys, bent on the destruction of every hidden germ and virus; she used sponge and cloth, mop and towel, wiper and broom in her pursuance of the excellence of cleanliness. She viewed cleaning as a dynamic that supplied her with several goals, to wit: it was a goal she could achieve every day with every wipe of her trusty sponge that ultimately resulted in admiration from her family and friends. Others, she often thought, as she cleaned during the silent night, pursue goals they may never reach or never understand or are unable to show, but my goal is one I can do all day and others can benefit from. Other women sewed or baked or gave gala parties, but her extraordinary ablution of her house was always apparent, and always praised, every time and by everyone. She gained comfort from this, and she would not be denied her reputation as someone who kept a fine home.

As Time Goes By

Time wept inexorably by for Oscine. She felt entombed, incarcerated, ineffectual; she felt buried alive by burdens and responsibilities, a prisoner in her own house and wherever she went by virtue of the long reach of wireless technology; she felt that whatever she did or said or wanted in the House of Heath did not matter, that she was merely another player in the unfurling play that was her husband, her lord and master, her overseer; but she would not yield to the idea that all of it was permanent, not now, not with yet another baby born and too many societal pressures to stay married; so, whenever she looked at her marriage and saw an empty cup, she filled it at least halfway with her resilient hope and optimism.

She was working longer hours at the hospital strictly for the money—it was what Heath wanted; and although her hours increased at work, her work hours at home did not decrease.

She still woke up early in the morning from a night of too little sleep and fixed breakfast for her three little ones and her husband and then started the laundry and then rushed to ready herself for work; she then swallowed bits of food as her children pranced about the house and her husband complained of something, and then soon he was out the door and she was ushering her boys into the car and dropping them off at school or daycare and then speeding down the road and breaking every known speed limit until she arrived at work. She was at the hospital for ten exhausting hours and every hour there she was not sure if she was going to make it to the end of her shift, but she always pushed herself onward, ever onward toward the hour of departure, when she would jump into her car and speed off to pick up her children at daycare and take them home and begin dinner and resume the laundry and check on the dinner again and then start the cleaning. And then there was the homework of her boys, and she did that, too, and after the homework was done and the dinner was done and the dishes put away she resumed her cleaning and the laundry; near ten o'clock at night she would watch a slice of television and then try to fall asleep, but she found herself too tired, so she would clean some more and watch a little more television until eleven o'clock and then she would slide quietly into bed and then lie there wide awake and frustrated beyond words.

At five o'clock in the a.m., she would awaken and start the cycle all over again, except on Saturday, when she could sleep in until seven o'clock. Saturday was a day to do more chores outside the house, and this meant shopping and taking the boys to events and cousins' houses and birthday parties and this and that and everything their little heart or Heath's little heart desired for them or himself: like barbecues and family get-togethers and T-ball for the boys and camping trips, and scouts, and team sports; on Sunday morning, she awoke tired, but arose and began the day with breakfast and cleaning and laundry, and playing with her boys. It was with her boys she began to feel what she had felt so long ago with the animals and the beautiful flowers, it was her boys that were the human glue that kept her together with Heath, it was all for them, the idea that they needed a man in their life, no matter how he treated her, it was this prevailing notion that kept her going and striving to better her marriage. It was through her boys that she could feel herself becoming renewed; that through her sweet, innocent children she was giving to the world three good men who would amount to a greater virtue than she.

Sometimes at night, sometimes on a Sunday night, when the boys and Heath were deep in slumber and she was alone in the kitchen and sitting on the white bamboo chairs and admiring the robust cleanliness of her house and thinking about her love for her children, that she would walk quietly up to the high brown cabinet doors and extract a large black bottle and bring it down and take out its oblong cork and pour out its substance into her best crystal glassware; she would sip the sweet, pink, alcoholic nectar therein, and look about the house and admire her handiwork and think about her beautiful children and how each of them were different but that the middle child was a little too much like Heath. At such times, she would close her eyes and try to imagine and hear the very breathing of the house, and she would truly bend her ear and feign that she could hear the melodic breathing of her precious boys, upon which every rise and fall of their little chests and every gentle breath in and gentle breath out she waited in joyful expectations, thinking that she was responsible for their very life-force and that she was alone responsible for them growing up straight and tall and true and that one day they would be fine young men and they would come home and upon greeting her kiss her sweetly and lovingly call her Mom; it was times such as these that solidified the idea that she could never leave, must not ever leave, that it would be impossible to leave Heath. She resolved to stay the course, if only for the children. It is all for them, she would muse, sipping the intoxicating wine and admiring the grandiloquence of the symmetrically arranged and extremely sanitized-smelling house. She felt noble, now, noble that she would sacrifice herself for her boys, that she wanted nothing for herself, nothing but work and struggle and burden, but it would all be worth it when they were finally fine young men and would bring their beautiful wives home to her and their handsome children and she would greet them all with a kiss and glow with pride and honor that she had done the right thing.

These are the virtuous thoughts she would have and then sometimes she would step out onto the porch that Heath had built in the backyard and she would look up at the silvery moon and the lustrous diamonds in the sky and she would look to the birds about the yard and she would whistle a gentle tune and beckon to them, but alas, they would not come; and then she would look to her fruit and vegetable garden, and alas, she knew they were not growing; and then she would look to her lazy dogs and cats, and alas, they would just raise their lazy heads and look at her and then lay their lazy heads down again and shut their lazy eyes.

So, she would resume the kitchen chair and sit again and think of the coming week and what she had to do, and then she would go to bed and would not truly fall asleep for an exasperatingly good while.

And so the next Monday morning she would awaken and she would feel like she was still exhausted but she would force herself up and begin the whole cycle once more, and by that night she was saying to herself that she needed a chance to truly rest herself; but no, she would convince herself, she would force herself onward, ever onward, for her boys, for her boys she would drive herself to the very end without complaint or capitulation or divorce.

And so it went, on and on and on, every day and every week and every month and every year and it never changed or was ever altered even for a single microsecond of time; and lo, she knew that her savior had still not come.

Ellen

Oscine, dressed in her white cotton nurse's uniform, sat next to the old woman who had a disease her old body could not put away. When Oscine attended to an infirm person she felt their sorrow and grief as if she, indeed, had their ailment, as if she were suffering the disruptions in their lives, as if she were experiencing their fear and horror of the unknown, and she aided them as if saw herself lying there on the sterile white linen sheets. "I might be lying there one day, and I would want the same kindness," she often thought. She never considered herself truly sick, a term she reserved only for those patients who were physically incapacitated or chronically ill or terribly handicapped. Here, at the hospital, she felt at home, for she considered these people her people, her own kind, the only ones capable of understanding her special emotional turmoil.

She was sitting next to Ellen, sweet and beautiful Ellen who was dying and had no visitors, Ellen who had lived the last forty years of her life seemingly ready to die but somehow continuing to live; Ellen, who had been abandoned by her husband because of her illness; Ellen, who was an old woman frightened of dying alone. Oscine felt she could tell this kind woman all, for telling secrets to a dying person was like burning your letters in a consuming fire.

"Life could have been so wonderful," Ellen whispered to Oscine as she lay on her white hospital bed, speaking in a halting, aching voice that echoed the tumult inside her decaying body. "If only I had just done what I knew was right but was too timid to do. It is as if," and here she coughed, a horrific spasm careening throughout her wilting form, "I have been condemned to suffer." She began to weep, her wrinkled, sundried, weary old face collapsing into streams of sorrow. "It is as if women are born to tragedy."

"Oh, no," Oscine said, pious tears wetting her smooth, rose-colored, high cheekbones, "that's not true." And even though she spoke this with great pathos, somewhere in the conflagration of her hurried life she knew that somehow it had merit in given circumstances. "Life can be wonderful for a woman."

"No," Ellen said, closing tight her tired, small grey eyes, which had no desire for life radiating from them, "we are condemned to suffer because that is who we are—we are here to suffer." She opened up these puffy, tired eyes that had no eyelashes, her countenance growing intense as she touched Oscine's arm. "It is one of the biggest lies of this world—oh, I believe very bad people started this lie; man or woman, I don't know, but it is a lie, for certain. We can't be happy because we love men no matter what and we see the good in bad men no matter what, and stay loyal to them, no matter what; it's all so tragic I can't stand to think about it, really, I cannot, and the ironic part is you can tell a woman what is going to happen to her—no, what is happening to her," and she cut the air with her old, fleshy arm that had the IV dangling from it and white gown sleeve hanging off it, "and she won't believe you—another tragedy. It's only when you're much older do you understand the Truth, but by then it can't help you, and it can't help those it might help. Tragic, tragic," she whispered, closing her sad eyes again. "And only the old, beaten women know, and some men know but they won't tell anybody—unless it's for money." She shook her head in disgust. "And younger women always think it won't happen to them—tragic." She presently fell to rest but woke up an hour later and was delighted to see that Oscine was still in attendance, holding Ellen's sweaty, small, weak fingers. "You're a good woman, Oscine; it's too bad you can't be happy—you deserve happiness."

"But I am happy," Oscine protested, meekly; "my husband loves me."

Ellen, a woman who had lived the lie and found the Truth, could see the subtle strokes of denial configured on the face of her pupil. Her visage grew animated, her eyes narrowed. "How often does he tell you that you're beautiful?"

Oscine smiled, as if to wash away the idea that the absence of such a compliment meant anything. "That doesn't matter," she shook her head, "I'm not that…"

"Oh, hush, child, you're a stunning woman! And yes, it does matter; and even if others see you as ugly—his love sees you as beautiful! Now, dear child, look into my eyes and tell me if he hugs you and listens to your troubles and lets you be a woman."

Oscine, as if caught in Ellen's powerful trance, nearly wept as she shook her head and then looked at the old Oracle. "Be a woman?"

"Getting all the dark mischief out of your cold heart so you can be warm again; you know, fits of rage."

"Oh, no, he doesn't like that at all."

She said in a bitter whisper, "He shuts you down as if you were a child."

"He words so hard, I don't want to burden him with my problems."

"Baby, your problems are his problems, and his, yours… and what about your problems? And you work harder than he does, girl, so quit making excuses for him."

"But he doesn't beat me," she said, shaking her head.

Ellen shook her head, letting it roll softly back and forth on the puffy white pillow; a little rustling noise came from the crinkling polyester. "He doesn't have to touch you to hurt you; and O, my beautiful, delicate Oscine, you're starving, you're emotionally starved; he doesn't understand you; he thinks you're just like a man but who looks like a woman; but honey, he's so wrong, so very, very wrong, he is killing you with his ignorance."

"It could be worse," she said, diffidently; "I could be living in a country where woman are treated like chattel."

"Don't ever think down," Ellen said, angrily. In the three weeks she had known her, Oscine had never seen her mad. "Don't be satisfied with half a loaf, always ask for the whole loaf; that is how a woman becomes happy—not putting up with the meager crumbs men give us."

"But all marriages can't sustain those first few years of passion, it's just not possible," Oscine said, shaking her head.

"Make the impossible possible; it can be done. It's called real Love, child—real genuine Love; it's very rare, like a rainbow cloud."

Oscine, startled by the memory of this chromatic mirage, imagined a vivid clip of her astonishing and seemingly limitless youth, and she felt a deep hurt and hollowness in her heart.

"You know, everyone thinks they know what Love is, but they're wrong." She tapped her chest. "I know otherwise because I have seen it, felt it," and she rolled her bony fingers with the shriveled black flesh together, "tasted it, too; O, Oscine, it's a dance with the golden sunshine, a dance," and she paused as she shut her eyes and remembered the sublime properties of virtuous Love, and her words became unstuck at the dam of disease and seeped through into the glimmering light, "a dance inside the lyrical poetry of music, a flight to the sky port to Heaven," but she hesitated again, having lost her lucid harvest of words; and then in a moment, continued, "but to recognize it and let go of those restraints," but she coughed, and then rested her voice from this long, uninterrupted speech.

"Restraints?" asked Oscine, after a little while.

"Yes, Oscine, restraints—men, job, money, career: it's all meaningless when you find True Love."

"You're not saying to abandon your husband," Oscine asked, frightened.

"Oh, yes, that is exactly what I am saying, because if you find True Love you aren't in Love now; yes, abandon every man you meet if it takes going through them like soft candy. Do it until you find True Love. But let me tell you something, girl, the husband you have now isn't worth saving any more than a stale chocolate—the sweetness gone right out of it. Once," and the old woman learned forward, with all of her remaining strength, "I found him but I let him go. Why, why…" and she fell back, exhausted, and closed her eyes once more and lay still for a short while, and then spoke, her voice captured by a cold sliver of darkness. "I wasted everything—my life, my love, my life, only one life to live from birth to death, one life, one life only." She opened her moist eyes, and placed her trembling hands on Oscine's soft, blonde head, and the two women looked at each other, as if they were looking through a mirror and seeing the reflection of the same soul, one young, one old. The old woman spoke with an increased urgency. "O, Oscine, if I could just get you to see into my thoughts, my memories," and her eyes glowed with a profound power, "O, Oscine, please, please, feel me, my wasted life, so far away, so far gone," and she sobbed, now, "so far away and here now, killing me from so long ago because I didn't make the right decision, because I let fear destroy me—fear, fear, O, fear, you killed me, fear and pride and shame, you killed me, and I killed me, too, I'm dead, I died when I walked away from his sacred Love," and she took Oscine's hands, and she spoke as if her entire life had been distilled into one final testament. "O, Oscine, when Love reaches out to you, please, please, for the sake of God, don't pull away; Love," she nearly sang it, so passionately did she adore it, "it wants to live in you, it begs life in you, it seeks to bring life to you, it," and she caught her breath and her mouth sputtered and her lips palpitated, and

Oscine let her head fall closer to hear these inviolate words, "it," she began, barely whispering, "wants to bring breath to you, to color your world, to," and she breathed calmly and then began again, "to give you shape, yes, that's it; to live in you, it needs sustenance like any living thing, it cannot live without us; we, Oscine, we create this earthly Love, and without us, there is no Love and its memory dies—and will feed us into a higher Love," and she squeezed shut her eyes and her pale lips trembled as her pious tears streamed down her wrinkled, ashen face, and she spoke no more, no more words released from the prison of time, no more ardent words dripping from her dying heart, but now only the moans of grief from a woman dying without peace, without True Love, with regret, with shame, her entire body sputtering and spasmodic and slowly churning toward a bleak, sad, empty death.

The next day, Ellen died.

Oscine went to the funeral, at which she was the only one in attendance outside of the cemetery workers. Oscine wept pious tears.

Heath called her six times while she was there.

Oscine came back to the cemetery every week for the next year, bringing a flower to put on Ellen's grave, sitting on the cool, verdant grass in front it and remembering what the wise old woman had said to her but always weaving a new tale in her own mind to dismiss the pessimism of the message and in its stead place her own version of optimism and hope based on the future of her blessed boys. She came faithfully every week and she felt good about it, that no matter what happened to her inside her home, she would be a good person outside it, and this was her way of balancing the injustices in her life.

Then one day, after receiving a phone call from Madelyn's sister to come to this cemetery, as she was waiting for her, she came across a grave that had a name she recognized engraved on a freshly carved grey cement slab. "Madelyn Windsor," she whispered, staring at it with a face drained of color, her mind slayed by the shock of the unexpected. She dropped to her knees, staring blankly at the freshly carved headstone, touching it with her trembling fingers. "No," she whispered, "no, it's not true," and she began to weep uncontrollably as her head fell upon her chest, "not Madelyn, no, it's not true, it can't be."

"It is true," a solemn voice sank into the gloom, blanketing everything with bitterness. It was Madelyn's younger sister. Oscine looked up at her. The woman's face was like a crumbling piece of stone. "He killed her. She is dead because she was a woman." She acknowledged Oscine. "She stayed with him for the children, though he beat her."

"No," Oscine sobbed, shaking her head in disbelief.

"You didn't know, she wouldn't tell you, she was so ashamed; he killed her, though, one night when she was finally ready to leave him with the children, he killed her." Oscine could see fresh blood on the woman's hands. "He made it look like self-defense because she had a gun, but we know he killed her; yes, he killed her, so I killed him, because who would avenge her death?" and she hugged Oscine, and whispered, with great conviction, "Nobody but family, so I killed him and I am proud of it and I confess it before God and Man," and she held up her bloodstained hands, fresh blood from her fresh kill, and she looked on high, "I killed your killer, baby sister, I killed him for you and Justice and Mom and Dad."

Oscine saw a commotion of colors black and blue, and red lights flashing, and she shook her head in disbelief as the uniformed men came running up to Madelyn's sister.

"Don't let it happen to you, Oscine," the woman raged as she was taken to the black-and-white squad car; "save yourself before it's too late."

When Heath learned what had happened at the cemetery, he was upset because Oscine had bloodstains on her expensive nurse's dress. She wanted to scream in his face and open up his ignorance and spit down the musty, dead space of his heart and pump it full of understanding, but she knew it was not to be.

And she went to the trial of Madelyn's sister, despite Heath's most strenuous objections, and later visited her in jail many times, and wrote many letters of hope and compassion to her.

Truly, she was now alone.

Dr. Argnine

The soul of music bursts forth with melody and rhythm, and the volume rises or falls, the tempo slows or increases, the meter is weak or strong; it is the same with Woman, who lives in the swirling heat of dissonance—she bursts forth with melody and rhythms, her volume rises or falls, her tempo slows or increases, her meter is weak or strong; but she needs to hear other grand songs when she has achieved, when she deserves, when she can find blessed and wondrous consonance—these times are crucial for her inner healing, and if she does not hear them, feel and hear and taste their rosy, honey-flavored hues and scents and musical chords, she slowly dies; a woman's flesh and muscle and tissue are sewn from the internal rhythms of her self-worth, her red blood flowing with the nutrients reaped from external harmony; a woman's body is made of twinkling stardust and vivacious atoms, but the fertile soil in her brain, and the sweet breath of love in her heart, all need a precious commodity from without, for a woman's soul is aligned with Nature—and Nature is a hard mistress, selfish for praise and glorification. A woman feels the pulse of life-giving forces in her, feels the burden of propagating her species, and of protecting, nourishing, and raising her own kind.

To give life is to be vulnerable to the ravages of the world, and Woman, instinctively understanding this, seeks shelter from harm, seeks a greater power to give her solace and security to soothe her fears, to caress her, to cuddle her, to stroke and love and keep her—this is Man's role. But Man must not only protect her, he must peek into her heart's nature, thus bringing his responsibilities to two levels, one who protects and one who praises. Yet, he must also be helper and lover and friend. To ignore the intense and intricate rhythm of the female soul is to slowly freeze her until she grows numb and withers away inside like a delicate rose planted in a dark cave that yearns and stretches for its savior, its power, its regenerative source, the sun. The woman begs to flourish and grow toward the man, her source of strength, but too often he shields all strength from her; nay, he molts his toxic covering onto her, wrapping her in a sticky, waxy dread. The woman will never dissolve this armor unless her savior comes and melts the potent poison in it and sets her free.

Oscine had so many layers of poisonous dread from Heath that she no longer remembered the warmth and the light that had once resided within her female heart.

And the birds still no longer obeyed her commands, and the flowers still slept even when she commanded them awake.

And she wept whenever she could find a private place and a private time.

Every bit of her feminine soul had been repressed to appease his dominate male nature, to be in rhythm and harmony with his male personality and cycles, to be in union with his likes and dislikes, his notions and prejudices; in essence, she had become more of a male in her actions around him, but still she retained those feminine qualities that pleased him.

He had carved out woman in his own image.

An episode would begin, in which her feminine psyche would attempt to expel certain undesirable emotional clutter from itself, a kind of internal, cyclical self-audit in which she sifted through her debris of memory. Some memories she would save, others she would discard, but she needed to rid herself of any perceived poisonous memory that might accumulate in her mind and inevitably bury her. The enlightened male understands this extraordinary occurrence because he himself experiences it in his own unique psyche, and so can guide her through the complex maze back to calm. The brutish male simply refuses her entrance, and this blocking of the exiting refuse will eventually lead to her psychological damage. But if she can dislodge it, she must aim her removed cargo at one she is emotionally involved with.

"Oh, I can't stand the way I look," Oscine said one Saturday morning to Heath; "my hair droops and I have bags under my eyes; and this house is a mess, and you're not helping." It was a gentle, benign pressure-releasing beginning in an attempt to flush out her excess emotional baggage.

"Hey, babe," Heath said, standing in the immaculate, sparkling kitchen, drinking a cool beer, "cut the rambling and fix me breakfast." He walked up to her. "Love you," he whispered, and kissed her soft cheek.

But she wasn't through, as the process was only at the beginning phase where the tempest storm within her whirled and loosened the outermost layers of grit and pain. She frowned. "Heath, I really need you to hear this," she said, "I just don't feel good."

"Babe," he shouted, so loudly that she jumped, "we've been through this female," and here he formed the "talking mouth" sign with his right hand, moving it rapidly up and down, "babbling nonsense before—I don't need to hear it; I mean, look, pop a pill, read a book on women's problems, get your nails done, talk to one of your crazy friends—isn't that what women do when they think they're going nuts? I don't know, but get over it, and do it soon; now, come on, babe," he urged her, gesturing forcefully, "be a doll and get me breakfast."

She smiled, automatically, expelling a fast breath. "Oh, I'm all right, really, don't worry. I'm fine, I just felt a little…"

"Gee, I'm so relieved," he mocked, rolling his eyes, "and honey, the breakfast? Dad is coming over to help with the fence." He smiled as if he meant it. It was all business to him.

She smiled, too, but she did not mean it. She felt the numbness collecting more weight, shoveling her mind and body and soul into a vast and widening, blaring abyss. She felt cold and dead inside when she looked at him. "Yet," she thought, "he doesn't beat me; he works so hard; he's a good provider." These were the very same words her mother often muttered to herself about her own husband when she thought Oscine was not listening.

Madelyn used to say to Oscine, "Quit boasting about what little good is in your husband; don't even evil people do some good? Look at the whole man; judge him thusly." Oscine pondered these thoughts, and she nearly cried as she turned away. "I suppose it will just take time for my love to change him. He's a good man, after all."

She spent inordinate amounts of time at the hospital, for there she could, at least, feel good, supplanting the deep sorrow that had burrowed into her life. Her disease, unchecked, increased its presence within her by minute fractions, disrupting her chores at work but still allowing her to complete her necessary tasks.

Oscine, at work one day, had once again returned from the bathroom, a chore she did twenty times a day.

Abraham Argnine, a doctor with sensitive brown eyes and a slender body and a kindly face that gave no secrets to beholders, observed Oscine with his wistful eyes. "Are you all right, Oscine?" he said, in his gentle tone. "Well, of course you're not." He smiled a little bit to let her know he understood he was touching the periphery of her personal business.

"Oh, I'm fine," Oscine said, blushing a light red, waving him off with her slender, white hands, and walking briskly past him with her sweet smile.

"You're not fine; so, let me help you." He had said this throughout the year, at times when he theorized she was feeling the weight of whatever illness she had but would not tell him.

She felt the warm, long-ago feeling of a man caring for her, and she said, "I have to pick up the kids from school, and then go to my mother-in-law's and pick up a carburetor kit for Heath, and go home and clean."

His face grew sober. "You know, I have never heard of a man having to leave work early and go pick up the kids from the babysitter or from school." He saw the shock on her face at his boldness, and then he steered the conversation away from controversy. "But you said you thoroughly cleaned the house a week ago."

"But we're having company," she smiled.

That night she did not sleep, as she scrubbed the sweat and grime and stain off every appliance and floor and wall. She used the vacuum to suck all the particles of dust off the white, furry rug, and wiped every piece of glass with cleanser; obsessed, she swept through every inch of the place while her husband slept in his warm, easy bed. He slept soundly and peacefully, knowing that his dutiful wife would sterilize the house even unto her own internal physical exhaustion. He knew she would do this to impress his friends and keep up the appearance of a finer palace that no ordinary mortal dwelled in. He also knew such immaculate splendor was a shining testament to his control over her.

Accumulation of dust and dirt, Heath understood, signaled a slippage of his absolute power over Oscine.

Oscine was sick that weekend, but she smiled her radiant loveliness, and all the guests marveled at the pristine conditions of the house and her boundless energy.

"How do you do it all, Oscine?" one of the female guests asked her.

"I don't sleep," Oscine replied, smiling, wearing her pink evening dress and her imitation white pearl necklace. She was in her element, and she glowed with pride, cooing to herself, "This is life." She saw the admiration on the faces of the guests. "Life is good." She uttered these eternal words of blood and life and strife and joy through the vision of her husband, from whom all things radiated, for without him, she was convinced, no good things could exist in her life.

Love

A curious thing began to happen to Oscine when she was near Dr. Argnine.

Just as the first rays of sunshine spread their silky wings and alight atop the frosted jewels of winter, slowly melting away the layers of thick, hard ice that has trapped life in its voracious grip, when Oscine spoke to Abraham or was near him or saw him coming, she felt a streak of illumination enter her heart and settle its magnificent emblem of love into the decaying, rusted chambers of her shrinking heart. These emotions both stirred and frightened her. She did not know what to do but she wanted to do something. She could hear Ellen's voice haunting her: "Wait for the one man and discard the rest."

When they would sit down in the staff lounge and talk about anything or anyone, she could feel his gentleness, his kindness, his great empathy for people who were ill or impoverished or experiencing injustice, and she could see herself in him, she could feel herself becoming him, she could hear herself saying his words and walking his walk and living his life. It was as if, when the two of them sat down next to each other at a conference or stood together at the back white counter and talked of social issues or when they drank tea together and merely chatted about work, it was as if it was not her mouth talking, not her ears listening, not her skin feeling his occasional playful touch, but her heart talking, her heart that heard his passionate words and felt his warm touch; her trampled-upon, scorned-upon, muted and blinded heart that had been buried for so long in the rubbish that Heath had thrown upon it, her heart that had lain smoldering in this purgatory, until now—until it felt the tall sail of a silver ship pass over its flattened form, and now it began to throb and ache and awaken to the possibilities of life renewed; and so it followed the savory scent of this perfumed mast and filled its depth and height and length with marvelous Love, and regained its pulse and regained its purpose and regained its knowledge of eternity. And its final act was to undress itself of past burdens and false claims and old, dried layers of encrusted bitterness, and reach out its delicate limbs that were covered now by freshly woven birth-robes of satin and lace and embrace the mighty heart that sat upon the silver ship. And lo, in Oscine's mind, she and her secret lover—she wearing a diamond crown and he with a crown of gold—sailed away toward the blossoming, ruby-red dawn.

He was the one whom she dreamed of, he was the one whom she thought of and wondered about when she was driving; it was he who she fancied was her paramour, it was him, not Heath, not anyone else she had ever met, not any other man she had ever dated, it was Abraham, it was his handsome face and charming wit and great intelligence that she thought of when she cooked and cleaned and washed and ironed; it was all Abraham, all of him filling her every waking moment and dreams, him, him she imagined long walks with at the briny seashore and on long, leisurely bike rides along gorgeous mountain paths and on summer picnics in verdant meadows; he was above everyone she had ever known, above every friend and relative and family member and even her own children— yea, she placed him in every way on every level on her own emotional and intellectual and spiritual and physical level. She was finally able to breathe as a woman should breathe and behave as a woman should behave and talk as a woman should talk, and it was all because he had allowed her to; for he had transcended time and space and physical boundaries to implant his Love into her heart, and she knew it was no ordinary Love, no Love as begotten by lust and infatuation, but a True Love begotten by honor and fidelity and friendship, a Love that could only have been born and nourished and flourished if she had truly loved him and he had truly loved her. Six months later, even though it frightened her, she now knew she was in love with Abraham Argnine, but she kept it as a warm treasure in her heart, never daring to speak of its inherent dangers to anyone.

"Let me help you," Dr. Argnine said one day, upon seeing her anguish. "I can't stand to see good people suffer."

"Oh," Oscine replied, waving him away with her hands, "I'm fine."

Abraham's nature was such that he loathed seeing anything or anybody suffer. He wondered why Oscine's husband did not worry about her illness. He had deduced long ago that a husband who did not care about the health of his wife was an unfeeling, selfish wretch, and that any man who allowed his wife to slowly drown in domestic chores was a callous, insensitive brute. He did not understand why women allowed men to whittle them down to fragile stick figures who sadly crumble before their time. He would often sit and imagine himself saying to his ladylove, "Your problems are my problems; my problems are your problems; whether we rise or fall, we do so together," and feel great solicitude in his heart.

Abraham understood Oscine because he understood the horror of disease. "Suffering creates real human beings," he used to say to himself while he studied in medical school, as he watched the pretty female students, wearing their cashmere sweaters and fresh faces, flirt with the handsome interns.

"Look past the slender reed to the inner, fertile juices of Love and Gentleness," he would oft think as he watched the young women walk by him. "Am I not close to your idea of perfection? Am I not willing to alleviate your burdens and honor you?" But he soon realized that these women did not want internal harmony or devotion from a man, but external prowess. "It must be in their genetic code," he reasoned, and thus was resigned to the dusty, dry places on the periphery of Love. "But one day I will meet my own kind, and our hearts will recognize each other." Abraham belonged to another group of humans, who owned a singular heartbeat, humans whose eyes were softer and whose heart was bigger, and whose small hands were never quiet as they were incessantly proffering succor to others. Such human beings labored to free people from squalor and from the oppression of tyrants and the furnace of disease, horrible disease whose bony enthusiasm with its sharp steel claws lit into the bulk of Mankind without remorse.

But Abraham suffered from a flaw fatal to men of the twentieth century, to wit: he idolized and worshipped and adored women and elevated them beyond his earthly reach, so much so that now he could not be with any woman unless he was in love with her; yes, it was true, he could not be with a woman simply to wrest physical pleasures from her, as he considered such acts unwholesome and socially unpalatable. And if he was with a woman he loved, he would not lie with her, for he thought this vulgar and liken to the desires of insect and animals. He yearned for marriage and romance and family, and he knew this was frowned upon by modern society, but he could not deny his own moral conscience, and so he waited for a woman who believed in the sacred idea of love and marriage and not just lust and random sexual unions; and so he was consequently shunned by many women who saw him as cowardly and unmanly, and he was alienated by women who scoffed at his idealized version of love, and he was verbally abused by men who thought him too meek to walk alongside their brawny bodies in their brawny shadows.

People who appeared to be of a higher quality of morality, and who devoted themselves to helping others in need, but who also were afflicted with disease, were Abraham's passion. "They are the very angels on Earth," he often said, "who, by their very nature, ask for no help; but by their good deeds, they shall surely receive it." Women who were like this he felt an abiding love for, women like this he loved, a woman like this he wanted as his wife and mother of his children. "I want to help and protect and reward women such as this, good women who understand what life really is and what true sorrow and pain is; I want to know such women and experience their love; it is not the flesh alone, but the mind and heart and soul, as well, that must carry her and the marriage and family."

He loved Oscine as much as he loved the cause of helping the poor and ill, for she was, to him, the symbol of undeserving victim, a victim who was pressed by her own conscience into the service of bringing solace to others. She was the one he had been searching for his entire life, a woman who was totally devoted to the succor of others, unselfish and caring and gentle. He loved her beyond himself.

And yet he knew it was a forbidden love, so he kept it veiled except through his loving manner toward her, where he treated her as if she were his Queen.

Oscine had been married for twelve years now, and she was the mother of three boys whose rise to manhood was questionable if it was based on their being weaned on the shriveled, narcissistic, caustic wisdom of Heath. She watched over the boys, ages eleven, nine and seven, who had the maturity levels of males much younger than they. She sometimes thought she saw the same physical mannerisms and arrogant swagger and disdain for weakness in her middle son that she saw in Heath, and she thought she would go mad if any of her precious boys ever turned out like her husband.

Oscine was sitting at the downstairs kitchen table in the middle of a hot summer night, sipping white wine, feeling the warm, bubbly sizzle delight her dry throat and sink into her inflamed stomach. White, rich, honey-tasting wine soothed the savage beats in her brain and relaxed her and eased the accelerated pace with which she raced through life. At night she could be alone to reflect on the madness that was hers alone, the innate madness born from endless chores and roles and duties and expectations. She would prop up her aching, bare feet on the white cushion that sat atop the bamboo chair, close her tired eyes and let her mind wander; she could not clear away the mangled clutter in her mind until she laid down her defenses and let her thoughts drift through the fierce mania, and then it would begin—she would see it all—from morning till night. The wine was the delivery agent from her woes, though it ultimately irritated her system, whereupon she paid the price for its potent elixir by rushing often to the bathroom and excreting copious amounts of waste. But before this last act she was at ease and not thinking about the strange slippages in memory the disease had newly deposited in her burdensome mind. Still, she was anxious about the lack of physical and emotional discipline her boys showed. During these times she did not think about Heath, who continued to do less while she did more. She labored without complaint, and she still hoped he would somehow decide to help. She did think of a man, though, but it was Abraham the Good and Kind, so noble in his ways and deeds that she loved him as if he were indeed a part of herself. Yet, it was a love she could only sow in infertile ground. "I love my husband," she often whispered to herself. "Things will get better; it will be like it once was."

But the way it once was, this filtered, glorified image of their past, she could not properly see anymore in her congested memories.

And then she awoke in the morning and showered and threw on her clothes and dabbed on her makeup—and sometimes moaned when she thought she looked older than she should—and then rushed downstairs and began breakfast for Heath and her boys, and then she ran to the laundry room and started a load of clothes in the washing machine and then hurried back to the kitchen to fix the food and lay it carefully out on the elegant white-frilled cover on the glass dining table and then rush back to throw the laundry into the dryer and then rush and lower the ironing board and grab the heavy black iron and quickly but efficiently iron Heath's shirts and pants—his mother had always ironed his clothes before he went to school and before he went to work and then ever afterward until he had been married; and now Oscine had inherited this particular sin of her mother-in-law so Heath could feel warm and smooth all over and look professional as he sold cars at the local Auto Mall; her boys would be coming down the stairs now and mumbling about the terrible chore of waking early, and none of them seemed to hear her kidding banter about the joy of an early morning sunrise and birds singing and the glory of a musical silence that pervaded the whole wide world before the mechanical beasts awoke; and then, sometimes, she would think of days that seemed too far gone and a storybook fantasy about a little diseased, flaxen-haired girl who had a special relationship with the idols and inhabitants of Nature, but then she would shake it clear out of her head and continue on with her manic chores and let her mind be sucked up once again into the whirling vortex of a never-ending family life.

Her disease, unchecked, moved onward, as was its practice in those bodies that did not receive the proper ingredients to impede its nefarious progress. The disease moved like an encroaching jungle in her body, steering its entangling yellow roots into the most vulnerable parts of her fragile anatomy; and consequently, she felt herself slipping away at times, falling into this acrid mist that cradled her waning senses in its bloody fangs. She would sometimes think of Abraham, and how her life would be with him. "But I must not think of that, for it is a betrayal to Heath, and besides," she would chastise herself, "it is always so good in the beginning of any relationship—it is all an illusion, after all. It's just something new. If I had married Abraham, it would be as it is now, and if I had met Heath, now, he would have seemed something so exciting and new; no, I must not falter in my sacred wedding vows." And she felt so good and pure thinking such thoughts of rebuke against her fantasies. This was the way, in the beginning, that she convinced herself that Abraham was nothing more than something merely different that would soon, given ample time, become stale and slowly pass away. She liked to say, "Like all things, once fresh," to drown out the echoing words of her sisters in pain, Ellen and Madelyn, whose very memories of rebellion against acceptance of bad marriage tore at her thoughts every day.

Oscine had no long-lasting friends outside her home life, for there was no time except to cook and clean and tend to the every want and whim of her family.

She was host to gala gatherings at her home where Heath proffered his wife as if she were a trophy and boasted of his immaculate, designer home as a reflection of his strong will.

She was nurse at work, wife and fellow conspirator to Heath's every whim, be it in travel or a movie or patronizing business acquaintances. She did it all, willingly, a loyalist to her husband, but her resentment about his refusal to help her in the daily chores and to help raise the children and his continued obstinacy to listen to her woes rose like a fuming volcano whose molten cap grew more volatile every day.

And Heath simply ignored her illness, as if her problems were her own; but, of course, as he saw it, his problems were hers, too.

Love Spreads Its Wings

Heath remembered, like a good pupil, what his father had taught him. "If you give equality to a women, if you treat them as if they are special, if you are nice and gentle, then it is in a woman's nature to attempt to dominate you, and she will sense, with her uncanny, wily brain, a power void. She will resent your benign attitude and even think you are a weak sister; therefore, you must purposely do things to teach her who is in command." This philosophy explained some of Heath's actions, but the rest of his behavior was simply insensitivity, an ideal toward women men have practiced since time immemorial.

Heath simply did less because he could, and she simply did more because she would.

Oscine and Abraham were at a conference in Los Angeles during the horrible, drenching heat of August, and while there, Oscine became ill, vomiting every hour until she was dehydrated and delirious. While Abraham sat at her bedside in her hotel room, she spoke those hitherto unmentionable words that have destroyed civilizations and founded others.

She was pale, her dry, powdery skin chafed, her body feeble, yet even in sickness she wept for others less fortunate than she. "O, Abraham, what happened to the child with the high fever?"

At the hospital he had taken her to, Oscine had managed to talk to a little girl who was sweating profusely as she lay in her mother's soft arms in the emergency room, and had given up her name in the rotation to get the child in ahead of her.

"She's fine," Abraham replied, in awe at Oscine's altruistic nature, and for a moment his visage soured as he thought of her life with Heath.

Oscine, feeling better now, smiled weakly. "You don't have to stay, I'm fine," she said.

"I know," he replied, shaking his head, "but you're not fine, and I want to help you get well—but I do not mean your usual subnormal health. Look, there is some exciting research I am engaged in that might help you." He was nearly weeping for joy.

"You're such a good man," Oscine said, passionately, and she realized that it was the first time she had ever told a man that he was good; and then her mind, without her wifely filter attached, thought aloud, "I love you."

His mind, in flights of wild ecstasy, flushed with the fever of a Fate realized after so long, directed his hand to take her small, delicate hand in his, but he refrained from doing this. "I love you," he murmured, passionately.

Oscine wanted to cry. "What are we going to do? This is awful. I love my husband." She said it dutifully, though her mind was still in a waxen casket of confusion.

As quickly as he felt rapture, he felt it drain away and spill onto his cold flesh. This sharp loss of euphoria excreted bitterness and irony into his veins, and the mixture bled shame into his mind. "But you can't love two people at the same time," he said, numb. This was a predigested and rehearsed speech he had decided on long ago. "If you loved your husband," he refused to say the man's name, "and he loved you, you would wear his love around you, like a special kind of armor, protecting you from all seducers. Temptation can't penetrate True Love."

He made the error of speaking derisively about the incumbent lover, a practice sure to bring him woe, for Oscine, like all emotionally starved women, knew the status of her relationship with her spouse, and now she became defensive.

"He's a good man," Oscine returned, frowning, taken aback by his emboldened speech. If she did not defend her husband, it would have been an admittance that she was married to a bad man, making her appear to be a cowardly wife and a bad mother for staying in a bad marriage. "This is a mistake," she murmured, about to weep—and lately, she was too often about to weep. "We can't be friends anymore."

Such severe words struck him unawares, but her austere attitude was not daunting to him.

"But we mustn't lose our blessed friendship, Oscine," he said, intent still on gaining her love. She reluctantly consented.

Thus began the affair of two human beings who by Fate had been revealed to each other as true soul mates, a singularity as rare as a rainbow cloud.

Oscine's guilt was the engine that drove the relationship.

"You must not touch me," she said one day as she and her beloved stood next to each other in the lounge of the hospital, "it would be adulterous." She wanted his thrilling touch not only because she loved him but because she was physically starved for passion. Her cellular phone, imbedded in her white leather purse, rang. "Hi, Heath!" she said, automatically smiling. "I love you, too," she said, finishing the short conversation.

Abraham cringed. "She isn't aware of his stranglehold on her," he mused, "but how can I walk away from a woman for whom I have waited my whole life?"

They met whenever they could, wherever they could, in parks with tall, dense trees to obscure them, in crowded parking lots, at the top of steep hills, and at the bottom of dirt roads—and here was the first time she allowed him to hold her sweet, slender white hand. He was alive for the first time in his life.

For weeks, despite her weak but waning protestations, they met, allowing their true selves to be expressed freely, without conventional restraints or niceties. They were more in love than ever.

It was on a Saturday afternoon when he heard the most powerful and provocative words yet spoken to him. He answered the phone, and after Oscine explained that Heath and his father were outside working on cars, she whispered tearfully, "O, Abraham, my love, I just needed to hear your voice or I thought I would go absolutely mad." When he was done talking to his beloved, he vowed again never to give up the fight for her.

He began to do everything he could to reduce the tremendous strains that had been placed upon her by her family.

In the fourth week of this strangled love affair, he met with his childhood friend, Eli, a man who had an inherent gift for attracting any female he desired. Eli, a surpassingly virile man with a strong and comely face—yes, the perfectly round head and thick black hair and the deep-set, coal-black eyes and the thick, slightly arched black eyebrows and the slightly square chin—could decipher the entrance code of any woman in a glance, arouse her natural curiosity with a few choice words, successfully court her, and make love to her all in the same day.

"And the sad part is," Eli was saying as he sat next to Abraham in the restaurant, "these women must know I'm just using them; it's a strange thing that somehow they think they are going to be that special one, especially when they know I have been with many other women."

"Maybe they're using you," Abraham said, as an absurd aside.

"Not likely," he said, smiling amusedly; "that isn't the way their minds work; they think by allowing me to make love to them I will love them in return. Most of them are in love with me in a week—and more than willing to have a baby, too." He frowned and shook his head, and a long lock of black, curly hair moved over his forehead. "You know something that is really odd, ol' buddy? Right after I pass my DNA to them, the thrill is gone," and he snapped his fingers, "just like that, it is as if the entire affair was simply the thrill of the chase—that is why I never give up the hunt: only the faces change, but the hunter remains the same."

"But haven't you caught your quota, ol' pal? How many trophy heads do you need on your wall? We mustn't be selfish—didn't your parents ever teach you to share?"

He smiled. "I'll just keep building more walls." He was over thirty years old and full of the male genes of domination and aggression and certitude, a virtual predator in the land of timid, helpless damsels. But what made Eli truly dangerous was the fact that he knew the way the world was meant to be. "Men are supposed to protect women," he said, already finding, by scanning the room, a stunning blonde at whom he could successfully cast his magnetic gaze, "it is up to Man to settle lands, and women, without a good man—why, without a good man, there really are no good women. Look at what happens to women who don't have a man—they run wild." His engaging smile suffused across the room like a hungry shark. "They all need to be mothers." He abruptly abated his effusion of wisdom to explore his new treasure find.

"And how many women have you hurried to motherhood, mister role model?"

"Abraham, such cynicism," he said, still smiling at the blonde beauty. "There must be a pattern in women's brains that looks like me, replete with blinking lights and arrows that point to a sign that says, 'mate with him'! Mother Nature is using me to perpetuate the species; I'm just a one-man biological stud farm to her." He watched with a large grin as the platinum blonde walked toward him.

"Tell her to go back to reading her Bazooka Joe Bubble Gum Cards," Abraham said, sighing, and then watched as his friend and the inveterate trollop exchanged frivolities.

Eli received a phone number from the fluttering little velvet butterfly, and then he looked again to Abraham. "The sacrifices I make for you, old buddy." His wry smile, the smile of the conqueror who has invaded the worlds of both men and women, came on. It was the charming smile of the usurper that lit his face like a runway for women. "Now, where were we? Ah yes, your little dove," he began again, in earnest, and candidly, as it must always be with true friends. "There is a window of time in which to take her from her husband; now, I know what you are thinking, 'But other mistresses stay for years with their man.' Yes, but not your little housewife, she's good for maybe a few months as she is wavering between her no risk, no strife, boring-but-safe marriage, and you. You are an unknown variable in marriage, my friend. This affair is a fuse; it's what is at the end of the fast-burning fuse that counts." He scrutinized Abraham's brown eyes. "You have to do it, boy," and he thrust his hand into the air, just as if it were a weapon. "You have to do it swiftly, or you'll lose her."

"But I want her to make up her own mind."

Eli laughed, uproariously. "Women are to be won," he said, leaning forward, "you make up their minds for them." He said it as easily as if he were telling a known fact.

But then Abraham stated, emphatically, "But they aren't children; I don't want a submissive little peasant girl who stands petrified, her head bowed before the master."

"They do," Eli said as if he knew it were truer than anything he had ever discovered. "They can lie to you all they want, but in the end, they want you to lead, and to lead means you being the master. But, of course, there are different kinds of masters."

"Not with her; perhaps with your cinnamon girls; I want an independent woman who won't put up with a man's authoritative arrogance."

"And Mr. Argnine, what kind of dress will you be wearing when you go to the ball tonight with your master?"

"She is my soul mate, Eli, I can't treat her like a pet. If I want an obedient companion, I can buy a German Shepherd."

"The pet argument is old, old friend, and not valid anymore because you know as well as I do that women who exert themselves do so at the expense of a man's declining power. Two people can't live together and both of them remain co-equal. I'll leave that mystery to God; but in the meantime, you need to act quickly." In his perpetually dreamy stare, certain invisible golden auras radiated out in concentric circles that, once touching the female retina, caused it to become infatuated with his tanned muscles and designer physical features with which Nature had so smoothly outfitted him. Once again, another young vixen was caught in the effulgent flood of his subtle charm, which seeped into women's open pores and planted its tyrannical seed. "Work beckons me, Abe," he said, smiling the white-toothed grin of the insatiable predator. He always called him "Abe" when he was euphoric. "This might be number four hundred and thirty-four."

Abraham pondered this wisdom gleaned from the practical experience of Eli, and he understood it intellectually, but not emotionally.

Oscine would sit next to Abraham in his white sedan and she would simply rest her silken, light blonde hair next to her shoulder and move her head against his to receive what she did not at home: the glow, the warmth, the joy of male flesh. Here, she refueled, felt alive, safe and secure. She knew it had never been this way with Heath, but still she hoped it would be.

In two months, the guilt she felt as she restored the depleted empty stores in her female psyche began to flow like a polluted river into her whirling brain. "My husband is supposed to be loving me," she would think, sitting by herself at her glass dining table, sipping her bubbly white wine, "not him." She began to resent the fact that Abraham filled her heart with gladness, for she felt the adulteress. She bemoaned the possibility that she was a bad woman, and began to search her anxious mind for foibles in her lover so as to abuse him in her thoughts; but, alas, she could not find many. The affair had burrowed deep into those protective spheres that guarded her sanity, and she could no longer reside there, within her mind, for peace, for even there was tumult, and waning and waxing images of Abraham and Heath. Soon, she would have to tear one image down or lose her sanity. "I cannot break my heart in twain; I need absolution. I need release," and she drank until she fell into a deep slumber.

It was Christmas Eve and Oscine was cooing from the rest her mind had received, for her and Heath's family were at her home, a home now joyful and festive, and all the families were marveling at her shining, clean house. "I love you so much," she said to Heath during dinner, he who had slept very nicely during the night while his obedient wife had scoured the house from top to bottom. "Things are good again," she thought as he hugged her, and he then walked away to watch the college football bowl games on the television with his sons and his father. "He loves me," she thought, and as she thought of Heath, she became angry, for she knew Abraham waited for a phone call from her. "He's invading my private, decent joy," she raged, internally.

She was enwrapped in the illusory web of family unity that was spun only through festive times, a fact she ignored to preserve her hopes of future harmony within the family unit she so craved. She did call Abraham the day after Christmas, and her wrath was flamed by his eager voice. "You know, I can't keep doing this; I love my husband."

Her words shred his joy. "But I must say something," he thought, "and nothing to upset her."

"But darling," he said, aloud, "I know how difficult this is for you."

"Oh, do you? If he ever found out about this I would kill myself. We can't do this anymore. I'm sorry, it's over. It's best that we never see each other again."

"No," he said, pleading, "don't do this, Oscine, we love each other; you can't love him."

"How dare you tell me that?" Her voice charged at him like a battering ram.

"You're right, but let's think about this, let's talk; we can't just destroy everything. It's not like we have committed adultery." This had always been the unspoken glue—the fact that they had not engaged in adulterous conduct—that kept the affair from finally slipping away.

There was no talking to her that day, for that day she was discharging all of her emotional waste onto him, the only man she could empty her full bowls of wrath upon, the only man who would allow it, the only man who had ever truly loved her. That moment, all of her confusion and pressures and burdens and bitterness surfaced, and he took it in, gorging himself on its hot breath and fragrant liquor. He begged and pleaded and nearly wept to give their relationship more time, to which, in the end, she agreed, though not before condemning his show of weakness, and stamping the inscription, with her thick and nasty vehemence, of "wimp" upon his vulnerable forehead. She said that he was indeed timorous compared with Heath, who would never have allowed her to treat him so.

Abraham attributed all her emotional upheaval to the unbridled terror of her situation with Heath; alas, he did not yet understand fully the psychology of the female mind, and so he retreated in his manly nature during this attack, creating an artificial territory upon which she might settle, an unwanted trespasser into his private sanctuary of manhood. "I must make allowances to ease her burdens," he reassured himself.

She, conversely, while talking to her secret lover, loved Heath, and hated Abraham, and then reversed her positions, changed direction again, admitted to herself that she loathed Heath but wished he would be more giving, admitted to herself that she loved Abraham but wished he was more like Heath. She desired that Abraham would take her away, by force if necessary, from her captor, and was so intoxicated with his sweet, gentle love that she was ready to abandon even her own children.

She shifted once again and wanted to cleave Heath and Abraham in two and devour them into her widening mouth and give birth to them and raise them to be who she wanted them to be, but also that she would be their masters. She felt persecuted, enchained, unloved, used, scorned; she hated, she idolized, she wanted to kill, she wanted to flee and hide and run about and have affairs with any handsome man. In the end, she let Abraham continue the masquerade, even though her mind was erupting with high degrees of consternation and madness. But, when the day was over, she did feel better, having regurgitated all of her wailings and horrors onto poor Abraham's head, where it would lie in decaying heaps until he knew how to properly dispose of it.

Dissolution

Oscine read magazines, written exclusively for women, that contained articles primarily for married couples. She wanted to explain her affair, to offer excuses for difficult periods in her marriage. "It doesn't mean you leave," she reassured herself, reading an article by a female who had the all-important "PhD" next to her name. Oscine sought to drown out the bitter words of Madelyn, "it won't get better, he'll never change," and the dangerous prophecy of Ellen, "don't be satisfied with losers—go through them as if they are scalding water through a paper cup; you must search until you find the one. Do not make just any man the One; for goodness' sake, girl, go until you find him and then experience real love, experience the miracle. Don't believe all this 'old-age-man's-world' philosophy that says Woman must stay with her man to the end and sacrifice everything to keep order in the world. Go find the new man; do it, girl, be strong!"

"They're all so wrong," Oscine said, lying upon her queen-sized bed, which was covered with green silken sheets, and as she looked up at the oak-wooden-framed pictures of her family in the hallway, she felt a warm feeling of love and unity in her breasts. "I'll make my marriage work; it's up to me. Heath works so hard. After all," she giggled, "we women are smarter than men on matters of the Heart." She was enraptured with the idea of one man and loyalty to him, forever. The notion of fidelity to her husband in the midst of temptation imparted pride to her feminine heart. "I'll fight for my man," she vowed, weeping, "he loves me so; I'll make things better, I just know it."

She labored harder than ever around the house, driving the yellow sponge deeper into the white tile, scrubbing harder against the grime, and being more vigilant than ever against any dirt or stain that appeared. She fixed more elaborate meals for her boys, planned family gatherings and read books on improving communication with one's spouse. As she surveyed the results a month later, she was more exasperated than ever, for she had failed. "Why, it's like pushing a boulder up a mountain every day, only to have it roll down again—my men are supposed to hold onto the boulder at the top," she thought, watching her boys eat at the dinner table. "But why won't they?" In the midst of her gloom, she thought of Abraham, with whom she had barely kept the affair going, he who had seemed already to possess the traits she desired in men, he who had vowed to alleviate her burdens. "What is wrong with him? He can't be a real man, to want to help me with so much—to even help me with my chores; to think like that is just not right!" But then her anger turned to Heath, but was bounced off his virile, stolid, intractable male flesh, and it landed on the sweet, sensitive, caring image of Abraham. "It must be Abraham's fault this isn't working; I can't think straight because of him."

Abraham bought Oscine gifts, helped with her duties at the hospital, worked with her on a college course she was taking, bought her books on the identity of Woman, and gave her nutritional and health advice on her illness; but it was all to no avail, for she resented the fact that he was not her husband.

"It's over," she said, that dark day inside winter's frosty cloak, "I can't see you anymore. I love my husband. What are you waiting around for, anyway? How dare you?" she said it to his face, right there in the car, in the cold, cruel rain, but he couldn't see the outline of her heart.

"But we love each other," he protested, passionately.

"Oh, that doesn't matter; these things happen. I'm transferring to another hospital." She spoke of her leaving with such a severe disruption he did not fully comprehend it at first. He sat motionless for the longest time after she drove away.

Weeks later, Eli sat with a sorrowful Abraham, and when he spoke, his voice was comforting, yet strong. "You simply cannot be passive with her; you can't treat her as if she has the mind of a man. I'm not saying that to be unkind to women; what I am saying is that she needs to be won, as I have told you. Look here," and he knit his black, thick brows, "remember Rudolph Valentino? Women loved the way he swept them off their feet, the way he was forceful with them—they love that; you must not be some sweet, gentle man all the time, because that will only hurt you."

"You want me to be something I am not," Abraham said, melancholy; "perhaps I am a genetic freak, destined not to mate."

"No, you can change," Eli said, so assuredly that Abraham nearly believed him.

"Maybe it is men like you who re-populate our species, and men like me who die off because no woman will have us."

"Don't be ridiculous, you can have plenty of women, but you can't sit back and wait; you have to adopt a new way of thinking concerning females; in love and marriage, you can't treat them like your best friend, believe me."

Abraham, doctor of internal medicine, placed his head onto his folded arms. "She is my goddess; I worship her; how can I hurt her?"

"The worship phase is useful when you discover the idea of woman when you are sixteen; women don't like the worship part when they are mature adults. Abraham," his words were no longer tinged with male power, "you must take charge, wrest her away from her husband."

"And have her condemn me later? I would rather she decide on her own."

Eli frowned. "You'll wait forever," he said, shaking his head; "you have to decide for her, and she'll thank you later. You must lead."

And Abraham did nothing but wait, and soon Oscine was away from him, but he distinctly remembered what Eli, the veteran of romantic affairs, had said on the topic of Love, "Believe me, as long as she loves you, and you love her, it will never be over."

It made no sense to Abraham for a woman to love another man with all of her heart and not love her husband, and turn away from the man she loved. "Perhaps if I were in her situation, I would do the same; certainly it is a difficult situation." He wanted to understand, and so he began to talk to other women, and to read many books on the secret lives of women. In the meantime, he wrote her many love letters, begging her to preserve their beautiful friendship, even if it meant to erase their love affair.

Eli, upon hearing Abraham's latest ideas on the affair, pronounced gravely, "That is all well and good, but you can't be friends with someone you were involved with and not show love to that person."

Abraham did not understand such wisdom, for he was limited in his experiences with women, and so he pursued Oscine's friendship until, quite unexpectedly, he won it back.

Abraham and Oscine once again met, in secret, the only way she could with a man not her husband, and they talked and laughed and celebrated their blessed friendship. They avoided past talk of love, and they both played the same game of feigning a casual relationship.

Oscine was now studying to attain her Bachelor of Science in Nursing, and Abraham, seeking to relieve her burdens, became her partner, helping her research and write numerous term papers.

"I think I would go crazy without your help," Oscine said one day, glowing as she looked at him as they sat in the medical library. Her burdens had increased once again, but, as always, Heath had not increased his percentage of duties.

"You would make the perfect husband," she thought, watching him as he walked up the aisles, "so caring, so kind, so gentle," but then her internal conflict came to her, and she felt the confusing thoughts overwhelm her, and so she shut her eyes to block them out.

Three months hence and her classes were complete, Abraham's good deeds for this task were done, and Oscine was more bitter than ever. "Why," she thought, "he isn't my husband; he should be, but instead I'm living with this bully who watches me disintegrate every day while he and his equally brutish father play with their idiotic toys."

It was a Sunday, and she was serving Heath and his father glasses of cool lemonade on a warm afternoon, all the while oozing a pleasant, robotic smile.

"Love you," Heath said, taking the glasses from her the way he would from a maid, without looking at her. But he had spoken the magic words, so, to him, all was good in his kingdom.

"And I love you," she said, smiling brightly, thinking all the while that Abraham should be here, her rightful soul mate, her passionate lover, a man who would be a good father to her children. She condemned Heath for being a selfish boor, and Abraham for being too timorous. "Abraham should rescue me, can't he see that? But I must stay married to my husband." She thought of the scandal of divorce, the financial woes, the lack of the natural father for her boys. "But I don't care; if he would just come; O, why won't he come? Do I have to tell him these things?" And later she wept bitter tears because the men in her life continued to fail her. She felt as if she had been born to suffer.

The next Monday, Abraham called her, for she had called him on Friday, and he enjoyed hearing her sweet voice before work.

"What do you want?" she asked, disapprovingly, holding her cellular phone at work.

He frowned. "Just called to say 'hello.'"

"Well, I'm sick of it; you're harassing me."

"What?" he fired back, as if her accusation had been shot at a mountain of rock, causing an avalanche of incredulity.

She was condemning his phone calls as worthless and tiresome because she wanted in its stead action, but would not, out of pride, say this. "You heard me; I keep calling you every morning to stop you from calling me." She wanted him more than ever, if only he would be strong; if only he were aggressive, she would leave everyone and everything to be with him, anywhere; but he was listless, and she had to punish him for this unforgivable transgression. "I love my husband," she uttered, which was the greatest lie of her sad life, for she loathed Heath with every inhale of his unrestrained effrontery, and with every exhale of her scorn, she hated him more. But she would not divorce Heath unless he had committed adultery, and she would not be defined as an adulteress, forever tarnishing her image—an image that was meaningless if she was unhappy, a fact she did not yet understand. She was about to weep.

"But what about your illness?" Abraham said, strongly. "It would be immoral of me to stop trying to help you, now."

"It isn't your concern; Heath looks after me," she returned, coldly. This was simply another lie—Heath accepted her disease as if it were simply the way things were.

Abraham hated hearing Heath's name, and especially now, for he knew she did not love him. "If he loved her, he would not rest until she was healed of her disease," he often thought.

"I won't call you anymore, then," Abraham said, numb, suddenly weary of the complexities of the affair, "but I want an explanation one day."

"Maybe," she returned, uttering that infernal, disturbing, nebulous word that females keep in their arsenal of verbal mayhem.

Thus, the affair of friendship ended, and the two were sev-
ered from each other like a united mind losing those thoughts
that once gave it solitude.

Abraham had no malice directed toward her after she
had abrogated the love affair, for he reasoned that he could
not cite her for being honorable to her husband and family;
but now, his bewilderment began to produce shoots and roots
that sucked nutrients in undesirable soil. Her angelic, shim-
mering vision had been anchored in his mind by his faithful,
unselfish, pure love for her, and when he thought of her, he
could only think of this sublime figure; but now, a stealthy,
cunning, dark shadow began to creep in.

"I need to talk to her," Abraham moaned, a week later,
sitting on Eli's silver sofa, his head buried in his open hands.

"You're in emotional pain; you're like an addict abstaining from a drug, and the worst thing you could possibly do
is have some," Eli said, holding his small glass of fine liquor
as he surveyed his friend's slouching body. His countenance
became one of compassion, a rare phenomenon for a man who
devoured women much as a hurricane devours a soap bubble.
"If she loves you, truly loves you, she will call you back. You
need to wait, which is easy to say and hard to do; believe me,
I know." And he did know. "If you call her, you'll just make it
worse; even if you get back together, it would fall apart because
you initiated the return—you see," and he was deep into his
philosophical harpooning, formed from the bleached bones of
those corpses from dead relationships, "she cut you off, so you
must not come back first, that would make you even weaker
in her eyes; no, my good friend, you wait, and if she loves you,
she will come back to you."

But Oscine did not call, and Abraham was as if one dead,
his heart stripped of its glorious armor. He sought refuge, but

found none, for his confused thoughts murdered him fiercely; so, he continued to read the collection of books that purported to explain the complicated workings of the female psyche. In the meantime, a piece of deceit fell onto his lap, a residue from the blood wound in his heart, and it began to grow, like a poisonous weed, behind the measureless community of mercy her divine image generated.

On the one hand, in which her glorious image resided, he tried to understand women; on the other hand, in which his reverie dwelled, he sought to quench his pain, and this he did, in its infancy, by questioning the legitimacy of her actions. Each side grew fiercely, each attempting to slay the other with no little humor.

Freed to be in Prison

Oscine, freed from her relationship with Abraham, tended to her family with an unbound zealousness, creating a world for her boys and Heath that existed only in those fables and myths dreamed of by the worst of unforgiving men.

Oscine became, in truth, a domestic and entertainer to her family, not that she wasn't already, but now she magnified these roles more than ever. For her boys, she cooked the most delicious meals, cleaned after them, played games with them, did their chores, took them to their favorite places, and bought them what they desired; and for Heath, she was in total obedience, cooking any meal to his exact liking, not complaining about anything he did, acting interested in all of his banal talk, keeping their home the way he wanted it, and agreeing with any view he expressed regardless of its absurdness.

And in the end, the boys and Heath said nothing, but simply accepted it all in stride, and she glowed, because she knew they had to love her because she evinced so much overwhelming love through the sacrificing of time for their every whim. She pampered them yet demanded nothing except their love. But, they said nothing, and nothing changed, nor did Heath say she was beautiful or smart or hardworking, nor did he release his iron grip on her whereabouts, nor refrain from frowning intensely on any excursion she made from the house while alone.

"I'm not a prisoner," she would tell herself, sitting on her closet floor, shaking her blonde head to and fro, as she looked through her island of shoes. "They just love me so much they want me here with them all the time." In her slender, blonde hands she held those sacred documents, extracted from the inside of some of her carefully hidden shoes, which caused her breath to become deep and luxurious and surging, sending a sweet fragrance to her emotionally starved heart.

"Dearest Oscine," Abraham had begun his words of passion to her, dozens of long, sensual essays expounding on their fated, eternal love. Here, fondling his love letters, she held onto her sanity, and she felt truly a woman, not an indentured servant to her cruel masters. She thought of her childhood and searched for happier times, but sorrow consumed her. "You were born to suffer, Oscine, it is the Fate of all women," echoed in her tormented mind. It was only when she was alone that she could speak to her real identity, to reflect upon her role as female, mother, wife, cook, nurse, seamstress, daughter-in-law, aunt, neighbor, friend; in it all she seemed to be lost, as if she had tumbled into a thick, abandoned mine in the deep recesses of her soul. But even in this comforting reverie, her disease, its gnawing strength growing, would not relent; indeed, she was getting sicker more often, and it was becoming more and more of a nuisance to Heath. Even now, she had to abruptly abandon her fortress of solace for the quest of the ceramic chambers of the bathroom.

Heath walked in, he who was supposed to be on a flight to another city, far, far away from the danger of Oscine's readings, which she carefully planned whenever she was absolutely certain he was miles and miles removed; nevertheless, he was in the room now, and she was, although emotionally distraught at this, certain that the letters were stuffed deep, deep back into their narrow and dark, dark protective shelters.

She was wrong.

Light and Dark

F ermentation is a strange yet necessary act of nature, for, in the end, it changes things, with results that are good or bad, depending, of course, on the perspective of those things involved.

Allow an array of weeds to grow within a bed of delicate flowers, and watch—as they grow, they slowly tunnel their way to domination by stealing the plants of precious sunlight, water and nutrients.

Now, plant a seed of poison that ferments in the mind of a human being whose heart has been boiled in grief, and whose mind is smeared with the sticky pap of disgrace, and the boundaries are endless, the potential destruction unlimited, the results beyond reason.

Abraham lay for days in a melancholy swoon over the loss of his beloved Oscine. He worked long hours at the hospital and every glance upward toward the door, or every look at the back of a blonde female, caused his heart to leap at the anticipation of her; but she never came, never came back as he reasoned she should have, never ran down the hard, white-tiled, glossy floor, crying and then leaping into his arms and he just standing there, holding her fast. No, it did not happen minute after hour, hour after day, day after week, week after month, and still whenever he looked up he expected to see her beautiful form coming gracefully toward him with that indefinable and inexpressible look of soul love.

He drove around to shops and stores and parks, hoping to see her, but he did not; he would not go to her house, though, for he said, most emphatically, "I will not be the stalker."

More often, he lay in dark seclusion at his house and mourned the loss of his sweet angel, whom he still adored. Her image was still sacred, she was still without sin in his mind; she was still a glorious image wrapped in a translucent halo as he yearned for her and imagined her and reached out to her and cried for her and dreamed of her; it was what he wanted, now, the romantic image of the lost true love, and he knew that their love was true and that she was still dying for him. "We are lovers kept apart by destiny," he would lament, lying as one dead on his tan sofa, and desired to weep to seal the glory of his forbidden love. Yes, he secretly desired this forbidden love; yes, it was what he wanted, it made him feel as much a man as any man, that such a fine woman would dare to love him while being married to a man who would look down upon him.

But then the realization that she was never going to call or send a letter began to haunt him and he found himself surrounded by grief, and the romantic images floundered and began to splinter and peel and reveal a darker and more sinister picture therein. He began to analyze his relationship with his lost love in every minute detail, to rationalize her seemingly insensate actions, to fantasize about her behavior at her home during their affair, and he began to look at her from every point of the compass, and to see through her and into her heart and clear through to her soul and imagine what it was like and what her heart was like and what her mind was like, and he began to imagine what she thought about and what she was thinking about now, and how she had truly felt and how she truly felt now; and lo, he began to create her in his own image according to his own limited construct of what he knew of her, and for every new idea about her he now formulated her image according to his reshaped idea of her, so that what she once was as a person was gone; so that she had become another person whose prior and present actions and roles and behavior were dictated by selfish and shameless gain for her family.

It took months but he finally created a living, breathing Oscine doll that would fully explain all of her inexplicable behavior during their romance; so now, for everything she had done that he had not understood, he could activate this living creature and program it so that it gave him the proper reasons for improper actions.

"How could she say I harassed her?" Abraham mused, sullen. "Is the woman mad?" This pronouncement of accusation, even quizzical, was the first such aspersion he had cast against her intemerate, ethereal image. "What did I do but treat her as if she were a goddess? And she spat upon our friendship, even with no love quotient in sight; did she do it to spite me? May it never be! She loves me still, of this I am certain. But did she do it out of bitterness because she could not have me?" He mocked her. "'I love my husband'…what are you waiting around for?" He draped her crumbling image in foul slander. He brooded on the undeniable fact that she had eliminated their friendship. "And for no good reason," he sneered, "she used me and cut me off." He suppressed the notion that it was all because of the great conflict in her head. "She used me and treated me horribly; she didn't have to betray me; and upon me, who treated her better than any person in existence, she heaped her disgusting bile." Poor Abraham did not understand that he was the only person upon whom he could deposit her excess emotional baggage, that she had to divest herself of all her toxic cargo to survive. He let his righteous indignation flourish against a mute defendant, Oscine, and an evil portent sat itself upon his head, like a black cloud, promising absolute victory.

To assuage his emotional pain, it was necessary to increase his discontent with the way he perceived that she had shamed him. He thought of little else except the sinister elements of her charade, which he clothed in wicked dress. "Instead of reciprocity toward me, she scorned me; she isn't a nice person, no; I can excuse her stopping the love affair—ha! Some affair!" But as the months went by, and her image melted into the black cauldron in his mind, even the forgiveness for abating the affair evaporated.

Yet, he still sent her letters of friendship, also pleading to let him help her heal from her illness, and at such times he was magnanimous in his forgiveness toward her in his mind, and stated that he was willing to take her back if only she would communicate with him in some way, if only she would send him a letter or give him a phone call or come by the hospital just for a moment; but no, she refused him, she rebuffed him, she shut him out, ruthlessly and utterly, and he did not know why and so it crushed his heart so completely that he could finally descend to the next level of bitterness.

Thus, his heart, having been lacerated and bruised and beaten by unfulfilled love, conspired to negotiate a path back to the light of romance for him, and this was easily done on any good summer day when the weather is hot and the women are plenty and the golden rays of the sun reveal their curvaceous shapes, therein; he saw so many beautiful women who were not Oscine, so many available women who had not her face nor figure nor family, that his heart leaped at the tingling thought of mining such an open treasure box of dazzling flesh. It was finalized in his brain and announced in his heart that she was dead and her sisters around the world were alive and willing and ready to be captured by a man who previously was frowned upon by men as weak, but a man who had indeed captured a sublime creature, and this transferred great confidence to him and he stood up taller. He began to physically condition his body, and noticed that women began to look his way. "Yes," he thought, looking back at these fascinating creatures, "soon, soon…" But in the meantime, there was still some tearing down of her sacred image while building up his own.

"The woman is not a good person," he mumbled to himself, massaging his black, curly hair, "she needs help, that one." Contempt, brother to hatred, incubated in his combustible brain as he still read the books that explained why men and women act and speak as they do. "Too late," he would whisper, reading treasure maps to the psyches of the sexes. "Women's minds have been opened to me," he shouted, "I will soon be their master, as all men should be of all women."

Abraham would soon unlock the secrets of the female mind; but for only one gender of the human species to understand the other's actions would be like fixing only the minute hand of a broken clock: the one hand would be correct and always working, while the broken hand would be right twice a day. But he no longer cared about such progressive niceties.

The Way Out

"I never would have hated her if she had not terminated our friendship," Abraham said to Eli, handing him the books he had mastered in the past six months. "Women use men because they know men need them, and so they prostitute themselves to get things they want from us because they know we hold the money and power; it's a game: men use women, women use men. And is anybody ever really happy?"

This exalted idea of bliss between man and woman had been violated in Eli, not only by his friend's sudden descent into depression but from his own failings with a woman whom he had truly loved. He said, soberly, "This is a natural course you're assuming, it's a safety device to block out the pain; believe me, in a few months you will be back to worshipping women, like me."

"No," Abraham said, his visage hard and blank, like stone carved from cold, harsh, grain-filled winds, "this will never end. They say people don't change, which may be true; this is simply the real me, uncovered by the treachery of Woman— they make the real man, you know," he said, as if he truly meant it. "I wasn't real yet until they completed me; this should happen to every man when he is very young."

"And if she called you right now?" he asked, as he had done many times before.

Abraham's face contorted into a malevolent mask. "Not a chance," he replied, as then stated, as he had many times before, "in fact, I would enjoy it so I could tell her to go away." But this time, he paused and reflected upon his words. "It's been too long; I know her, she will never call again."

The phone rang.

Abraham's callous righteousness became an easily extinguishable vapor, and Eli could see Abraham's face, as well as his voice, soften, and gush maudlin pap, as his friend whispered into the phone, "Hi." Abraham's wounded heart miraculously healed because of the luminous sparkle that elicited from the sweet voice of the woman on the other end.

Oscine called to thank Abraham for his hard labor on the essays for her classes; but no, she would not weaken and continue their relationship. The charm of the metamorphosis in Abraham's countenance continued even after she bid him farewell.

"What a mistake," Eli said, "to call now."

"Yes, I suppose so," Abraham said, timidly.

Abraham was in such emotional pain that he would have accepted her back, even then.

"One day you will not be so susceptible," Eli thought; "wait for that day and know true hatred." He picked up the book of psychology on men and women. "How could these books possibly enlighten me? What troubles have I getting dates?" he mused.

The next day, Abraham, weakened by Oscine's unexpected assault upon his hardening defenses, began to speculate on the nature of her phone call. "Is she still in love with me? Of course. Did she want me to say that I still loved her, or that I was still her friend? What does she want?" He wrote more letters, glorifying their special relationship, praising her, but not writing about their past love. But he received no reply, and again he felt the weight of injustice fill his mind like a dark cloud. He begged to forget her, but thought of her always, when awake, when asleep, when happy or sad, in victory or sorrow, in crisis at the hospital, in attendance at festivities, while watching lovers, while breathing the precious molecules in the air she may have exhaled. She was ever omnipotent in his mind, her angelic image resting silently in his benighted mind.

"Why, I shall drive out the one image with the many," he thought to himself after concluding the twentieth book on female and male psychology. "I have the match now, and I have only to light the fuse," he said to Eli, months after Oscine's last phone call.

"So, you will understand women, but they will not understand you," Eli said, frowning, "just a dog on a leash."

"No," he responded, quickly, and with great certitude, "a very obedient dog on a very tight leash."

"Yet, still you grieve."

The visage of his friend was unmoved, as if the heart that operated upon it was enchained by ice. "Grieving can be assuaged by pleasure."

Eli shook his head. "What about the women you are going to use as therapy?"

"You're humoring me, of course; you, who have been with, how many—over four hundred women?"

"Ever since I lost Charlotte and I began to use other women to forget her, I began to think about how they must feel after they knew I used them."

He frowned, heavily. "Let's see—thirty-five years old and developing a conscience? How quaint, but as for me, I am trying to dismantle mine. It is rather burdensome to have a conscience from the beginning because it compelled me to treat women right, and look where it got me; but now, I am in devolution; now, I start anew, climbing down the lofty tree of the moralists to join my brother savages. But," he pointed to his library of books on female and male psychology, "an intellectual savage, the most dangerous kind."

Although Abraham, intellectually, had resolved to use women for his own sordid devices, his heart was not so easily absorbed by this idea that was antithetical to him, and the result was that the first three women he dated, he respected, and he began to have feelings for them and to treat them specially, all the while practicing his newfound methods upon them. However, as they, each in their own way, attempted to control him, he gained more power from his bitterness against women. "Why, they merely think me a plow horse, something to use—but no, that is the receding shadow of the weak fool they are glimpsing."

And so, after setting free his female lab rats, he began to prosper afresh, and began to manipulate, as well as exercise, his natural dominance over women, and in return, he laughingly told Eli, "They exercised their natural submissive nature, and I merely turned it on, like it was a master key in a rusty lock; I give it a few shakes, used some gentle force, and, there you have it, a simple theorem proved."

Eli frowned and shook his head, thinking of days past when he fashioned a conscience out of the copious tears of his female victims. "And who could tell me I was wrong?" he mused. "Even now, I am not certain if I was in error; after all, these women have free will in these relationships; it isn't like we're forcing them to acquiesce to us."

Women Women, Everywhere

I t was with Rebecca, a young nurse, an educated woman, a diamond-studded, candy-coated, honey-sweet vixen, that Abraham began to flex his shiny, new, pink male muscles which resided in that peculiar region of his mind known as the power arena of aggression and domination.

"Rebecca," he said, standing next to her on a warm, April night, when the great expanse of silky clouds drifted about in a silvery moon bath, "you look so incredible tonight; I don't want to take my eyes from you, for fear that I might not behold every moment of your luminous beauty." He watched as she gazed into his dark, hard eyes, watched as she grew limp in his strong grip—a deliberately strong grip, one he readily applied because he knew that evincing a kind of physical prowess was part of the process in winning women over. "Follow the steps and they are mine," he thought, "connect the dots and you complete the circuits in their brains that disable their common sense; why, they fall in love with any fool who deliberately or accidentally fills out the cryptic order correctly.

"The secrets of a woman's universe hath been revealed to me," he mused, watching Rebecca glow and purr with contentment. "I am certainly their master, the riddle of the centuries mastered in a mere span of time. Ah, science! I hail thou, thou art our true god on Earth." He smelled the sweet aroma of this physical perfection of a woman, and saw the peaches and crème complexion, the silky smooth, slender figure of tender flesh. "It seems a lifetime ago that I would have been actually frightened by her sublime appearance, as if she were, indeed, above me; but now I know that all women are a treasure with certain inherent traps within, and whoever can decipher these snares and reach the highly valued prize that resides within her heart tastes the fragrant juices of union with her. I now have the pick of the elite litter, for no woman is above me or beside me; nay, they are below, far below, like strange, confused creatures who wait for someone to solve a rudimentary puzzle even they don't understand."

The recital of the formula was the same for every woman he met, no matter her social status, education, career, past or present conditions, appearance, wealth, age, marital status, geographical location, color, creed, religion, or intelligence. "It is a master key that unlocks every woman's vault of secrets," Abraham often thought, smiling like a very greedy child in a very large and sumptuous store of diverse sweets.

"Oh, Rebecca, you're so absolutely beautiful today," he said, kissing her luxurious, chestnut-colored hair with complete conviction, thinking all the while that it was hardwiring her brain to love and serve him. "You must," he thought, massaging her slender shoulder, "praise those things they consider virtuous, and spend inordinate amounts of time complimenting things such as their hair and nails and consideration of clothes, and you will continue to carve your initials into their walled fortress of love."

"You're so sweet and loving," he said, and then he proffered reasons to her; otherwise he knew the praise would be vacuous and apt to bring doubt from his little dove. "You're so intelligent and clever," he continued, and then dissected several things she had told him about her job as a nurse, and built up her behavior and action at her job to make her seem more cunning and astute than she was. To consummate this flood of good feelings he gave her, he put a string of imitation pearls, not the best luminous white eggs of the oyster, but those created artificially by forcing a foreign object into the poor creatures' homes while they reside in large vats of water. "Her neck will never know the difference," Abraham thought, thinking of the future. He once told Eli, "I like these cultured pearls because they remind me of people: shove something that naturally irritates a person down their consciousness, and they might, after ample suffering, produce a magnificent pearl; reminds me of myself."

Abraham now had five such delicate beauties like said pearls on a short string. "I have no more time than that," he thought, listening to Felice on the phone, whom he had named, in his secure, shadowy mind, as "number three." She continued to dislodge the content of her feminine mind onto his eager table. "I listen," he mused, "and know when to comment, when to offer advice, when to be silent, when to simply say, 'I love you.' It's quite odd, really; it's like programming a fembot," and he chuckled, for he had just said to her, automatically, "Terrible, how awful for you," when she had decried how her boss had ill-treated her. "I'm a clay maker," he continued to muse; "it's too easy, really; I step hard upon the pedal, and the clay I mold goes one way; I step softly, and it goes another way. Volatile clay never feels my master hands; truly remarkable."

His empire of women began to encroach upon the territory of Eli, an occurrence hitherto considered impossible by the latter, who said one day, while observing this phenomenon, "The balance of Nature has been forever upset, and there will be furious repercussions as She rights herself."

Oscine of the Sorrows

Oscine was looking in the bathroom mirror, which shone like it was newly installed, and she noticed, for a brief moment, how old she looked, and then she sat down on the pristine, white ceramic toilet with the polished, varnished, brand-new-looking wooden seat. It was then that Heath walked into the room.

"What a mess," he said, looking at her disheveled shoes in the closet.

Oscine, attempting to distract him, began to talk of other things. "Heath, oh, I'm so sorry you missed your flight, darling; I'll be right out, Heath…oh, tell me what happened, won't you, dear?" She felt perspiration flooding her flesh and smelled its waxy, foul, yellow scent as silence greeted her for two full, agonizing minutes; and then Heath came into the bathroom, his meaty face blazing like a red fire as he pounded his hulking form up to Oscine, who shrank away from him in terror.

"Whore," he yelled, and taking her straw-colored hair in his right hand, dragged her off the toilet to the closet, and threw her into the bulk of the shoes. "Adulteress! You wicked woman!"

She was still trying to pull up her white slacks, still conscious of her dignity.

He had never used violence upon her, and he didn't particularly care for it unless it was absolutely necessary, but now he wanted to use it on her because his obedient indentured servant had displeased him, and because the violence gave him over to a sense of sensual pleasure to degrade and humiliate her as she pleaded for forgiveness. In fact, the more she pleaded for forgiveness, which, to him, admitted guilt, the more intense his pleasure to punish and debase this woman who everyone thought was so innocent and pure and loving. He wanted to rub her nose in her sins just the way a master rubs the nose of a newborn kitten in its own misplaced excrement. Heath was still training Oscine and he was about to become her absolute lord and master. He sensed this and it stimulated him to punish her without boundaries. He knew that now, guilty and imploring mercy as she was, she would take punishment without complaint, no matter how full of animosity and shame it was. His father had raised him well.

Oscine's mind was shaken and placed upside down in a black, oily fog, hearing eerie, accursed noises and promises of destruction, and she felt fear creep through her every pore onto her wet, tingling skin. In the language of this tribulation, she formed only one message, "I love you," but she didn't mean to address Heath, but Abraham, whom she prayed would appear at that very moment to rescue her. "I love you," she whispered, again, to Abraham, as she crashed against the cold skins of the shoes. Her brain externally sought to appease the monster who owned her ill flesh, and so she said, again, "I love you," but this time meaning Heath, yet he never knew the distinction. Abraham would have discerned which declaration of love was for him, for he truly loved her and knew her thoughts and ways; but Heath, only living with her and not loving her, could not distinguish it any more than a stranger could distinguish between a set of identical twins.

"Shut up, you harlot," Heath cried, and he threw the passionate letters on her trembling body.

Oscine's instinct for survival in the marriage prevailed and usurped the ebbing cry of love for Abraham. "But I didn't do anything," she wept, "I never committed adultery." She tried to look at him, but turned away to shield her eyes from his accusatory scowl.

"You cheated on me! And I've been faithful to you all these years, never complaining about your illness or your frail body! I've turned down many women to be loyal to you! You, you filthy whore!"

She felt the urgent compulsion to divest herself of waste, a matter she had never completed in the bathroom. "Please, Heath."

"Don't say my name, adulteress."

"I have to go to the bathroom," she begged now, as if she were a child again and talking to her vengeful father.

Heath gesticulated about the place. "Everywhere you go is a toilet, so," and he spat on her, "go here," and he stood guard over her until, squirming all the while, she let go. She sobbed like a trapped, wounded animal. Disgust lay like vomit on Heath's face, his visage screwed up as if he breathed the vile fumes of it, as if he felt its wet, dark slime on his crawling face. "You soiled yourself—good," he said, sneering, "now, you wear your shame for everyone to see."

Feeling emboldened and totally impervious to sin, Heath grabbed his wife's sweaty, matted hair and pulled her along the fine, crisp, clean fibers of the silver carpet and down the long and torturous stairs. Oscine was sobbing and pleading, "Please let me explain, I didn't do anything wrong; forgive me; O, I love you."

If she could have produced proof positive that she was innocent, that would have mattered nothing at all to her master, for the letters were the excuse he finally needed to own all of her and smash the last bit of womanly resistance to his male dominance. Now he would live, he reasoned, as his forefathers had, with women not merely in a willing abeyance as it relates to power in the home, as they sometimes were, but with women in total subjection and harmony to his andro-centric universe.

Heath released her from his grip as he sat on the fine brown sofa with the lustrous shine, and she lay sprawled before him, and then he excitedly ran to the backyard to summon his little men. The thought of leaving Heath right there and then did not occur to her; to leave and avoid more shame, to avoid the evil augury her feminine intuition prophesized, to join Abraham, never entered her mind; for in her swirling thoughts was the idea to resolve the misunderstanding and to make it all work because of all the time she had spent with her man and her precious children.

Her image as revered and suffering saint dangled like prize game on a sharp hook, rotting in the hot, smoldering sun. Her mind began to shift into the mode that activates survival in a marriage. "We've overcome worse," she thought, shaking, her head bowed as she sat in her own stinking excrement. Her beloved boys, whom she had raised, walked in. "They love me, they'll understand their mother," Oscine whispered, and she was raising her head to repeat it when her master shouted a harsh order for her to avert her eyes in the presence of men, an order she quickly acquiesced to as she lowered her trembling head.

"Boys, behold your mother, the queen harlot," Heath said to them, mocking the designation "queen" that Abraham had used so often in his letters. He began to strut around the room, reading the love letters to them. He then took a dictionary from the dust-free, mahogany bookcase and read aloud the definition of "harlot" to his bewildered children.

Oscine's children, her boys, truly her sons, for she had attempted to raise them in her own image to be gentle, kind, selfless and forgiving beings who cherished the light and hated the darkness, saw a mother sitting before them as if she were a very naughty child who was being severely punished by her parent. The youngest one began to cry when his innocent eyes began to take in the full picture of the hallowed image of his mother: for her silky, golden crown of delicate strands was soaked in perspiration; her body reeked of the acrid scent of sweat produced during fright, and her white slacks and pink pullover top were streaked with wet and brown stains. Her entire fragile body trembled, her slender legs knocked together, her small hands twitched, her head bobbed up and down. Then there was the horrible stench of the fresh excrement wrapped in an aroma of shame that spoke horrors to her little worshippers.

She looked like a prisoner of war, thoroughly beaten, and then threw up her pleading arms toward her smallest child as he ran outside.

"Your mother had an affair, boys, she has been making love to another man, like a prostitute," he said, smirking, and he commenced to dump an inordinate amount of verbal sewage upon her person through the base and profane description of the sordid lives of prostitutes and easy women.

"But I never did anything wrong," Oscine protested, summoning all her strength in a meek reply.

"Shut up, whore," Heath returned, shouting directly in her bowed face as he bent down, "when you're in the presence of a man." He stood up fully erect, feeling every bit a man, as much a man as his father. His chest heaved, his breast swelled with pride, his crimson face flushed with the sinister ambitions of conquest. "There are going to be some changes around here, boys," he cried, walking about like a general, "from now on, she," and he pointed to her—with an outstretched arm that was more like a sword forged and sharpened on the murdered images of women past—and then shouted, careful not to say "mother," "is your servant."

Oscine whimpered as if she had been kicked in the stomach by heavy boots. "But this isn't right," she whispered in her thoughts.

"We give her orders, boys; we," and he shouted, "we are her superiors, lords and masters! All men are superior to all women!"

"But that's not true," Oscine thought, who really couldn't think in a coherent manner but managed to direct a few ideas into clarity. "I've worked hard to make my boys gentle; aren't they gentle? Heath, why are you being so contrary? Why won't you let me explain? I must look horrible to my precious darlings. They will understand after I explain, won't they? If I had a daughter, she wouldn't betray me; no; she and I would be friends." For a passing moment, too brief to be able to form in her spinning mind, was the vapor trail of that idea whose origin was long ago, that of a shining, esoteric creature whose noble face seemed chiseled by the hands of God, a savior who would rescue her from stress and woe, cure her pains, calm her fears, cradle her in his strong arms to protect her from all harm. She thought of Abraham, good and kind Abraham, who was the only person alive who understood her and was willing to make her happy; and then all of it was quashed, just as if it had no real foundation at all, for its base was made of dead dreams and loose sand.

"I love my husband," she reasoned, "I'll make it all work out. I hate you, Abraham, you're so weak." She tried to weep but her face felt so cold and her thoughts so distant that she could not summon the absolving agent. "My head feels like it weighs so much," she mused. Her head was numb, her thinking numb, her heart numb, her love numb.

"Ethan," Heath commanded, feeling very much a leader now that he had absolute power and obedience over all of his family, "get up, boy."

Ethan, the eldest, who possessed a cherubic face and a kind disposition, a child who could not even, not too long ago, find the proper venom within himself to punish a wasp that had stung him. He had cried when the wasp died, and now he was forced to stand before his mother, whom he idolized, and mock her in his father's image.

"Slap her, boy," Heath commanded, and banged his hands together so hard that Oscine's entire body jumped. "Let her know who is the boss; put her in her place, now; pay her back for all the times she wouldn't let you be a man. Go on, do it, boy."

It was impossible for Heath to impose his will upon the boy, for a continuous, solid, luminous mural of reverence for his mother lit his heart, and he could not, by any command, hurt that which he was nurtured on. Consequently, he began to weep, and he ran upstairs to sanctuary.

"You made the boy into a sissy," Heath grunted, and then looked at Wyatt, who was age ten, the middle child, "come now, Wyatt, show your father you're a man now and teach this slut a lesson; you do know what a slut is, don't you, boy?" And then he expounded on the abhorrent word, going into absurd, hyperbolic language about the life of a fantasy whore, and then he raged on with a sooty stream of unprofitable maledictions that painted Oscine to be a very busy prostitute who ate fresh, pink babies. "Do it, boy, slap the harlot, but good."

Wyatt was the child born with a unique set of characteristics resistant to his external environment, traits uniform in their grand goal to terrorize all things smaller, weaker, and more vulnerable than himself; consequently, Wyatt had given Oscine her daily grief. Oscine, sobbing now, so helpless, so loving in her countenance, looked up at her precious boy, and then, with a malicious face smeared like fresh blood from a fresh kill, he reared his hand back and slapped her tear-stained face with a great bang. He watched in ecstasy as his mother did not scold him nor promise him further discipline, but instead she continued to cry, and so he slapped her again. A huge grin of revelation was painted large upon his gleaming face, and then he began to laugh hysterically as he slapped her again and again, and he felt the power of control over another human being flood into his tiny male-dominant-aggressive brain.

"Good boy," Heath cried, slapping the boy on his shoulders.

Feeling the pride of his father instilled in the boy through the condoning of this aberrational act, Wyatt, his brute's brain now activated, spat largely into his mother's shamed visage. "Whore," he yelled, disgusted, and slapped her hard again.

"I love my husband," Oscine thought, "I'll make this marriage work."

The Temptress

A week later, Oscine remembered waking up while she was vacuuming the house at the end of a six-hour cleaning session. She, for some inexplicable reason, sat down next to the phone, while the boys were outside playing football with their beloved father, and she called Abraham.

"Hi, it's me." She always began conversations with him in this way, finishing her first words with a soft expulsion of breath and a pleasant smile.

Abraham spoke to her as if he had never hated her, and indeed, he never had, for his had been only a false hatred to protect his wounded heart. "Hi, how have you been?" His voice was joyous and free of resentment. He would have taken her back without hesitation or conditions or discussion.

To be in Love, sayeth the philosopher, "surpasseth all things, and the need to Love is cleansed of all obstacles by the desire of that Love."

Her voice was sweet and whispery. "I just wanted to thank you for all your help on the exams. I just passed my last class. I couldn't have done it without you."

"Oh, how wonderful," Abraham returned, "and I just guided you, really; you're so smart. I'm so proud of you! Your family must be so proud of you, too!"

Her family was not proud of her, any more than a master would be proud of any slave who achieves some grand distinction the master does not care about. Heath never understood Oscine's career choice to be a nurse nor her obsession with helping the infirm and the elderly. His reply to her news a month ago that she had passed these tests was dipped in the stagnant pool in his brain wherein resided all things self-serving: "Does that mean more money?"

Abraham and Oscine talked as two lovers talk who are hiding their love from listeners, each afraid to speak what their hearts felt.

"May I see you again?" Abraham asked, like a boy after his first date.

"No, I think it's best this way."

"How about if I send a letter?"

"Maybe; well, yes."

The conversation ended with a small patch of hope for Abraham, and indeed he wrote many letters of friendship, always threatening himself to write a proclamation of love to her. "But no, I gave her my promise not to speak of it again," he thought. It is true, to keep their friendship alive, he had promised never to speak of their Love again. "She must be able to rely on one person in this world who is honorable." And so he kept the letters of passion in his wooden desk, unsent for now.

Oscine waited for the love letters, every day watching for the mailman, trying not to evince too much excitement as she walked hurriedly to the mailboxes in her lounge at work. She was disappointed when no love letters from him came, happy but sad when she read his friendship letters, and in time, bitter, when she realized no letters would ever come. "Doesn't he know I am waiting for him to rescue me? Must I tell him everything?"

In public, Oscine and her family played the game of harmony to perfection, and no one would have speculated, even for a moment, that she was their willing slave.

"Oh, women are much more assertive now," several of the nurses at the hospital would say upon discussing such horrible topics as the "old days of repression" with Oscine.

"Today's modern women would never put with the way men treated women long ago," said Cynthia, one of the youngest nurses, "and you know how bad it is in some countries, where they openly beat their wives and where wives cannot leave their homes unless accompanied by another man; what suffering these women endure, silently; why, they must be going mad."

"How horrible," Oscine said, refusing to think that she was like these women. "I feel so badly for them," she thought, and she nearly wept because she felt the pain of these martyred women.

"And in America," said one of the nurses, a young woman who had a sharp mind as well as a sharp-looking face, "men use their minds and mouths as whips. It is all the same."

"Oh, Clarisse, you're so cynical," said one of the older women at the round, wooden lunch table.

"No. I just know human begins, and strong men exploit weak things—like animals, the land, weaker men and weak women."

"But not me, she is not talking about me," Oscine mused, looking at Clarisse's knitted brows, "she has obviously been hurt by men. I just need to work harder with my boys, and soon, everything will be the way it used to be." Yet, it was never the way it used to be, for she had drawn in her mind a past with Heath that had never existed.

At dinner that night, Oscine served her children and Heath a scrumptious meal at the dinner table, walking back and forth from the kitchen, and by Heath's orders, she was unable to eat until the males had quenched their appetite. It was one of his ways of separating her from the boys, and already, three months after the discovery of the love letters, Oscine noticed how Wyatt had begun to pull more away from her.

"Oh, it must be because Wyatt is nearly an adolescent," she would think as she watched her boys go with Heath on another outdoor adventure, this time an all-day event while she was left to concentrate on cleaning and laundry for the men of the castle.

With this goal in mind, she felt secure and had an easy direction to go. "With success easily attained," she thought.

In her mind, having been given a task to be fulfilled, she expected a reward, and in this case, forgiveness and better treatment from Heath.

A month later, it was autumn, and the idea of a cyclical change of color, and the passage of living things falling to a state of abeyance, the movement of life to warmer areas, the somber mood of Nature, the anxiousness of human beings to ride the crest of ebb and flow, pervaded every molecule and thought and gave excuses for new things, new directions, new ideas and new beginnings.

Oscine came home late from work on a Thursday night and upon opening the door, heard the comfortable laugh of a woman's voice, and immediately her female intuition burned the thin thread in her heart that rested upon the delicate hook that hung from the flame of jealousy.

"This is Vivian," Heath said, sneering; "she is going to stay with us awhile." Wyatt had a rapturous smile carved on his radiant face.

"Oh," Oscine replied, aware of her new role as compliant wife in all things, "is she a relative I have never met?"

"No," Heath said, unashamed, "she is my mistress."

Oscine's face flushed a nervous, disturbing pink mask as she shook her head. "Now wait a minute, I don't..."

"Hey," Heath shouted, rising quickly from the sofa, watching Oscine drop her head obediently, "you don't have to understand." He walked up to her and cried, "You will treat Vivian with total respect, and if you don't, you're out. Understand?"

"Yes," she said, trying not to weep.

"I was thinking," Vivian said, she who was ten years younger than Oscine, "we should like breakfast in bed. Wouldn't that be yummy, Heath?"

"I like that," Heath said, turning toward the deep-black-haired beauty, and turning back his attention toward Oscine, he said, with authority in his thick voice, "Now, go to your room, the spare bedroom, and don't come out until I call for you. The boys and I have some things to discuss with Vivian."

That night Oscine had to endure the noises she considered so egregious coming from Heath's bedroom. At two o'clock in the a.m. she was sitting quietly, like a mouse, in the kitchen, with only the silver moonlight streaming from the window to show her how much red wine to pour into the crystal glass so it would not overflow.

"And you're a lush, too," a voice interrupted Oscine's reverie, "so it is amazing that you held onto Heath so long and kept this house barely acceptable to live in." Vivian stood behind Oscine, adorned in Oscine's white negligee.

Oscine turned round. "How dare you! I work hard at keeping this house very clean, and who do you think you are, coming to my home?" she returned.

"Who do I think I am?" Vivian said, laughing, standing next to her, her slender arms crossed over her fabulous figure. "I'm sharing your husband's bed, that's who. You're a loser, girlfriend, and you're old and sickly and you lost your man. Put me out on the street if I wind up like you, an old hag before her time."

"Is that where he found you?" Oscine said, emboldened by the alcohol.

"No, but that's where you'll soon be—know why? Because you don't know your place, and I know mine; and, by the way, the only reason I don't call Heath right now is because I don't need him for everything, like you apparently do," and she laughed as she knocked over Oscine's glass. "Now, clean this mess up, drunk," she sneered, "he said you're like an automated machine—one spill and your program compels you to clean without question." She watched as Oscine sponged up the mess, and then said, with sufficient scorn, "How pathetic. Is this what happens when you get older and desperate?" and as she turned away, she said, eerily, "And I like your older boy, too."

"You leave him alone," Oscine nearly shouted, still on her knees, trembling from rancor.

"And what," Vivian said, standing still, but with her back to Oscine, "will you do, you lush? Tell on me? You're on your way out, sister," and she walked back to her new room in her new house wherein resided her new lover.

"It's not right," Oscine whispered, lying in her new bed that night, "she shouldn't be here; but I brought it upon myself by being so wicked. But isn't he doing the same thing? Oh, he can't mean it; but he is—no, he's trying to make me jealous; he's testing me. But what if he isn't? Should I leave? What will everyone think if I abandon my children? Will my boys come with me? What if Heath tells everyone about my affair? Oh, it isn't right. Abraham, where are you?"

The next morning she heard the bell that Vivian rang at seven o'clock, and Oscine, having not slept, was knocking at the bedroom door, carrying the simmering gourmet meal on the metal breakfast tray, a meal she had prepared from a list Vivian had left for her before Vivian retired to bed the night before.

"Breakfast in bed," Vivian said, excitedly, lying next to Heath.

"Where is the smile?" Heath demanded, sitting up.

Oscine smiled obediently and watched Heath taste the fresh eggs and whole-wheat toast with the sweet butter and marmalade. "Good, you did good, now go." But before she was gone, he said, sweetly, "Love you."

"And I love you," Oscine said, turning, as if, for a moment, it had all been a terrible nightmare.

Vivian started laughed, hysterically. "She's pathetic, Heath; she is just like a trained dog; no self-respect at all."

Heath, irritated by Oscine's whimpering countenance, motioned for her to go. "Get out, go, go away—go clean, adulteress; go, go—shoo, shoo." Vulgar laughter stained the door as Oscine closed it behind herself.

In a moment Oscine was in the bathroom, gushing waste into the toilet. Her illness had increased in its relentless, gnawing ferociousness. She felt as if she were going mad.

The next morning Vivian rang the cute gold-colored metallic bell, and when her maid-in-waiting did not appear, she angrily searched the house, but gradually her wrath subsided, as she thought she had already driven out Oscine; but her anger quickly returned when she realized she would have to assume the duties Oscine performed; and so, when she found Oscine outside, she was relieved, but then she cried out, "Heath, come quickly." There, amongst the splendid garden of pink Icebergs and a rich trove of multi-colored roses, Oscine sat, with five birds, of snow-white- and cherry-red- and deep-blue-colored bodies, sitting upon her shoulder. "My goodness, Heath, she's a nut," Vivian said, incredulously. The boys peered out of the window, and shame burrowed into their hearts, and they felt more detached than ever from their mother, who seemed so weak and frail now that she seemed useless to them. Wyatt openly mocked her.

"Oscine, get out of there, you little fool," Heath shouted.

Oscine, sitting in her own excrement and urine, and wearing her white robe, seemed disoriented; indeed, she did not remember how she had come to be there.

She was thirty-six years old, now, and that night, on her birthday, a day no one cared to remember, except Abraham, who sent her a card, Oscine lay in bed, trying desperately to sort out the rambling chaos that brewed in her mind. "Where is he," she whispered, weeping, "where is he? O, how I have waited."

The next day she was sitting in her car, in the park where she used to meet Abraham, and she was staring at young couples strolling arm in arm under the tall elm trees. "Are they truly happy? Or is it all an illusion, a brief interlude, a fancy never truly realized?" The conflict in her head concerning Abraham, her boys and Vivian, and whether to leave or stay was smothering her. She thought of her disease, her inability to focus her thoughts as of late, the bouts of blackness where she awoke hours later without memory, and she felt that going insane might be a more honorable resolution. She felt in her feminine soul that all of these woes were amassing for one final push of her consciousness into the yawning mouth of that dark leviathan, the utter monolith of hell that is the slipping away from reality into a cold, distant madness. Every day she felt her frail grip on sanity slipping through the weakened barriers in her mind, and she could not impede its progress.

She felt quite the martyr.

Together Again

E li walked into Abraham's house, only to find his friend sitting in the collapsing, sooty darkness, engulfed in a dreary gloom, his face expressionless, his eyes staring at an unearthly picture no one else could see.

"The hospital called me to find out why you didn't come to work," Eli began, somewhat irritated that his compatriot could not let lose the emotion of the past.

"I saw her," Abraham said, as if dying, "I held her, and still I am stone."

"What?" Eli said, bewildered that Abraham would see her, and that the elusive paramour would manifest herself in his presence.

"I told myself I didn't love her, that I hated her and I hated all women because she betrayed me, and as long as she was out of sight, I was not to be undone in my vow to exploit women's weaknesses; but then I saw her in the park, and I am all undone. What is this thing, love? It haunts me, it burns in my brain like an eternal fire. What good is love if its end is not just? Men search the world over for love when they would be better to marry a peasant girl and hear nothing but the wind brought by her low bow."

Eli stood still in the cool darkness, knowing that his silence was his friend's best ally right now.

"I did not mean to see her, certainly, as I thought I had successfully driven her out of my head, like a nest of vipers smoked from the attic," he cried, holding tight his throbbing head.

That day in the park, Oscine had been sitting in her car when she beheld, to her utter astonishment and dismay, Abraham walking in front of her, to which she shook her head to admonish herself of the consequences of his discovery of her; but then he turned his head and saw her and held fast to the sunburnt sidewalk, transfixed.

All of his sinewy manifestos against her memory, all of his sweaty, violent tirades against her deeds and inaction now dissolved when he saw her beauteous image there. He could murder her character only in her absence.

"Hi," he said, softly, betraying all of his passionate vows never to speak to her.

"Hi," she said, smiling, as if they had never been apart.

"May I sit with you, mademoiselle?" he asked politely, as his newly christened persona of the aggressive, dominant male slipped into a monk's humble sackcloth.

"Of course," she said, without hesitation or worry.

"I want you but I don't want you," Abraham mused, his mind all asunder; "don't think," but then he decided, quickly, "it only ruins you."

He wanted to tell her how much he had hated her and how he had tried to forget her but how he had dreamed about her and thought about her all these last days, every sable or bright morning, every bright or sable night, only her, no one else, everything else rendered meaningless, and in his transcendent dreams only she, she above all others. "Don't think," he raged, "just feel."

"I love you," he said, with passion and urgency, "I love you; O, how I love you, Oscine."

"I love you," she said, before her mind could object.

They embraced each other and did not speak during the greatest moment of their tortured lives, for they felt complete, meaningful, alive, when all had seemed irretrievably lost.

Oscine had been starved her entire life, for physical affection and love and attention; she yearned for a man to tell her she was smart and beautiful and capable and clever and good. She was emotionally starved and she was dying, dying because she did not receive something so basic as the touch of a husband for his wife, the touch of affection; she was truly dying—but no, she was dead, numb without the soft, gentle touch of her lover, and her heart was cold and sterile because of the grey, dead color of her flesh and the lack of verbal passion that could infuse life into her.

Heath purposefully accelerated her premature internal death.

Abraham was the only man who had ever offered her true love that sought to appease all of her needs—physical, spiritual, emotional and intellectual.

When she held Abraham, she felt womanly, truly a woman who was doing as Nature intended her to do, he being a man who adored her and yearned for her and protected her.

"I want you, now," Abraham said, speaking from the raw, exposed insides of his heart, her head snug against his now-brawny shoulder. "I need you to live; I am the walking dead without you; let's get married, Oscine, my love, let's begin to live. You know we need each other. Oscine, I love you like no other man ever could because you and I are the same. O, Oscine, for you I would gladly die."

She loved him, dearly, truly, passionately, loved him as she had loved no other nor ever would love, and she never wanted to leave his warm flesh and good and loyal heart. To go back to the rusty slums of her home, where in a deep, desperate dungeon her shriveled heart lay, was unimaginable.

"No," she said on a sudden, her female intuition bursting forth to rob her intellectual champion, common sense, "I can't do this," and she pulled away from him, shaking her head, her long, blonde hair brushing against her flushed face.

"I love you, and you love me; this is right," Abraham protested, frantic now as he felt his emotional grip on her fading.

"That doesn't change things; I'm married," she said proudly.

His voice was saturated with the blood of despair, and he fought everything he had learned. "You love me, not him; he will never change, and your love won't change him."

"I love my husband," she replied, defiant, desperate to believe in the blessed institution of marriage.

He became aggressive in all manners he despised. "Your husband is a human monster, he uses you. He doesn't love you any more than he loves his precious cars. He offers you nothing but misery; to him, you are a slave. Set yourself free, Oscine, be strong."

"Get out," she cried, not wanting to hear the truth from him, "you don't know Heath. He has good qualities."

"Even evil people do good things, but they're still evil; why are you punishing yourself? Why?"

She felt a shudder as he said this, for Madelyn had said the same. "I'm sorry, but you need to go; somebody might see us. I would kill myself if Heath found out." Her face was crimson with trepidation.

His countenance was grim. "You're throwing your life away."

"Go," she said, shaking her head, about to weep. "I'll make it work. What kind of world would it be if every time a marriage was in trouble, the couple divorced? How horrible! No, I won't do it!" She sat fully erect, her head held on high.

He looked at her for the longest time. "O, Oscine, don't you see," but his words became gentle, "we're our own world. You are your own world, and when you meet a man, you create a world with him, a special world, and the outside world doesn't matter anymore; and when you have children, you create a truly special world; but, O my precious Oscine, when that world collapses forever, you don't stay in it, buried, you get out; you survive and rebuild a world with someone else until you build one not on a foundation of sand but of rock, and that rock is love." He looked at her with all the love in his heart. "We could have been truly happy together; you and I could have done what few others have done: we could have achieved true bliss."

"Please go," she said; her eyes welled up with the pain of regret.

"I will go, forever; I will go," and he kissed her on her smooth forehead. "Once, this kiss would have protected you from all harm; now, it is the kiss that leads to an unjust death, our love; and still, I would wait for you forever because no earthly thing can separate those ideas destined to find each other's heart." He turned away from her, not once looking upon her trembling form. She did not cry, for she felt so numb with uncertainty and confusion.

"I must make my marriage work, I must; Heath loves me," she thought on her way home that night. "Things have to get better; he's just testing our marriage. He doesn't really love that woman; he's just punishing me for my wicked affair. He's right to punish me. I've been so bad."

She walked into her house full of contrition for the past, and full of boundless love and hope for the future. "My love will win them back; I will show them what a good woman's love can do," she vowed, looking for them, nearly singing their names. There was a noise coming from Heath's bedroom, human voices emitting profane sounds and fury, and when she opened the door, she beheld a scene that gashed her gentle spirit. She stood there like one dead as she saw but did not comprehend, for her mind had changed the particulars of the scene of acts of carnal excess Heath and Vivian and their female guests were practicing. "Ethan," Vivian called loudly, "come to me, baby."

Oscine lost her senses.

"How dare you," Oscine cried, "with my baby?"

"Come and join in," Vivian said, pleasure dripping from her sweaty face, "come and see your boy become a man," and she gestured to Ethan, who had recently come downstairs and now stood outside the door.

"Where are Wyatt and Luke?" Oscine screamed, holding her head, as if to prevent her surging thoughts from exploding. Her chest heaved as she walked in, horrified, looking frantically about this den of iniquity.

"Another year for Wyatt," Vivian said, smiling foolishly.

"Get out, harlot," Oscine shouted, shaking her head in shock.

"You should talk," Vivian laughed, "pot calling the kettle black."

"Ethan, you shouldn't be here, baby," Oscine said, her face ashen.

"Mother, how could you allow this wickedness in our own house?" he said, full of anguish and sorrow.

"Ethan," Oscine said, not hearing her son, "are my babies here?"

"You had better leave," Heath said, standing now.

"I want my babies," Oscine said defiantly, "I'm their mother; how dare you!"

Heath shook up his male indignation and leaped toward her with a promise of violence. "I haven't beat you, yet," he said, his hot breath on her, and then he abruptly slapped her, and waved to the participants of this vulgar scene. "All of this is your legacy, you filthy whore."

"Whore," the participants echoed.

Oscine stood firm, yielding nothing, as the image of her blessed children loomed in front of her.

Heath, his countenance now tender, suddenly smiled. "Oh, honey, you've come through. I was just testing our relationship; I just lost my head for a while; oh, sweetheart, everything will be as it once was. Oscine, darling, I love you."

Oscine hesitated for the first time in her career as his handmaiden, stepping back in obedience to feminine instinct, although her face evinced receptivity, and said, in profound revelation, "You're a liar—you're crazy." And then she stepped back, looking at him as if for the first time, as if all the images she had seen of him and stitched together in her mind until this very moment were false; as if right now, here and now in this house of suffering and sorrow, her good heart had unmasked him and could see past this artifice and into a small, petty soul that was a cesspool, a structure willingly and happily built to harbor any kind of residue and repercussion that fell from his freely executed will, that being: he had greedily and happily collected the rot, the dung, the waste of human failure to be good, and had fed off its nutrients and allowed it to replenish his heart and mind with its unnatural tenets.

"A few moments," Heath had earlier mused, "and the little fool who can't say 'I hate you' to anyone will say 'I love you' again; my father was right when he said 'a woman without a man is like a runaway horse: put a horse to a cart, and the horse slows down and has direction and discipline and obeys; so it is the same with women.'"

A knock at the door interrupted this drama, and soon Oscine was opening it, only to see a uniformed man standing before her, to which she blushed deeply, and began to babble to, insensibly. "Oh, officer, I assure you, it isn't what it seems; you see, these people are not welcome here." She wanted to bring the man in the dark blue uniform into the house, but she also wanted to stall, hoping that Heath had heard this and the illicit performers had clothed themselves. But more than that, she wanted the officer to arrest Heath, yet she thought of Ethan, and so she hesitated. "And what of my reputation?" she wondered. "And O, Abraham, we will be so happy together;

you were so right, we were meant to be together. Soon, my darling; and p.s., my darling," she smiled, inwardly, thinking of the postscripts he so cleverly attached to all of his love letters. "You were right, Heath is a bad man." She was as happy as she could ever hope to be, for it was the beginning of a new life, and her savior had finally come.

"But it isn't about a party, ma'am," the officer said, solemnly, "it's about your two boys." Oscine's heart abated its happy chorus. "There was an accident." Oscine's face blanched with an eerie mask of painful, hurtful horror as she began to scream, shaking her head violently. "I'm sorry, but both of your sons, Wyatt and Luke, were killed in a car accident."

Oscine's brain no longer perceived those things in the world that did not relate to her precious children, and she was striking Heath, spitting, wailing, running about the house babbling insane epithets, gurgling like a madwoman.

For three days she was committed to a place where people go to rest their swelled, boiling brains.

And the boys were not even dead. It had all been a hoax.

Darla

"So," Eli said, after Abraham finished telling him what had transpired at the park, "it is over, once more."

"I offered her everything she needs to be fulfilled, and yet she goes back to that loser; why, why do women think they must be such martyrs?"

"Forget her, she's had her chance; weak women are a burden on a strong man if you care for them."

Abraham lifted his head, sorrow upon his weary face. "What are you saying?"

"I'm telling you to get a woman you can control completely, and be done with it; they're the best kind; they serve you well, they know their place and they cause minimal stress for you."

"How can I marry a slave after I have tasted real love? I loathe men who subjugate their wives."

Eli smiled. "You've been doing it for months, and believe me, women need it; they're happier being told rather than leading, and they're not being a slave, they're just being who they are."

And so it was, as Abraham embarked once more upon a crusade to romance every woman he desired, and to treat them according to the dictates of his research, which provided invaluable insight into the female mind, allowing a man like Abraham to secure the keys to women's closely guarded modus operandi. His attitude was brazen with these lovely women, his intent plain and bold, and they did not seem to care as they bowed their heads in servility, even nurturing his arrogance the more he treated them with authority and discipline.

Abraham was buried in this avalanche of ripe beauties who were bursting with enthusiasm to gain his love. "It's all so pathetic—why, they're all still little girls playing with makeup," he mused, thinking about it all as he checked his list of potential mates. "It's like breeding pedigrees; and to think, I was once in awe of such women," and to this reflection he laughed loud and hard and long.

So it was that he selected the finest and youngest of the breed, a passing-fair lady with intelligence and common sense, a companion, a mother for his future children, but not a woman he could love. "Love is an aberration," he concluded, "when you love, you hurt someone; this way, with Darla, I will treat her civilly, nothing more, nothing less." Yet, his casual plans could not be executed if two people were to simply live together. He was married three months after he had seen Oscine in the park. "Goodbye," he said to Oscine in his benighted mind, unable to speak her name, "stay with your man; let him take care of you; let him worry about you and heal you and protect you."

A few weeks after his wedding, he was in his house, sitting on a black stool, watching Darla faithfully mowing the lawn in the backyard, when the phone rang.

"Hi, it's me." It was Oscine, sweet and gentle.

For a moment Abraham's insular, muscular fortress erected against her memory weakened, but then quickly strengthened itself. "Hello."

"I just wanted to tell you why I acted the way I did in the park."

"Not necessary," his voice was cold, and he looked at Darla. "Good girl," he whispered.

"I've been thinking about us," Oscine said, her voice quivering. "Us?"

"Yes; look, I understand why you're still angry, but I want you to know that I'm ready now."

He sneered, as does the hunter whose long-sought prey suddenly capitulates to him. "Revenge upon thee," he grumbled, though he loved her still. "Ready?" he said aloud to her. "For what?"

There was a slight pause, a barely imperceptible break in the response time that only he could detect. "You love me, and you want to marry me."

"You're a married woman, and to a great man, might I add," Abraham said, innocently, "you love your husband, as you should."

"You're hurt, and I understand that, but you can forgive me. I was confused."

"You're still confused," and he paused, savoring the rich, perfumed aroma of inflicting pain upon her who tormented him. "I am married," he said with joy, imagining the weighty impact of the revelation exploding in her mind, "and I love my wife." He cherished the very saying of the words to her, but, concurrently, he felt ill to his stomach. "You betrayed me," he raged, internally, "and then you want me back; well, it isn't that easy. You hurt me, and now I will—no, I must hurt you."

After the dreadful silence, her wounded voice, failing now, began, "You promised me you would wait, forever."

"That was before you terminated our love, and now our friendship. You threw me out of your life in every way. That wasn't right."

Darla called to him, asking him if he wanted a cool lemonade.

"Is that her?" Oscine asked, feigning interest.

"Yes, it is," his voice was bitter, "and she adores me and appreciates the fact that I care for her in so many ways. She got tired of the Heaths in the world."

"I made a mistake," Oscine said, weeping, choking on regret.

"Yes," he replied, softly, "you did; now, go back to that wonderful man of yours and make it work."

"But I think there is something wrong. Heath is up to something."

He loathed hearing Heath's name, and that was sufficient impetus to terminate the call. "Just remember, he loves you so. You love your husband, remember?" and as he set down the phone on the receiver, the world seemed smaller to him. "Phones aren't right; they should make people talk in person," he said, closing his eyes, his mind all asunder.

Darla came in, she who had a master's degree in education, she who taught high school English, and who was very glad to be obedient to her man as long as he did not physically beat or verbally abuse her. "Hi, honey," she said, kissing him on the cheek, "was that the hospital? Someone sick?"

"Yes," he said, numb, "someone very sick."

"Oh, how awful; well, I hope they get better. Lemonade for my husband?" It was still that fresh part in her marriage where she loved to hear the word "husband" fall from her pious, pouty lips. It gave her direction and identity.

"Oscine, why so long?" he mused. "Yes, dear, thank you," he said aloud to Darla, and it sounded so false to him, he winced. "Oscine would know how false I am with Darla," he mused. "Darla, you poor, pathetic woman; the right man could love you, but you sold yourself for a man with security; to you, I am a feudal lord for whom you debased yourself. It is always the same."

Abraham now understood women better than nearly any man and most women, and yet, despite this privileged knowledge, he let Darla slide down the same old abyss Oscine had traveled with Heath. His crime was that he knew when Darla needed him, and yet he often turned away from her.

"I could never love you," he would say to himself later, as he watched her emotional state suffer, "you are ordinary, and your fate is to serve man, head bowed, three steps behind him. Perhaps only those women who find their true love can truly be loved and treated right."

Going Away

Oscine woke up in a white room that was reserved for those select few whose brains have left their homestead without a forwarding address. She remembered nothing except that she had had an eerie, foggy dream that she was living in a universe where men ruled women with their explicit permission.

The doctors were observing her with care, for they had been apprised of her recent disturbing behavior, which had worried her family, and so she lay sedated for three days in the white-linen-covered bed.

"I'm fine," she said to the nurse, after she found out why she was at the hospital.

The nurse assumed that anyone who came here was guilty. In that respect, she was like a judge in a courtroom. "You're here to rest, dear."

"But I am a nurse, too," Oscine said, bewildered, "I want to go home by my own will."

And so it was that she went home, only to find all of her boys alive, which brought great joy to her heart. Vivian was gone, which gave her over to ecstasy; and she felt as if life would begin anew. Abraham became a memory.

She was sure now that by laboring harder without complaint, and by assenting to her boys' and Heath's every whim, surely they would love her and forgive her. Around the neighborhood she displayed boundless enthusiasm, bringing succor to neighbors in their distress, as she had always done, but even more so. She aided the elderly people in their daily chores, smiling brightly at the menfolk as they attended to their landscaping duties, chatted with the womenfolk about babies and schools and the latest fashions; and yet, she did not neglect her own family, for she in fact simply slept less. "If people treat me unkindly, why," she said to herself one day, her bosom swelled with pride, "I will just be even nicer. They won't change me!" To her, her goodness was her mother protector, an inner shield built by deliberate good acts, selfless dedication to family and friends, and by abstaining from bringing injustice upon the meek and innocent.

"Who will save you when those whom you trust turn upon you," Ellen had once said to her, suggesting she look toward God for Truth.

"God is cruel," she had responded; "he lets people suffer."

"No," Ellen had said as she lay on her hospital bed, "people let people suffer."

As it was, Oscine felt as if life's vital forces were streaming back into her tired body; yet, her inherent disease, that plague which Abraham had implored her to let him help her defeat, continued its course—meeting, incidentally, no resistance from Heath, of whom Abraham had once spoke thusly, "He knows you are ill, and shows not only no concern, but no desire to bring you relief, has thus forfeited his right to you, and has dissolved the sacred bonds of marriage."

One day Oscine woke up, kneeling down in the corner of the living room, steel-bristled toothbrush in hand, and glanced at the clock, realizing she had been asleep for an hour. "I must be tired," she reassured herself, and indeed, these blackout spells often happened while she cleaned during the early morning hours. But then these bouts of unconsciousness began to occur during the day. "My goodness will save me," she would recite to her herself when the horror of the disease seemed to be dismantling her sanity, and she would lie in a cold, clammy sweat on the white-tiled floor, thinking of circumstances she could not control.

One particular night she awoke and found herself on the sofa in the living room, feeling uncomfortable about her body, as she had on many such occasions recently, but she reasoned it was her illness wreaking havoc upon her various organs. "It is like a rapacious vulture, preying upon the innocent while they sleep," Abraham had once commented to her about her disease.

For a moment she froze, terrified, thinking she heard the low cackle of Vivian's smooth, arrogant voice. "Could it be? Has the witch returned from her haunts so soon? Have I failed?" She sharpened her hearing, but nothing came to her. "O, I am so wicked to pronounce judgment upon you; Vivian, you were just doing what you were taught," and satisfied that her rival had not returned, she was magnified in her desire to clean, as if with every stroke of her hard labor she was that much closer to winning back Heath and her boys.

Nearly three months after the incident with the hoax involving the death of Oscine's children—which Vivian had orchestrated but which Oscine never asked about, for she was simply overjoyed to find her two boys alive—Oscine began to suspect something was amiss. The men in the neighborhood looked at her differently, as if they had seen her in another way, indeed, in a unique way, in her womanly way. She felt chilled to the very marrow of her thinning bones at the salacious, devouring stares the menfolk gave her.

A week later, she awoke again in the middle of the night, after she had passed out on the sofa, and again she felt a strange sensation over her body, and she smelled a strong scent on her; and once more, she thought she heard Vivian's voice; and so she crawled, circumspectly, in the direction of the hushed voices and soon confirmed one of the voices as belonging to the seductress.

"The fool wore his cologne, she might suspect."

"No," Heath said, whispering, "Oscine is a little fool, she trusts everybody; and, anyway, if we have to, we can show her the tapes and threaten her with exposure."

But then the voices abated, suddenly, and Oscine, emitting a greasy sweat, crawled away, wide awake and horrified at her suspicions. She sat in her room till rosy-colored dawn took its perch on the far horizon, and she contemplated the future. She called Abraham in the early morning but he was not suscep-tible to her condition. "Oh," she screamed, internally, holding fast her head, "I feel as if I am losing my mind." Indeed, her thoughts about who she was and what she had become, the role of men and women in the wide world, the sacred bond of marriage, fidelity, honor, family—all these ideas began to congeal in her confused mind, and she could not sort out the distemper this hallucinogenic mess propagated. "I need time to think," she said, weeping as she scrubbed the floors, and then she threw down the cloth in disgust. "What am I doing here? Who am I," and then she lost consciousness.

That night, she awoke, lying on the couch, again feel-ing as if her body had been disturbed. She had asked Heath about the strange sensations she felt, and he had told her he had made love to her on several occasions while she was in this lethargic state.

Once more, she heard voices, and once again, she crept silently to the bedroom.

"Women have been sacrificed for centuries to appease the gods," Vivian's voice said, harshly; "why, virgins and young girls have always been given to kings and lords and wealthy men as gifts, or simply taken. This idea that a woman's body is her own is a new one, and mostly a Western idea. She's lucky to live in a nice house you provide for her." She was talking as if she were not a woman.

Oscine could hear kisses exchanged.

"You really think so? I mean, she is my wife."

"Look at the money we're making off that little fool; look at her reputation around here: the bright, innocent, angelic, righteous beautiful woman whom every man fantasizes about raping and degrading and humiliating because he cannot possess her; we have a gold mine here."

"But the law…"

"Oh, phooey on the law; we have the tapes showing her—shh…"

Oscine crept away, delirious, ill to her stomach, her thoughts incoherent. Finding her way to the bathroom, she spent an hour there excreting waste and vomiting. The next three nights, she drank full-bodied, rich red wine: a half bottle the first night, one the second, and one and a half on the third, and it was then that she called Abraham again.

"Hi, it's me," she said, whispering into the phone at two o'clock in the a.m., "how are you?" She still believed that he loved her.

"What do you want? You woke up my wife." It was a lie, but he thought she would believe it.

Oscine felt hurt, as if his vows to be there for her, always, had been breached. "I need you. I'm in trouble."

"Maybe you don't remember," he said, coldly, "but I'm married now; and by the way, I love my wife. What are you waiting for?" and he hung up the phone with a great deal of satisfaction.

Oscine wept. "I must find those tapes," she said to herself, and began to hunt where she had not looked. "I'm not an alcoholic, the wine just tastes so good right now; it soothes me, it calms me," she thought, crawling about the various living rooms with the bottle of red wine in her hand, from which she occasionally stopped and drank. Finally, she found a false panel in the wall that delivered five tapes to her, which she immediately put into the video-recording machine. There, on the television screen, Heath stood, while Vivian encouraged numerous men from the neighborhood to sexually violate Oscine during her blackouts. She vomited on the carpet.

But a casual observer might never know Oscine was unconscious on the tapes.

"She's found out our little secret," Vivian cackled, coming from the bedroom, and walking in an arrogant strut in front of Heath. "Men have lusted for you for years around here, and you thought they were your friends, but all the time they were just animals kept at bay because of your sham marriage. So, when we offered you to them, even at exorbitant prices, they all leaped at the chance to rape you, like wolves on a delicate, tasty lamb."

"You're sick," Oscine said, feeling so weak she could barely sit up. "Heath, how could you?

"Economics," he said, indifferently, "you're a commodity." As he stood there with Vivian, his loathing of Oscine seemed to grow stronger. "Eh, and why not, car sales have been low lately."

"Well, we can't let a good thing die," Vivian said, as if Oscine was not there, "now, there will be a new, exciting twist—she will be awake when they rape her, and this time they will pay dearly to look into her begging eyes."

"No," Oscine cried, attempting to stand, but Vivian slapped her hard to the ground.

"She'll obey or die," Vivian said, sneering.

"I'll tell everybody," Oscine said, thinking of her savior.

"And we will just show those tapes to the PTA," said Vivian, laughing now; "be a good girl and cooperate," and she commenced to beat Oscine with her fists and feet, and then tied her to the bed in Oscine's new room. "The customers will pay dearly for a protesting saint; they love raping their heroines, especially slender beauties," Vivian finished, scowling, and proceeded to make the final preparations.

One drooling, slithering, ecstatic customer came, one after another, sometimes alone, sometimes in pairs, sometimes in groups, week after week after week, to rape the conscious, weeping, and protesting Oscine.

One month later, Vivian and Heath, deciding against placing a babbling, incoherent Oscine in an asylum—and also because Heath was afraid to murder her, despite Vivian's insistence—they agreed to transport Oscine to a far, faraway city and supply her with plenty of cheap wine and a cornucopia of illegal drugs. They dropped Oscine's lethargic body in an abandoned, remote alley in a seedy part of the town, hoping to use her documented mental lapses as a reason for her disappearance once they contacted the authorities.

"Your new home, harlot," Vivian said, sneering as she looked at the mumbling woman groveling on the cold, grimy pavement. "Your goodness didn't save you, whore; we made you into a whore, so easily—where is your precious goodness now? I spit on your goodness," and she did spit on Oscine, and became so enraged by Oscine's whimpering that she began to violently punch her, and for a very long time, kick her, and then proceeded to urinate upon the feeble woman and even defecate upon her; and then she shouted so hard and loud in a such a shrieking, soul-emptying voice that her face bled a dark, crimson rage, and then became a scowling, black, iron mask that glowed in rapture at the unremitting pain it visited upon its helpless victim, as if the torture of this Innocent stoked its prodigious power. "There, harlot; and don't forget, you love your husband," she cried, her strong, youthful body trembling in the fever of unbound ecstasy, and then she laughed a laugh so wicked that even Heath was afraid of her.

Bitterness

T he longer Abraham was married to Darla, the more the intensity of his hatred grew for Oscine and Darla; nay, for all women. "Whores, one and all," he would say, musing upon the stealthy tactics females used to gain a man. Darla served him well, cleaning and cooking, all the while smiling and never complaining. "The little fool doesn't have the intellect to complain; why, she fears me, the pathetic creature, how perfectly tragic."

Abraham prayed every day that Oscine would call him so he might scold her for meekness in the wake of palpable evil, and for allowing it to grow and encouraging it to flourish by doing nothing. Yet, every time the phone rang, his wrath subsided, and he was ready to forgive her and love her and marry her and forget the past. But every time the phone rang and it was not her, his bitterness grew, like a disease, fed on the poisons of enmity.

"It is true," he mused one night as he lay next to Darla, "women are here to serve men; they are weak and easily persuaded or dissuaded; what a disappointment. I waited my whole life for an equal, and in the end I got what the brutes get, a submissive mate who will stay with me whether I beat her or not." He closed his eyes. "I offered her the world and she turned me away; how could she, how?" He still could not utter her name, so deep were the wounds of love in his heart. "I want her to beg me to come back; I want her to crawl so I can make her suffer." He looked at Darla. "Even now, would I take her over you? No longer," and he sneered a vicious smile.

The phone rang at two o'clock in the a.m. It was Oscine.

He chastised her for waking up Darla and after hanging up the phone, he felt gleeful. "I feel ten years younger," he thought, gloating, "now, just call back once more and we will see…"

New Things

"Well," Eli said, after hearing the news of Oscine's latest call, "it sounds like she is having trouble in her marriage—no, enough trouble that she is calling you about it. But this sounds like a revolving door. Ditch her. You're married, boy." He knew it was the right thing to say, though he still did not believe it.

"She's the only one I'll ever marry," Abraham said, stone-faced.

"And what of Darla?"

"Compassion? From a man who uses women like candy?"

"But you're not me; you would not wear it well."

"Darla was merely an interlude because I was anxious."

"Put that on her gravestone." He paused, knowing it was time to speak of other things. "I read those books you gave me; very interesting. I've had a few test cases, and I regret to inform you that I may be developing a conscience, again."

"Why?"

"Because I tried to understand women, and, consequently, by listening, I began to have genuine feelings for them; and so, I let these women linger longer than normal, and I found myself feeling slightly rotten after I dumped them."

"You poor fool," Abraham said, smiling, "go back," he motioned with his hands, "go back to the dark side."

"Too late," Eli said, and realizing the topic of himself had begun to wear upon his own unique sense of self, he shifted the topic. "And what if she doesn't call?"

"She'll call."

But Oscine did not call, and for the next three months Abraham, ready to divorce Darla, was ferocious in his attitude toward her, pouring out his frustrations upon her, scolding her, belittling her, and watching her forgive him for it all; he hated her the more for it.

And then Abraham began to hate Oscine again, and he turned his feigned affection toward Darla, who soon became pregnant. "Through you I will have many babies," he thought, observing her stomach rise and fall as she lay next to him on their bed during the night, "and I will live through them, and they, my own flesh, shall surely love me." And he hardened his heart against Oscine, vowing never to think of her again, yet a vow impossible for him to keep.

Now, we turn to Eli, who began to form a true conscience, concerning his ill treatment of women.

He would lie in bed at night and think of his latest female companion who would debase and humiliate herself to be with him. "Is this all there is?" he mused, and he would think of all the women he had been with who had begun to mean something to him, especially those women of late, and how he simply had terminated these affairs, or simply, with a phone call, temporarily brought them back for physical pleasure or to help him forget another woman. "These women have been tools I have used to fill a void; I suppose they have feelings, too." He had said this exact sentiment to Abraham but had not emotionally or intellectually understood it.

The idea that women have lasting feelings was a new concept to him.

The very fact that women submitted to his every whim had, in his mind, plunged their human status below the level of Man.

"They are so easily manipulated by expensive gifts and dinners and praise, are they not like little children to be guided and complimented lest they stray and have violent fits?" He mused upon the idea of Woman and decided to experiment further with three of them who were currently within his tight orbit.

Eli soon met a young woman, named Corrine, who was as beautiful as she was intelligent, and he, at first, did not exert his dominance over her; but after a few months, when he felt as if she were exerting her own will, thus distorting what he considered the natural order of things, he exerted his will and sought to dominate her, though he loved her greatly. In due time, she rebelled against his authority, though she loved him dearly; but she would not be controlled by men, and so she left him, and it wounded Eli deeply in his heart. All of his prowess as a lover could not sway her to come back, and so he fell into a profound funk, often unable to speak or eat properly or have lucid thoughts for days. He thought of Oscine and Abraham, and how tragic it was that their authentic love could not be. "True love conquers all things," he reflected, "but not an unrighteous man's arrogance. I have destroyed what God has placed before us as a miracle." At such times he often prayed to God, though truly he believed more in the idea of God than God himself, a God in Eli's own image and agreeable to his own thoughts.

"You should be with Oscine," Eli had said to Abraham in many ways, many times, during the last few months, but now he said it with great conviction, and at the end of a long conversation when two competing philosophies were smashing like warships against each other.

"Darla is pregnant," Abraham said, as if one dead, "and Oscine can rot in her own stupidity and weakness."

"You have to rescue her, she's waiting for you. You know as well as I do that women need to be won, and in this case, saved from the black knight. Be a hero."

He stepped back in a feigned surprise, and imparted an exaggerated look at his friend. "What was that, again? And coming from you?" He nodded his head as if he were now the master. "She will come only if she wishes."

"No," Eli said, angrily, "she needs your strength."

His angry resolve began to weaken. "And what about Corrine?"

"I destroyed my love for Corrine. There is no rescuing what is dead. Your love is alive. Go and take her. Go."

"Go," Abraham repeated, as if in a trance, wanting to believe all of it. "What about Darla?"

"Darla will be fine. Go."

"But what about the baby?"

"The baby will be fine. Go."

"Go," Abraham said, summoning up his lost passion for what he thought he could never have, "and when I get there, what do I do?"

"You will know when you are there. Let your sacred love guide you. Now, get going."

"Yes," Abraham said, as if he were looking into a future dreamscape no other person could see.

And he went.

The First Tale Endeth

A braham, after hearing Oscine had been reported missing, accessed hospital records to study her stay in the mental ward. "She lost her mind over me," he thought, embalmed in grief, and he began to search the town and the local cities, but could not discover her whereabouts. Consequently, he began to lose days at the hospital, until, finally, he quit to attend to the search full time, financing his mission with his savings, entirely neglecting Darla.

Darla called Eli, one night, in desperation. "You are his best friend, Eli, you must do something. He sits in the dark and won't talk to me; he doesn't eat, he doesn't sleep, he doesn't listen. Eli, I am so worried. He is carrying a gun." She wept as does the wife who knows her husband is attending to business of a consuming nature that is more important than her.

But there was no talking to Abraham, as he was one possessed now of a single purpose, and no human barrier would stop him, nor was any human shield able to prevent his finding Oscine. Eli could do nothing but join the search.

For three more months they walked the dirty streets of every city near them, and then the cities far away, bribing every bartender and homeless hobo, contacting every police station, hiring private detectives and passing out thousands of flyers with Oscine's face on them.

One night, in the hotel of a city one hundred miles north of their homes, Eli lay in bed, thinking aloud. "Doesn't it bother you that Heath isn't looking?"

"No," Abraham said, scowling, "he never loved her."

"Still, I don't like it. I smell a rat."

"I'm going to get some food," Abraham said, and he walked out of the room, down the old, faded wooden stairs and out into the icy air of winter.

"Hey, aren't you that fellow looking for that woman on the flyer?" asked the man at the local convenience store.

"What of it?" Abraham said, now inured to such questions, not even thinking of success anymore based on hearsay.

"I know this fellow, a bum, really, who says he knows her."

"Where?" Abraham asked, stone-faced.

The man behind the counter stroked his black-stubble chin. "I know there is a reward involved somewhere," he said, narrowing his greedy eyes.

Abraham, accustomed to the process, handed the man a twenty-dollar bill. "Where?"

There was an ordinary hobo, ubiquitous to the world, who lived in a typical hovel under a typical concrete highway bridge. He smelled like cheap wine and dried urine. "Know where your woman is," he said, smiling through black gaps in his rotting, yellowish and chipped teeth, "know where the whore is." Abraham, shaking his head, turned to leave, but the old beggar began to describe the woman. "Slender, golden-haired, got troubles with her bowels; might be a beauty." The wily bum noticed the interest in his customer. "You must want her real bad; truth is, so do many round here, and we've had her, too," and he smiled, sickeningly, stroking his bearded grey chin, "many times."

"Where is she?" Abraham said, not wanting to know the meaning of this cryptic language.

"Tell you more about her; she's a lush, bad case, too, do anything for the wine, the whore. If you want her all you got to do is promise her a bottle, and she offers herself to you, the pretty little thing; kind of sad, though," and he laughed, "but I like it, 'cause I know where I can always get a woman even though she is a filthy whore." Abraham's face was flaming with wrath, but the bum rambled on. "One time, one of my brothers, after taking her, decided to put her in her place just because he felt like it, and he—oh, what shall I say—to remember my high school education—evacuated his bowels upon her," and he smiled in satisfaction that his memory was not totally annihilated, and then proceeded, cocky and full of himself, "and then he urinated on her; and what do you know, eh? Don't you know she got excited about the whole affair! So, he gives the signal, and lo, within a day, twenty of the brethren had taken her, then defecated and urinated on her. What a mess she was, covered in that heap of waste; wonder what kind of woman she once was…" He leaned closer to Abraham and let his alcoholic breath flush out with a harsh whisper, "Hope she ain't sane."

Although he was certain the woman the bum described could not be Oscine, the thought that any woman could be treated in such a vile manner gave him over to a boundless rage. "Where is she?" he said, his words dripping in righteous vengeance.

"What about the reward, eh?" The bum laughed, as does the man who has done wrong and who is willing to betray others of the same wrong, for money.

Abraham, without mediating upon the subject, brought the tip of the black barrel of his gun to the loose folds of the red, meaty throat of the vagrant. "Your reward will be to live; now, talk." In a moment the bum, who now smelled of freshly spilt urine, was yapping like a beaten dog.

In an hour, Abraham, alone, entered the dark alley the derelict had described in astonishing detail. There was covert activity going on in its long stretch of filth, behind a group of abandoned couches. There, on a bed of stained mattresses, seven men were gathered round a blonde-haired woman, some of them lying with her, others casually drinking alcoholic beverages.

"Get along, mister, we're all full now; come back in an hour," one of them said, indifferently; "this whore is being used."

Abraham could see her face, plainly.

It was his beloved, his love, his innocent, sweet darling, Oscine.

He easily pulled out the gun and began firing the bullets not around or over or under the flock of human vultures to frighten them but into their diseased minds and bodies. Soon, after the screaming was over, he stood next to her, looking at her bewildered, bruised, puffy face, and beheld her clothes, rags now, covered with excrement and urine, and blood and beer; he stood, transfixed, for he knew his life was at an end. He began to weep uncontrollably as his body trembled. "I loved you, Oscine, O, how I loved you; I would have given up the world for you but you rejected my love. You proved yourself weak and foolish. Why, why do women stay with monsters? I loved you, loved you like no other man could ever love you because we were the same, and you turned away from my love; you killed yourself for him, that monster, that vile creature who did this to you. He needs to die, too." He looked at the dead bodies of the miscreants around him. "I killed for you. Who else would do this? I will die for you, who else would do this for you?" He heard sirens approaching and he looked at her matted, greasy hair, and saw her emerald-colored eyes flitting about as if she were a wild animal in a steel snare.

"I love my husband," she mumbled, staring up at him, shaking her head.

"I loved you," Abraham said, falling to his knees. "Oscine, O, my poor Oscine, why, why couldn't you allow yourself to be happy? I hated you but I loved you, loved you more than Love."

He heard the police car door slam, and the urgent orders of the officers for Abraham to drop the gun.

"I love my husband," Oscine repeated, narrowing her eyes as she stared at him, and then said, in a tone too low for humans to hear, "my husband, Abraham."

"My love," Abraham said, kneeling next to her, stroking her face, "I love you, I love you true, forever and always, my darling, my sweet, sweet Oscine." And he kissed her for the first time, a long, luxurious, intoxicating, rejuvenating kiss.

And then he placed the point of the gun barrel to her head and pulled the trigger, ending her life on Earth, and then pointing the gun to his own head, pulled the trigger, ending too his life on Earth.

A Nightingale with brown feathers and a whitish, tan breast flew into the alley and landed next to the two lovers, and began to sing its melodious song.

Soon, Eli stood at the entrance of the alley, identifying the bodies of the man and woman to the police.

He had followed Abraham's path. "This can't be the end," he wept.

Book Two

Once at home, Eli devised a plan to discover the truth behind Oscine's disappearance; after scouting Oscine's old neighborhood, he found the place of employment for several of the women who lived there. He easily became friends with two of these women, and then became their paramours, regardless of their marital status. The women of the men who had violated Oscine's physical sanctuary were very willing to tell him the sordid secrets of the raping of Oscine, as they had, being subservient to their husbands, and feeling inferior in beauty and goodness to Oscine, relished the idea of her being physically assaulted.

Eli, upon attaining this knowledge, sought out the men, and began to drink with them, for all of the men involved were abusers of alcohol and everything narcotic-like, and full of various kinds of addictions, and he easily gained knowledge of their role in the rapes. Yea, the men boasted about it, as if the rapes were the pinnacle of their misbegotten lives. Thus, did Eli match the list from the women to the list of the men, and soon, he knew who had taken part in the slow, torturous murder of Oscine. To think of what they had done to a cherished and good woman gave him over to weeping anywhere he happened to be, and unashamedly so. "How could men do such things," he would rage, "but I know now, and Justice sits upon my shoulder like an avenging Angel."

One night, months after he had quit relations with the nefarious horde of Heath's neighborhood, he decided, after the investigation into Oscine and Abraham's murders by the police brought forth no guilty parties, that the time to cleanse the neighborhood of this black scourge was nigh.

Eli sat at home for many months after this, pondering over the fate of Abraham and Oscine. He took no phone calls or answered no knock on the door from friends or lovers or acquaintances, as he wished to expend nearly all of his energies on the proper disposal of his enemies. But he was a pragmatist, too, so he rose early and attended to his business that had gained him several million dollars a year, which he oft used for recreation and amusement; but he no longer cared about the business that he had built from a particle of an idea to a financially solvent cash machine; he no longer put in eighty-hour weeks and partied on the weekend and then went back to work and put in a seventy-hour week and partied on the weekend. No, it was all over, evanescent, dead, a frivolous mirage that seemed a distant cry from a broken mirror from a distant parallel universe that was rushing too quickly past his emerging consciousness.

He knew he had to proceed with caution or all would be lost, but he also knew that he was smarter than those whom he hunted, smarter and more cunning and more willing to take chances that would ensure their complete and utter dislocation from their lofty perches in life.

And then one day he decided to listen to the messages from his multitude of lovers, past and present, and as he sat in the smoky gloom of his back room, it was as if he heard the voices of these women for the first time. "Why," he marveled, "it is as if they are like those in the neighborhood of Oscine," but the very mention of her blessed name nearly crumpled him to the cold tile. "These women, they are like—well, what are they like—who are they? What are they, and what are they after?" And he began to analyze the sum and substance of these women, and he began to feel as if he were dissolving his own soul into the bottomless abyss with every reverie and reflection. "Am I no different from these pathetic creatures; am I not complicit in their guilt? Am I nothing more than a pimp to their prostitution; am I nothing more?" His skin was crawling now with shame, his mind numb with repugnance, his heart filled with sorrow, but he could not accept this revelation, and so he called up these women, each and every one, and met them and lay with them, and then went to nightclubs and bars and through a newly installed filter in his heart, he saw these female creatures trail him as if he were a prince. He marveled at the ease with which they gave themselves to him and were willing to submit to his every whim and fancy if only he would subsidize their lifestyle.

"But who am I that I have such power over these women?" he lamented, some weeks later as he sat in the glare of a dark seclusion in his magnificent home. "What have I become to attract such women; am I no better than the Heaths of the world? Are there no better women in the world than these, so easily willing to give up their bodies for money? Am I merely to them but a man?" And he thought of Oscine, and her virtuous image propelled him to his knees and he wept like a child who realizes for the first time that he has practiced mischief his whole life.

The phone messages from his lovers, past and present, piled up like dung on a rubbish heap, but he still had not the will to purge the flashing red lights from his life.

On a caprice he went down to his red Corvette and fell into it and put in the key and started the engine and then drove to the street and down to the freeway and out into the dark night that was fringed with twinkling white lights and populated by gliding cars and sedate passengers, and he drove toward the east.

On his cross-country journey he met a great multitude of women of diverse backgrounds and creeds and religions, and his mind, as if watching this sweet-smelling, sweet-tasting female candy show through a dark veil, lured the women into its master lair, just as the ultraviolet stripes of a flower lure a bee to its sweet nectar or yellow pollen; and Eli lay with these women, too many women, too easily, too often, prevailing against their sense of decency and morality through the power of his handsome visage and his handsome money and his handsome wit. In a month he returned home, bewildered and depressed.

He sat for three more months in the dead silence of his home, which had once been the hub of promiscuity and a perpetual harem of willing women, gorgeous, physically superior superhuman creatures of infinite beauty who were willing to become pregnant or live with him or readily leave their husbands on his word that he would take care of them financially. This, he now saw not only as an anomaly, but a perversion of the natural order of things between males and females.

He wept at night over the realization of his role in the destruction of these women, and he wept over the loss of two lovers he considered innocent and above the torment and sin of his world. "But I must atone for my sins," he decided, and he looked to the west, "and there I shall begin my cleansing."

Eli is Coming

There are men who possess a dark, brooding, enigmatic, handsome talent that causes them to stand out amongst a crowd of ordinary men, a burning enigma that lights a fire in the hearts of women and reduces them to willing captives; some men who own it turn it inside and out and explore its unique nature and capture its essence and exploit its fullest potential, this mysterious It that allows one man to separate himself from the scurrying masses with his style and grace and look and manner; but in this kind of man, there is no acting, nor staged rehearsals needed in front of full-length mirrors, nor books read on how to harness its wonder, for it is simply his true self laid bare.

Eli had it and used it like an expert craftsman on his willing prey.

His jet-black hair was thick and curly and his head was round and his body large and naturally muscular; his eyes were large and coal-black and his nose straight and his teeth strikingly white; his light skin was clear and his manly scent was an intoxicant to women; his grin was genuine and dazzling in his effort to project confidence and trust; his easy gait and his easy laugh and self-assurance were fertile ground laid at the feet of his prey; but it was his smooth and even, deep voice that was a lubricant to the hesitant limbs of women, and his very reassuring words, spiced with humor and wit and intelligence, soaked the women in a lusty aroma and dripped down to the very resilient core of their reluctance to yield up their fleshly treasures and knead it until it was a soft putty. He could do it freely every night to nearly any woman and he had known it from an early age and had perfected it early on and now he was the grand master in his field.

This night, he was standing at the jukebox and observing three young and beautiful women laughing and drinking at the maple wood high-counter bar. He nodded his head as if in agreement with his instincts, and smiled a brief smile of remembrance and fidelity; he was attired in a black silk collar shirt and a black leather jacket and tailored blue jeans that showed off his trim legs, and he wore a diamond-studded, woman-piercing smile that preceded him like a laser beam as he walked across the darkened room.

He could see the effect his virile form had on the three women he was nearing; he saw their subtle glances and low, head-down whispering and nervous hand movements, and he was pleased; he slid next to them and allowed his lustful cologne to penetrate their heavy perfume and then he casually ordered a small alcoholic beverage. He knew the women would not leave, even if they were married, even if they had boyfriends, for he knew the game as well as they, and it stated that once the handsome male approaches and holds his ground, the female waits to listen to his story and then either decides against his advances or flirts with him.

He drained his crystal shot glass of hard liquor and turned to them. "Hello, ladies," he began, affecting a voracious smile that probed their inner psyches.

"Hi," they said, nearly in unison, their heads bobbing up and down on the hot columns of concentric waves that his comely looks generated.

"So," he continued, as casual as a man asking for directions, "what modeling agencies are you beautiful women with?"

The taller one, the one with the almond-shaped eyes and long, black, thick hair and the curvaceous figure, said, casually, "And what makes you think we are?"

"Well, I heard there was a plumbers' convention and a models' convention in town," and he looked them up and down so that they would know he looked them up and down, "and I don't take you for plumbers," he smiled, nodding his head, "but just in case you are, I do have a leaky faucet."

"What a line," one of the other women said, smiling admiringly at him, "boldness without shame." She raised her blonde eyebrows. "I like it."

"You don't believe me—for shame," he answered, shaking his head, and then summoned over the bartender. "Joe, what two conventions are in town this weekend?"

"Models and plumbers, I heard," he said, quickly, and motioned to a group of men bellowing and baying over in the corner seats.

"For shame," Eli restated, feigning disappointment, "a fellow can't even tell the truth to beautiful women these days without them thinking he is telling a fib."

"It doesn't matter, anyway," replied the one with the deep brunette hair, holding up her left hand and wiggling her middle fingers, "I belong to the married woman agency, and we don't take outside solicitors."

Her two female companions held up their left hands and wiggled their middle fingers, and then the gorgeous redhead said, her voice dipped in honey and wine, "But we belong to the single ladies' club, and we welcome new members."

"Bartenders live on bribes," the raven-haired woman said, suspiciously.

"Tsk, tsk," Eli returned, frowning, and then turning his attention to the hustle and hum of the bees buzzing around the honeypot, cried out, good-naturedly, "Gentlemen! How many plumbers from the convention are here?" Four young and three old men raised their beer mugs and shouted related affirmative responses. "And good ladies, how many of you are here from the models' convention?" Three very pretty and fragile-looking young women raised their beer glasses and flashed their smiles in unison. Eli turned to his inquisitor. "You would make a good lawyer."

She smiled at him and slowly looked him up and down so that he would know she looked him up and down, and read his body language and the mass of certitude awash across his roguish face, and she smiled, "You're either very, very bad, or very, very good."

He smiled and let his head fall forward toward his prey, and whispered, "I reckon I'm both," and he leaned his face closer to her and she did not flinch nor move away. "And I am wondering which one you are right now."

Her cell phone rang, and she picked it up, acknowledged the number, and carefully replaced it in her leather black purse.

"Duty calls?" Eli said.

"My old man," she said, and she lit a cigarette, and he let her.

"She just had twins, you see," the redhead said.

"And she needs to breathe adult air," the blonde woman finished.

The raven-haired beauty shot them a glance of disdain, but she knew they were simply vying for their greedy share of the genetically superior hunk of man before them, as she had done the same in her time.

"Playing hooky, are we?" Eli said

"A girl has to have some fun sometime or she stops being a girl, and she just becomes a mother," the black-haired woman answered, blowing smoke out of the side of her sensuous, full lips.

"And what about you two," Eli said, looking at other two women, "up past your bedtime?"

"Why, sometimes we don't go to bed at all," the redhead replied, parting her sensuous, glossy mouth and then biting her bottom lip.

"And I just hate to sleep alone, at least not without my teddy," the blonde said, twirling the curly locks of her hair, her face aglow with that come-hither look men on the prowl desired to see.

But Eli had seen this tiresome provocative invitation for mating so many times by so many willing and eager women that he was now bored with it and repelled by it. "Where is the challenge in that?" he now often thought.

The cell phone of the black-haired woman rang once more, and once more she checked the number flashing on the screen, and she rolled her luminous black eyes and shook her head.

Eli purposely exaggerated a look at her neck and then turned to the other two. "Well, I think we need to get going; this place is too busy for me." He introduced himself to the two fine ladies and ignored the other.

Aggravated now, the black-haired woman said, angrily, "So, you three think you're leaving?"

"And you're leaving too, going back home," Eli said, casually, looking again at her slender white neck.

"Why do you keep looking at my neck!" she cried.

He never lost his wry grin. "It's that noose of your master forming around you and dragging you back home," he said, and then laughed and looked to the other women and then back to her, "come on, they didn't have to tell their husbands they went to a Tupperware party tonight, right?" He smiled so sincerely and with such silliness that she relented in her wrath.

"How did you know?" the raven-haired one cried out.

"Oh, I've had experience in this sort of thing," he said, and raised his eyebrows and nodded his head and smiled at the redhead and the pretty blonde, and then they knew the night was wrapped up, that the sexual-teasing circle begun would be the sexual union circle completed by the morning, and all of the participants therein would have had their lusts satiated and then would begin the cycle anew the next available night. These women were merely like insects and animals, now, obedient to their biological nature to seek out and mate within their own species; there was no other deeper thought involved at all, no hesitancy about the affair based on moral restraint of societal condemnation or worries about judgment from Heaven or anything other than the fulfillment of their wanton desires, and the handsomer the man or the richer the man or the more skilled the man as lover, the better and the more exciting.

Eli departed the building with the blonde and the red-head, leaving the raven-haired woman to sulk and once again check her irksome ringing cell phone. She cursed like a woman scorned.

In the Palace of the Romance King

U p in the palace wherein Eli lived, up on the high hill where the rich and the powerful dwelled in the rarefied clouds, existed a world hitherto unknown to the two women he had picked to adorn his luxurious bedchamber for the night. It was a world they had heard about and read about and yearned about and knew they would never have through their own labor, so they decided early on in their adult lives that they would gain such a world and such a life through the hard labor of men, and they knew what men wanted, and that rich and powerful men wanted the most beautiful and young-est women. These two women knew that life had begun for them this night, in this prince's palace, where they might begin to learn the enigmatic nature and habits of such men, where they might profit from it as they ascended the golden stairway to their final destination, within the magical caste of a king.

And as they walked amongst the outside, finely manicured yard and the high statue waterfalls and the ornate swimming pool and the richly decorated yellow clubhouse and past the Olympic-sized indoor pool and gazed at the giant sauna and the giant recreation room and the theater room, which was replete with a one-hundred-inch high-definition plasma television and surround-sound speakers, and as they toured the master bedroom and walked on the plush white carpet and walked past the immigrant gardeners and the busy maids and touched the silver BMWs and the cherry-red Corvette and the black Lamborghini, they decided that they would do whatever women in such circumstances do to keep inside the fortressed walls of such a spectacular place; they would do whatever the men wanted and whenever the men wanted it and with whomever the men wanted it, and they would do it gladly and for whatever reason and all day or all night or here and there or anything that made any kind of sense or not, for now that they had put their nose into the honey jar, they could not possibly live another day in their pathetic little apartments knowing such a regal life awaited them if only they acquiesced to the demands of such men. And, they reasoned, were these men so bad, these wealthy men? They could not imagine these aristocrats asking them to do things that were so horrible that they would balk and leave. Why, these women had decided, it is the way of the world for a rich man to have a beautiful woman at his side, and they would be that woman, and for now, Eli would be that man.

And he was that man, now, he was good to them and fun and full of humor and generous with his money and his time with them; he required nothing in return, not loyalty or love, not gifts or friendship, only that they were his personal and private living and breathing pleasure dolls whenever and wherever he desired them. They had mined society for years and finally they had acquired a tiny streak of yellow gold that would lead to the mother lode, and they would not be deterred.

Two months hence and he was back at the bar where he had met the two women, who were now in the exalted orbit of other prosperous men they had met in his company, and he was drinking a hard drink in the corner booth and eyeing the raven-haired woman who was standing alone with a small glass of beer in her hands. He stared at her for the longest time, his face straining and grimacing as if he were interrogating her very soul, for this one he wanted more than the others, the elusive one, the married one who evinced fidelity to her husband; this one he wanted to break open and pour her guts and heart onto his waiting hands so he could mold her into what he wanted and then stuff it back into her body and watch her dance to his private tune. The two women had told him about her and he knew what he wanted and why he wanted it and so he stood up and drained his glass and walked up to the bar, heralded by his consuming and sensuous beam of male swagger and arrogance. He slid next to her and looked her up and down just as if he were examining a new car for defects. "Tupperware party tonight?" He barely smiled, as he knew she would be exhausted by the same ploy.

She acknowledged his presence with a small smile and then put down her drink on the wooden counter and sat on the shiny leather barstool. "My friends have told me quite a bit about you."

He looked to the door and back to her again. "And you didn't run away? How perfectly courageous of you."

"Please," she said, shaking her head, "nothing men do surprises me at all."

He leaned over and kissed her quickly and then leaned back. "Nothing?"

She slapped him gently. "I had to," and she smiled, coyly, "no men are allowed at my Tupperware parties." She wasn't smiling nor was she frowning, and then she held up her left hand and let it do the married wriggle dance. "Remember?"

"Oh, yes, my little sparkling friend that sometimes seems to get in the way of my conquests; but merely a diversion along the road, I assure you."

"Is that what women are to you, a conquest?"

"Wasn't your husband your conquest until you married him? Well, it's all the same, isn't it, it's just that I am still climbing the mountain and you are coming down it, or, sliding down it, actually."

She shook her head and smiled. "Your little word games won't work on me, I'm not one of your candy girls who is looking for their sugar daddy; my husband has plenty, and he treats me…" But her cell phone rang and she automatically looked at it and now she frowned, and she cursed underneath her hot breath. "I have to go."

He reached into his shirt pocket and pulled out a business card and handed it to her. "If you ever need a friend to talk to…"

He saw her study the card for a long while and then she ripped it up and placed it back into his hands. "You just want me because I'm unavailable, that's all," she said, rather smugly, and turned to leave.

"No, that isn't why I want you," he began, and watched her stop and turn around, "I want you because you are available—you just don't know it, yet." Now, he smiled that handsome, dangerous smile of the male sexual conqueror, and she felt an enthralling chill sweep into her breasts and tingle throughout her gorgeous figure. She smiled and nodded her head and walked away. "It is only a matter of time," he whispered, and ordered another strong drink from the bartender.

For months he toured the bars and the nightclubs and found many willing women and mated with them easily but he was constantly looking right and then left and behind himself for the raven-haired woman; he would meet the redhead and the blonde in their rotation between their generous benefactors and he would hear bits and pieces about her, and he heard them tell their stories about their life on the trail with them and the perversions therein, and he listened to their stories about how they told the raven-haired woman about how great a lover Eli was and how fabulously wealthy he was and how she should sneak away from her husband, and how different he, Eli, was from the other donors in their rotation. He was pleased to hear this and he acknowledged it in his mind and then he would satisfy their fleshly lusts and fly with them to Las Vegas and then fly with them to New York and then fly back with them back to California just in time for their next rotation. He would bid them goodbye and the next night he would put on his dashing and daring handsome man clothes and slap on his musky cologne and speed to the first nightclub. The music was loud and the beat was fast, the lights were splashing glittery silver and iridescent white, and these hard-driving rhythms, like the biological pulse of nature, and these penetrating, translucent beams, like the piercing shafts from Cupid's arrow, traveled to the very cells of the hot and sweaty creatures therein and switched on their lusty hormones, and soon these aroused bodies set out to search for the most fertile and seductive mates in this tantalizing flesh market.

When Eli walked through the gyrating sea of dancers, he was able, through the magic of superior male pheromones and astonishing good looks, to attract women to himself, just as if he were a magnet and they were bits of helpless metal; everywhere he went, he turned female heads, and by the time he was at the bar, he had two or three women trailing him to see what they could see. It was the age of female boldness, it was the time of reins loosened on their restraints concerning modesty and chastity, and Eli knew this and exploited it and helped the women feel empowered as he rewarded them for such behavior. Yes, three women stood next to him at the bar, and four more gazed at him from a distance, their faces disturbed with jealousy. At the bar, Eli read from the same scroll he had embraced once he realized he had this great power over the female species; it was a script composed by other men in other times all over the world, and it consisted in smooth words and smooth actions and effusive praise for the beauty of his prey, but with no promises to keep nor hints of the future, as it was a conversation of the now that promised thrilling delights. These women fed off these erotic currents just as they did off the sweet aroma of steaming apple pies or the pleasing warm rays of a spring day.

His cell phone rang and he answered it, and lo, it was her, the raven-haired one. He smiled as does the hunter who finally seizes his elusive game.

"So," he began, with a mischievous smile, "we have quite the memory for numbers, do we?"

She laughed. "I was bored."

He nodded his head and held up the cell phone so she could hear the three women jealously inquire as to the identity of the caller. "Yeah, me too." He grinned.

There was a marked silence punctuated by a heavy expulsion of breath. "Don't you ever get tired of weak whores?"

He held the phone up near his face as he, in turn, and with a slow deliberateness, kissed each of the now sexually slain women, and then, after clicking the speakerphone capability on the rectangular machine, spoke once more. "Whores are the best of women because they don't pretend to be virtuous."

One of the females, outraged, grabbed the cell phone from him and laid down a steady stream of profane mortar and brick against her unknown verbal assailant, much to the delight of the other giggling females; but then the response came from the eerie dead zone inside the thin piece of intrusive machinery, a savage rebuke shooting agile missiles of promised physical mayhem and hostile retribution against her competitors; the shocked women stood there naked and defenseless and dripping with an anxious dread, their mental fortress having been shredded to spittle and dust and then stuffed down their choking throats by this unnatural female predator. The trembling woman handed Eli back the phone and she and her two huntresses slunk away into the safe shadows of acceptable chaos and the unknown.

"You are a mean one," Eli said, amused.

"That is what happens when little girls who play 'slut' mess with a real whore."

He was pleased. "So, where are you?"

"Home; my old man is at a car convention, and he took his kids with him, and I just tucked in the twins, and I am," and then said, with great emphasis, "bored."

He was there in ten minutes, and having parked his car some two blocks away, he surreptitiously made his way toward her two-story home and soon found the doorway and knocked upon it. She came to the door and slowly opened it to reveal a voluptuous figure that was ovulating and bursting with willing desire, and he went in and she closed the door.

But now he merely stood there, the Love god about to initiate his newest disciple in the temple of beauty and lust. "I do have three questions for you," he began, slyly, with the confident visage of the conqueror of all things female, his rugged visage displaying a faint shade of smugness that could only be deciphered by the most experienced of women. She stood silent, as if to evince her willingness to indulge his puerile male rituals. "First," he said, with a wry smile, the kind that anticipates mutual enjoyment from his formidable partner, "are you," he continued, following a successful script he had used hundreds of times, "insane?"

She smiled broadly, staring into his handsome landscape, and then carefully enunciated, with exceeding facileness, "No."

His grin vanished, his demeanor became serious, as if he were in fact interviewing a job applicant, and then he said rather smoothly, "Have you, at any time, been diagnosed by a state-licensed, board-approved medical practitioner to have an addiction that is recognized and accepted by the science community, and one that would not allow you to lead a normal life?" Now, his sober face was washed clean by a mischievous grin.

She let out a small "Hmm," nodded her head as if to offer her amusement at this query, took a long drag on her cigarette, blew the smoke to her right side while staring into his deep black eyes, which were free of inhibition and worry, the strong, confident eyes of what a real man was to her; and then, with arms crossed as she flicked her long, sharp, colorless fingernails against each other with her free hand, opened her sensuous mouth, hesitated, smiled, and then softly murmured, "Everybody's crazy," and then tapped some cigarette ash onto the tiled floor, "the smart ones just know how to hide it better than everyone else."

He nodded his head, his black eyebrows raised, and murmured, "Hmm," while barely able to suppress the hilarity in his mind; and then proceeded on, seemingly unperturbed. "Are you now," he said, nearly in a whisper, looking right into her smoldering eyes, which were as black as an-absent-stars-and-moon-night, "or have you ever been…a man?"

She almost laughed, but righted her equilibrium, moved so close to him that her fragrant breath splashed like velvet temptation upon his waiting lips. "It will only take you the rest of the night to find out."

And so the torrid affair began.

Her Story

Their spent forms, lying next to each other, and having already exchanged bodily fluids and the fiery cocktail of hormonal chemicals therein, were fueling a memory unto themselves, of days past filled with unbound savagery and sexual instincts now unveiled and flown before them in a blood-red emblem; this recovered memory spoke of endless mating and endless carousing; this memory, ignited by the melting of two bodies into one through an unrestrained physical union, ushered in the revelation that unrepressed men need to be with unrepressed women, no matter how much violence they suffer, for the ecstasy gained from it is life-giving.

It was as if, the woman thought, the two of them had been wild caught and forced into a steel cage to mate. She looked at her male lover and felt she was seeing the best parts of her secret self, and then she closed her wild black eyes and felt his vast wealth seeping into her sweaty pores, and it pricked a sensation in her that awoke her slumbering soul. "I must have it all," she pondered, gazing at her handsome prince, "and he is my stairway to Heaven." She went to check on the twins, and came back.

"Dolores," Eli began, and then looking about the spacious room, continued in a playful manner, "could you be more specific about the return of your husband; I just hate that uncomfortable moment when he comes home and his wife and her lover are in bed together; it's just so hard to explain your way out of that circumstance."

"You worry about little things like that, really? I'm disappointed." She leaped out of her small chair and stood before him, condemnation written arrogantly across the light complexion of her face.

He folded his arms and placed them behind his head and then laid his head back on the white pillow, curiosity upon his countenance. "I'm just worried about you, that's all; hey, it's your marriage, I'm the interloper."

"Well, don't worry," she said, scowling, "I can handle him. I know him; it's you I don't know."

"So, here you are, the real you," he said, casually; "I suppose it's my own fault, since I have known you for a total of about three hours," and he reached into his pants pocket to check for messages on his cell phone.

She pushed him back down onto the bed, and lay upon him. "Men," she whispered, seductively, "they're such babies; you can't take criticism at all; well, if you're going to be with me, you had better like it, because I always speak my mind," and she kissed him hard on the mouth. "If you want one of your little 'yes' girls who just want your money and will do anything for it, leave right now, because who I am now I will still be one week from now."

A car could be distinctively heard coming into the driveway. "Plumber?" he said, his face as smooth as polished glass.

She jumped up and threw him his shirt. "You had better leave through the window," she whispered.

He frowned, slowly took out a cigarette, lit it, took a long drag on it, and then exhaled the smoke toward the white stucco ceiling. "I came in through the front door, and I will leave through the front door." He crossed his bare feet. "It doesn't matter to me who I walk out with."

The front door opened and voices were heard echoing in the pantry way. "You've got to leave before my husband comes in here, he'll kill us both!"

"Well," he replied, and then inhaled slowly and exhaled even slower, "I suppose he will."

Dolores crouched down and looked out through a small crack in the door, and presently stood up and walked out into the front room; more voices were heard, and then the door opened and shut, and a car engine started up, and then was heard the distinct sound of a car driving away. She came back in, smiling.

He was feigning praise as he pointed his right hand—the one that contained the cigarette—at her as he spoke, "You have powers of persuasion that dwarf the common man," and he let go a small laugh and a shake of his head.

"Oh, it was the contractor for the house," she began moving toward him, "they wanted to do some work on it today; I forgot they were going to come when we were on vacation, but since I didn't go, I was going to call…"

But he had already reached out to her extended arms and pulled her onto him. "You're either very, very bad, or very, very good," he breathed into her smirking face. "Maybe those stupid ploys work on little boys who play pimp with you, but not on men such as I." He pulled her hair hard toward him and kissed her mouth even harder.

"You knew it wasn't my family," she said, smiling largely, "from the beginning?"

He smiled. "I know women like you, I have always known women like you, and they don't make mistakes; no, they don't, not when they have plans in mind like you have, not women like you who are industrious, women who want more than their husbands can possibly give them, or anyone they know can possibly give them; no, I know women like you, and so has society, and history," he laughed, "you see, I don't play with words, either; you are what you are and don't make apologies about it; why, look at me, I am not about to preach about your bad conduct while I lie in another man's bed; no, I am what I am and you are what you are, and we both like it that way, and we both don't hide it." He kissed her passionately on the mouth. "Maybe we do have a future together, baby."

They would not leave the bedroom for another two hours.

Two weeks hence, and they had talked on the phone dozens of times, every chance she had when she was home and away from her husband, and always when she was away from home; and whenever she was away from home and could manage it, she met with him and they engaged in prolonged and lustful acts of unrestrained sexual congress for whatever spare amount of time they had—and over three months' time it amounted to sixty-four times. After three months, they met again, this time at his mansion, and after he had given her the walking tour and they visited the bedroom for a lengthy stay, they swam in the extravagantly built outdoor pool and then lay on their tanned backs together in the colorful rock garden, holding hands, eyes closed, cuddled by the silky rays of the yellow giver of light.

"Where do you get all of your energy from? I mean, I know you work long hours, but you seem never to get tired."

He smiled inwardly. "A secret," he said, and let it go at that.

"I feel alive here," she whispered to him, holding his hand, "as if I was meant to be here."

"Every woman feels she should be with money," he replied, "as if they were dead until they fell into it."

"But it's more than that; yes, it is the money, but it's you, and you without me seems so wrong."

"So I have heard from every woman I have ever had up here."

"Has every woman up here been the lover I am?"

"Nope, you're the best."

She smiled in glee. "Are there any better at reading your mind?"

"Nope, you're the best there, too."

"So, what is it, then; I mean, why don't you tell me things..."

He opened his eyes, grabbed her left hand and shook it up and down, and then said, "Remember, the little dance of the diamond ring? You're only as good as you are while you're married, and once you are not, you will revert back to who you are with him; it's just nature, it isn't your fault, no," and he let go of her hand, "just enjoy this forbidden fruit while you can and don't worry about what will never be." He shut his eyes again.

"What do you mean?" she charged, eyes screwed up as she propped herself up on her right elbow.

"I mean, that you are a different woman when you have an affair; you are the best lover and confidante and friend and anything else because that is all you have to be with me, the best of what you are not with him; whatever passion is missing in a marriage is resurrected during these affairs; it isn't hard, believe me; if I were to marry any one of the women I have had such affairs with, I would be cheating on her with some-one like you in a year's time; I am afraid it's just squeezing all the rich juices out of the ripe fruit in the beginning, and when that is all gone, at least for me, it's time to move on."

"Are you saying you will be moving on with me, soon?"

"I thought we weren't going to lie to each other." He never even opened his eyes.

She fumed for a moment, and then said, reluctantly, "Yes, but how do I know where we are going if we don't talk about us."

"There is no 'us,' Dolores, there is only you and me, and your husband at home who thinks you're driving up to your cousins' for a visit, that's it; you aren't going to leave him and I'm not going to ask you to."

She was silent for a long time, and then said, angrily, "You don't know me, at all; you don't know what I am capable of."

His cell phone rang and he took the phone call, and he smiled and laughed when he announced the name of the red-head; his tone was bathed in affection and delight as he spoke to her and promised to see her soon; he disconnected the phone and put his sunglasses back on and lay down on the white wicker recliner and let a silly, resplendent grin rise from his inner thoughts to his handsome visage.

"I don't believe you, Eli; you have no class at all."

He shook his head and looked over at her, and then spoke, his sharp words tipped with genuine uncaring, "Maybe you're not getting this, Dolores—you are married; you go home to your husband when you leave here and I go to my mis-tresses; this is what we are, now, you are just another frustrated housewife cheating on her husband, a woman who hasn't the wherewithal to go the distance, and I am living in the best of both worlds, just like the wild stallion that mates with the best of its herd, but also steals the best mares of another one;

that's just the way it is, baby, there are men like me in the world who have what a lot of women want and we take them whenever we please, and there are men who are just ordinary Joes and they have ordinary wives; and you, well, you are neither hot or cold, you're just tepid, because you don't really want to burn or freeze anyone's hand for fear that you might lose the hand that feeds you, because, if that happens—save us all—you might have to work for a living."

She stared at him hard for the longest time, and then stood up and walked away and disappeared through the back door.

"She'll be back," he mused, smiling, "they all come back, no matter what I say to them or what I do to them, because it is better being treated this way by a rich man than being treated this way by a poor man." He laughed and nodded his head in recognition of his youthful sagacity.

In fifteen minutes she came back crashing through the back door and walked quickly up to him and ripped off his sunglasses and threw them into the Olympic-sized pool. "You have some nerve telling me who I am," she cried, her lithe but strong hands on her shapely hips; "you never once asked about where I came from."

He pointed to the sunglasses, which were floating in the water. "Are you going to replace those if they're damaged?"

She cursed him as if he meant something to her beyond an affair. "I have risked everything for you!"

He frowned. "Dolores, you never risk anything, you are always playing both sides of the monetary fence."

"That's a lie! If my husband found out about this…"

"And what would you do, then? Why, you would just find another man to sell your body to."

She slapped him hard on the face and he reached over and pulled her down next to him and slapped her hard on her face, and then she slapped him hard on his face and then he slapped her harder on her face; and then she sat down on her fading white wicker recliner and looked at him with her reddened countenance and held up her fine round head.

"You don't know me," she growled, not massaging her physical pain, "you don't know what I will do to take what I think I deserve…"

"Dolores," he said, disgusted now, "I don't need you, I don't need this; you can just leave anytime…"

"You don't know me!" she screamed, as her very heavy words were fusing a steel casket over the dark deeds of her past, entombing them from probing minds. "I never had a chance to live like you," she cried again, her face crimson with rage; "I lived in filth and rats and trailer-trash parks and abandoned cars and with my insane mother and drunken father until I ran away from home at age thirteen and lived on the streets in LA and learned to survive; I stole and took drugs and turned tricks and turned in friends and shot at cops and robbed people and I never once apologized for it because I had to survive or die." She was not weeping, no; her face was strong and full of pride. "I did what I had to do and I would do it again, and I fought my way out of the ghetto and found a man and did what I had to do to hold him, and now I have you and I want you and I will do whatever it takes to hold you, too."

"Is that supposed to impress me, really?" he said, frowning and then smiling. "Come on, I know women who did the same things you did and ran away from rich families; you are what you are, Dolores, don't make excuses for your past; why, I am seeing a woman now who ran away from a father who was molesting her and she lived on the streets and found a homeless shelter and eventually helped run it and never once got in trouble with the law, and now she has a good job and a nice house because that is what she wants, right now; but that is not what you want, right now; even if you had been born in her house or anyone else's house, you would want the same thing because what is inside you is unique in all the world, and that cannot be stopped, so just accept it."

She cursed him again. "You have an answer for everything, don't you?"

"No, I just know people, and more importantly, I know myself, and I don't make any apologies for who and what I am; I've had a good life, parents who loved me and a good upbringing, but I am a louse who will take his best friend's girl if I want her."

She smiled and moved next to him. "You think you're bad, but you're not; I am bad, and I know it, and I am proud of it, because I can't stand weak people, especially weak women, they make me sick, all of them," and she turned aside and spat, and then let her full, wet lips linger on his mouth and then she kissed him. "I'll do whatever it takes to hold my man and keep him."

He smiled largely. "I'll take that as a promise."

They did not leave the backyard for three more hours.

Closer and Closer

B ut there was always the problem of the importunate husband tracking her every movement and action with his incessant phone calls, and repeated inquiries once she was back from her errands. He secretly installed a GPS device in her cell phone but Eli, being an electronics wizard, detected the device, and disabled it in a way her husband would never be able to detect; he took great pride in such acts, as he was continually amazed at how easily husbands were duped into abandoning their intuitive ideas about their wives' infidelity by simple acts of misdirection and duplicity.

Soon, the husband of Dolores demanded that she acquire a job, and when she informed Eli of this decision, on her cell phone, as she was driving with her beloved twins to the store, he laughed inwardly; but outwardly, he calmly replied that she could begin work at his electronics business, in the shipping and receiving department. A week later she was hired and she soon thereafter became the first employee to arrive and the last to leave; her husband was happy because more money was coming in and Dolores was happy because she was able to spend amorous moments with her lover before and after work and on long lunch breaks in clandestine places away from work and in hidden places at work; she enjoyed the perils inherent in their physical rendezvous, and she thrived on it as if it were necessary for her well-being.

One day, some three months hence, she was in the front office and was observing middle-aged and obese Martha work her secretarial position, and Dolores walked up to her and sat down and took a memo that the woman had been typing and she instead typed it in a very short while at greater speeds and with greater accuracy, and all the while Martha sat there, her large mouth agape and her response silent. Dolores then tossed the paper back to the secretary and leaned in and said, coolly, "You ought to be in a tree, old woman," and she nodded to the back rooms behind her, "that's right, in a tree, and the rest of us with thick branches," she nodded her head and smiled. "Do you know what the Indians used to do to old people when they suspected them of being too much of a burden? Well, they put them in a tree and then surrounded it as they held big, thick branches and then they pounded on the tree trunk," and she slammed her fisted right hand down so hard on the ceramic counter that Martha jumped a bit out of her brown, leather-covered swivel chair, "and they pounded on it, and if the old person had the strength," and here she balled up her left hand into a tight fist and stuck it in the secretary's face as it bled a vibrant fiery red, "to hang on, why, they could rejoin the tribe and live another day; but if the old fool did not have the strength to hold tight," and she let both of her hands slap palms-down on the brown counters, "why, then, the old bag of bones was left to be eaten by the wolves." She reared back and disgust pushed her pretty face into a heap of scorn. "You, you make me sick, people like you who society carries, fat and greasy and barely moving old fossils who are just mounds of decaying blubber, all of you ought to be in trees," and she laughed a laugh so wicked and empty of human strains that the woman moved nervously away from her tormentor, "you ought to be made into food for the young and strong, like me; yes, I would like to see you ground into meat and salted and be eaten, at least by dogs; yes, at least feed you to the dogs, so your last miserable years on Earth aren't a total waste."

It was as if Martha was caught in the stare of a swaying and poised-to-strike young cobra, unable to speak, but she slowly regained her faculties, and said, her voice blistered with outrage, "How dare you speak that way to…"

"Because," Dolores shouted straight into the face of the secretary, "I can, and I will every day until you leave and I am sitting in your place and I learn the business like you never could, you fat, ugly, old cow!" And she stood up and began to walk away but turned abruptly and screamed, "So, watch out, because it's a long way down!" and she laughed long and hard as she disappeared through the door leading to the large warehouse.

Martha complained to Eli about the behavior of Dolores, and that night, Dolores and Eli left work two hours late. Her husband accused her of abandoning her twins and having an affair, and the two of them screamed and shouted and she struck him and he struck her. The husband called his father and the father came over and the two men conversed in private for hours and when they were finished the husband summoned his wife and delivered his final decree that she must abandon her job and take full charge of her twins and his children. Dolores rebelled against this and her wrath against the meddlesome father grew.

Eli, after hearing this story, instructed her to arrive on time to work and leave on time from work to dissuade her husband from further suspicion, but the father-in-law was not satisfied, and he persuaded his son to hire a private detective to follow Dolores about town and also spy on her at her job; but Dolores, ever the eavesdropper, had become suspicious of her husband, and had left several micro-recorders about the house and soon discovered this information, and immediately relayed it to Eli, who met with her the next day at work.

He could see the frustration in her face and her need for a man to lighten her burden, and he was pleased. "Leave him," he said, casually; "it's time."

"But I can't," she complained, bitterly, "I can't leave the twins, they're my life; if I left he would get custody of them," and her voice became icy cold, and then inflamed with wrath, "and I will never let that happen, I would rather they die first than have them be raised by him and his mule of a father and his stupid, weak mother." She shook with fury.

After three more months' time, the private investigator was released from his duties by the husband, and Eli and Dolores resumed their affair outside the workplace.

It was a dark winter day, when the sky is a black shroud that casts the land in streams of dark shadows, and the cold rain flows in a heavy current and the frozen breath of the wind chills the land, that Dolores walked up behind Martha in the early morning and slipped a DVD into the secretary's computer; and lo, Martha, gazing upon the brazen images therein, felt her mind befuddled, and her soul become barren, and her forehead throbbed with agony and her heart ached so that she clutched her breasts.

Dolores leaned in and whispered near her tilting head, "You see, you old, stupid cow, I will do whatever I need to win, I will show the world your private warts and sins; you would never think of such an act, because you have your stupid rules of morality," and she laughed a sordid laugh, and rose up and let her mind fall onto the steel cage into which she had thrown her victim. "You quit or I'll play this on the Internet; you do know what that is, don't you, you stupid old tree hugger?" She expelled a long breath of arrogance and released the DVD from its sheath. "I'll expect your resignation in the morning."

"I'll tell the boss," Martha breathed, erratically, her head swaying from side to side.

"Go ahead, and you know what will happen," Dolores replied, and left by the back door. The next morning Martha had resigned and Dolores had applied for the secretarial job.

Later that day, Eli sat across from Dolores in the front office and stared at her. The other twenty employees had gone home. "Did you think I would not find out about your little ploy?" he began, his voice resting on a dangerous and blustery precipice.

"I don't know what you're talking…"

He inhaled all the power of his building temper and expelled his bitterest gall at her. "I'm not your husband, don't lie to me; you're not hustling your tricks and drug addicts, now; remember," and he leaned toward, "I know you better than any man, because we are the same." His breath was fast and furious. "Tell me," he shouted, nearly begging, "and don't disappoint me."

She clenched her teeth and sucked in her thick lips. "Yes, yes, I blackmailed your stupid secretary," and she cursed her, "what of it? You've done the same thing to get where you are; she's slow and stupid and fat, and she is in my…"

His magnificent shout stripped her of any impetus. "This is my business, this is my livelihood, this isn't the streets, you don't do those things here," and he pointed toward the brown carpet, "we have rules of conduct here," and then he pointed toward the outside world, "out there you can do whatever you like, but not in here; are you listening to me, Dolores!" Her muted response elicited more shouts from him. "I cannot trust you if you don't have a fundamental grasp of business ethics in the workplace," and he shoved his chair so close to her that she nearly had to lean backwards, "if you are a crazy woman who cannot distinguish between two totally and easily distinguishable worlds, then you need to leave."

Her face was fuming a fiery wrath, and her breath was quick and powerful, but the ripples of defeat soon spread over her body, and she relaxed, and presently relented. "All right, I'm sorry…"

"No, that isn't the correct response, the correct response is 'yes, Eli, what I did was wrong,' not that I am sorry I got caught." He shook his head and leaned back. "I don't know about you anymore, Dolores, I don't know if I can trust you if you continue to do such stupid things; I can't be looking over my back all the time."

"It's him," she began, angrily, "Bill." It was her husband's father. "He wants me to quit this job and be a full-time mother, and I know you don't play favorites at work; I know you are all business, here, and I wanted this new position to show his stupid family I could work a real job…" But she broke off as she gazed at his shaking head and incredulous visage, and then she sighed. "All right, I wanted this job because I wanted this job and I hated that fat old cow, Martha," and then she screamed, "are you happy? But that old fool Bill does want me to quit my job and my idiot husband is going along with it…" She looked up and gasped as she saw her husband pulling into the parking lot.

"Here," Eli said, quickly, "stall him," and handed her a raft of memos that needed typing, and he hastily retreated to the back room.

The husband walked in and Dolores burst out in a smile and waved at him, set down the papers, and then ran around the counter and leaped into his arms. "Can you believe it? I have been promoted to secretary! This means more money and benefits, too; aren't you proud of me?"

"Where is Eli?" the husband demanded, his face grim with a weighty purpose.

She responded with a frivolous conversation about work, and when she sensed that he would no longer tolerate this dodge, she said, casually, "He is in the back, working."

The husband barreled through the front office and slammed open the back door and walked swiftly into the large warehouse, shouting the name of Eli.

"Patrick," Eli said, coming from a far corner of the warehouse, and walking up to him, extended his hand but found himself rebuffed. "Well, what can I do for you?"

His words were curt and impatient. "Dolores is quitting her job." He turned to his wife. "Let's go."

"Would you walk with me a moment, Patrick? I would like to show you…"

"No, I won't walk with you," he answered, "let's go," he shouted to his wife, who was walking slowly behind him.

"I understand completely, I really do," Eli responded, deflecting the intense heat of his antagonist, "I just want Dolores to finish some documents so we can finish the biggest account we have, and then I'll have to have her sign some papers so she won't get the bonus money that was coming for employees who were still employed by the first of next month." He walked ahead and allowed the infusion of monetary reward sift into the brain of the husband, and he had the papers in his hand and then extended them toward Dolores as she and her husband walked into the front office. "Here, finish this draft fast and then sign at the bottom of the papers." He looked at Patrick. "I agree totally with what you're doing; I hope you don't mind that Dolores has agonized over keeping this job while it kept her away from her family; in fact, she threatened to quit many times and I talked her out of it; no, I am partially to blame and I believe this is the best course; a mother needs to be with her family."

"Whatever," Patrick said, scrutinizing his wife's movements, and then nodding his head, "you will pay her what she is owed…"

"Oh, of course, up to this very day," Eli said, and reached into a drawer to retrieve a box of checks. "I'll make this out right now," and he prepared the check and handed it to Patrick. He reached out his hand and Patrick reached out his and the two men shook hands. "Are you nearly done?" he said, looking to Dolores. "I have a date tonight." He looked to Patrick. "All work and no play make Jack a dull boy." He smiled. Everyone in attendance heard a honk and then they saw a most gorgeous female exit a black Ferrari and walk with an exuding sensuality up to the doors and enter the silent fray.

"Hey, baby," Eli said, coming round the counter and kissing the youthful redhead. He turned to Patrick. "This is my fiancée, Eliza." He watched with great satisfaction as Eliza and Patrick shared their brief time of flesh together by slowly shaking hands; he carefully analyzed the face of his antagonist and kept his moves and countermoves on the virtual chess board in his mind far ahead of his contestant.

Dolores blushed a red-hot jealousy.

"Well, everything is done, here," Dolores said, then stood up, put her arm inside the muscular arm of her husband, and then tenderly kissed him. "Love you," she whispered, to assume the role of the demure spouse who readily accepts the authority of her husband.

"Well, I'll be sorry to see Dolores go; she was a valuable employee," Eli said, turning to go with Eliza, "and she can go now—I'll finish the memos on my own."

"Well," Patrick interjected, "how much was the bonus?" He picked up the papers Dolores had been working with and began to inspect them.

"There you go, I have toppled your false pride with mammon," Eli thought. "Oh," he said aloud, "ten thousand dollars," but he proceeded out and around the counter and toward the glass entry doors.

"That's a lot," Patrick said, still standing behind the counter, and his nodding head evinced that he believed in the authenticity of the documents, "don't you prorate it if the employee quits early?"

Eli, frowning, turned. "No, and I am surprised, that you, being a man with such great business acumen, would think that a company would reward an employee who leaves, and certainly someone who leaves without any advance warning; no, I will have to find someone, and soon, to replace her, and hope it will be someone as competent and dedicated to the job. This time, I think I will find a single woman," and he turned to leave.

"Well," Patrick said, "what if she finishes out the year?"

Eli stopped again, and turned around, frustration wearing his calm expression. "Look," he began, his voice commanding now, "I didn't ask her resign, nor did I ask for this—you did this; it's done; she signed the papers and that is that." He shook his head. "Patrick, you are a businessman, you have your own dealership—would you allow an employee to simply stay another two weeks just so you could give away money?"

"Well, what if she stays past the first of the month?"

"I can't keep an employee I cannot rely on."

"Honey, my parents are waiting," Eliza said.

Eli turned and kissed her, and then looked back to Patrick. "I don't know what you want, but you are the man, and she'll obviously do whatever you want; but it has to be soon, I am sure you can appreciate that. This has been the biggest year for my company, and we're in the process of acquiring another business and nearly tripling our accounts, and I'll need the best people I can find."

"Maybe she can stay…"

"I don't need 'maybes,' I need a 'yes,' Patrick, I need a commitment from both of you; look," he assumed a softer tone and came around behind the counter. "I don't want to come in between you and your wife and kids; take your time and think about it."

"No, I have thought about it, she'll stay."

"Are you sure, dear?" Dolores asked, coyly.

"Yes," Patrick nearly shouted. And that was that.

Eli departed with Eliza and left Dolores to close up the business. When Patrick and Dolores were alone, she aroused his sexual passion and took him to the back room and engaged in fiery marital relations with him to seal her silent victory.

After the unfortunate incursion of Patrick into the secret lives of the two lovers, Eli instructed Dolores on how to surreptitiously place a GPS device inside the cell phone of her husband, so that they might properly track his every movement hence.

The Human Blemish

E li came back two hours later, and having paid Eliza—whom he had kept, one of many, on the ready for such emergencies—handsomely for her role in the ruse, he found Dolores hard at work at the front counter. She cursed him as he approached her and then they fell through the back doors and onto the white cot in the workroom and did not leave for one hour.

"So, the only reason you came back hours later was that you just had to be with Eliza?" she said, walking around nervously now.

"You were with Patrick."

She shook her head. "Where do you get the energy, really?"

He smiled. "My little secret, which I will show you, one day."

She slammed back down next to him on the cot. "So, you had those ridiculous papers sitting around just in case Patrick came in one day? You are so clever, you remind me of myself," she laughed, and then lay on her back; "it is so easy to manipulate people when it comes to sex and money." Her face assumed an unchaste shadow cast from her infected human soul. "I could corrupt anybody—I want to corrupt everybody," it was as if she were talking to the world, now, "I want to show everyone that no one is above me, that they're all just no good like me—but pretend they're not." And then she looked at him and seemed to focus upon the present. "I don't like the way Eliza came so quickly; I don't like her hanging around waiting for your phone calls."

"And this is from the girl who goes home to her husband every night."

She stood up, vexed. "I don't know how much longer I can do this, especially with his father against me; I need him gone. You're not doing your part to help."

He frowned. "Why are we talking about this? You're obviously not ready to leave your husband."

"I told you, I won't abandon my babies, ever," she said, firmly; "they're the only good thing in my life, other than you," and she bent down and kissed him passionately.

"I can't believe he let you stay longer tonight."

"The fool thinks only of money and his precious muscle cars and the stupid car shows he and his kids and father go to; he is fooled for now but he won't be fooled forever because of his meddlesome father." Her voice acquired a darker tone and a violent twitch. "His father needs to be put down for good." Eli laughed long and hard until tears were welling up in his eyes. "What," she smiled, "what is it?"

"You," he said, exploding with an exploratory laugh that was posed to deconstruct her hardness, "all you do is talk about how bad you are and all you are is an adulteress, which doesn't qualify as much, these days."

She stood up with her temper rising with her. "You are always mocking me on that, you don't know what…"

"Talk, talk, talk…"

"I'll show you, I'll show you how bad I have been," she shouted, her chest heaving, and she began to walk toward the door; "tomorrow, tomorrow I will show you who you are really sleeping with and why you should be afraid of me."

She came in the next day and Eli sat her and Martha down and explained to both of them the need to work as a team; neither of the women liked it but they accepted it and the workday soon transpired and all of the regular employees went home except the two irregular employees.

Dolores approached him in the back workroom and slipped out a DVD that she had been wearing against her soft white belly, and held it up on high, and said, her face beaming with pride, "See this? This will make you a believer in me."

Eli feigned ignorance and merely stood with a casual look on his face as Dolores placed the metallic silver disc into the DVD player and then turned on the machine. "Sit down with me," she said, and took his hand and led him to the white cot as the crowded, hazy images appeared. She squeezed his hands and her face became agitated with fervor as the sounds of human noises and the figures of human beings became sharper and clearer on the fifty-four-inch high-definition LCD television.

He beheld the human massacre on the screen and he could not divulge his human revulsion; he was staring straight into the maelstrom of abomination and he could not allow his body to betray his mental agony; he was witnessing the inner depths of immorality, seeing the encrusted seed of iniquity flowering before him like a malignant tumor, singing proudly its dreaded song of war on Virtue, and he had to ingest it and smother it and not allow the tiniest ripple of his moral decency to surface, lest the heinous creature who lay with him sense it. Yes, he saw this smirking sin that wore a crown of slain hearts upon it boasting of itself, full of itself, proud of itself as the fallen saint was devoured by those treacherous villains whose hearts had been worm-eaten and their souls tarred by unfettered wickedness.

His false woman was amorous as she narrated the history of this carnival of debauchery, and she pulled him down and kissed him, still laughing over the plight of the fallen heroine. There, up on the screen, he saw what he did not want to see but had to see, to be sure so he could inflict his mind with conviction that what he must do next was a fitting and proper judgment for those accused of this abominable crime; yes, he saw her, he saw Oscine, he saw her mind being dismantled moment by moment by the slobbering, wailing, pounding monsters that labored and grunted and groaned as they attacked her and scrubbed her consciousness clean from her disintegrating mind. He saw it, he saw it all and took it all in and his mind was set ablaze by the horror of what unprovoked human beings do to Innocents, and he watched as the men were paraded in front of the camera and how they strutted around their helpless victim and how Heath encouraged them and how Vivian laughed and laughed and cursed her vanquished nemesis. He saw it, he saw all the basest nature of Man rise up, not in a time of war or in unstable economic times or in any other troubled time, but in a time of idleness and sloth, and wealth and ease, when all was right with the world for these malefactors and when they were not beset or pursued by any bad thing, and when they simply lusted for a human sacrifice because it was the way they were and what they wanted for the present, without regard to tomorrow for anyone but themselves. He saw it, he saw the father-in-law, strutting around in his ugly, naked and sagging flesh, and he saw the camera pan to the mother-in-law, who was giving advice on how to film the better part of the assaults.

And he knew what he had to do, he was certain what he had to do and nothing on Earth could stop him now; yes, his plan would go forward and he would risk it all and he would be victorious because he had never been like these people, never dwelled in the house of habitual, unrepentant, unfettered sin and embraced it and drunk its fiery pestilence, because he had always known there was a limit to his physical lusts.

When the video was over and the temptress Vivian was in the bathroom cleaning up and Eli was standing and looking at the bathroom door, he lifted his head toward Heaven and shut his eyes and let his body grow limp as his thoughts arose in a great clamor of righteousness and honor, "Vivian, you harlot, Vivian, you witch, I will cut open your veins, yes, I will cut them open and drain your vampire's black blood and replace it with a bitter-tasting gall, and it will drive you to insanity, and you will do my will, and it will destroy your own kind; yea, I will make a slayer of you, a slayer of your own people, and when you have looked around and have seen what you have done, you will abandon your own life, gladly; this, then, is the Justice I invoke of a higher law; this, then, is the destiny you and your kind have carved for each other with every wicked thought and every wicked deed; O, Abraham, O, Oscine, I swear to you, I swear to you right here and now that I will have them all dead if I have to die with them." He fought back pious tears and let his head come down as he opened his misty eyes. "I swear this thing," he whispered, his words bursting with passion, "I will avenge you both."

The Clock Ticks

T he next day at work, Vivian was all aglow as she bathed in the waters of a glittering victory; she had her promotion and she had her rich boyfriend and she reasoned she had convinced him that she was like him and was willing to do anything for him. When they were alone after work, she was a fount of shameless boasting and gushing sensuality. "So, do you think I am so weak," she said with a playful wink, "now that you have watched what we did to that little fool? Oh, if Patrick found out that I had a copy of the video, he would kill me; he destroyed the original, you know, and he was paranoid for months after his stupid wife was found murdered—those stupid police, they always think the husband is somehow involved—and especially when the insurance men came and told us how much sweet money we were getting from the policy on her," and she twirled around the warehouse, humming and giggling. She raised her black and arched eyebrows and put out her finely manicured hands to him and he took them and the couple danced to her joyful rant. "Well, I had to live away from him for a few months because he was so nervous about everything; and after he moved to another neighborhood, then we got married; oh, and with the money we got, Patrick bought that dealership and we bought ourselves a good life, for a while, anyway; and then the money ran out and he became a bore and then a pest, and then he wanted me to be like she was, and that was when the trouble started, and then I met you, my love, my sweet, wonderful Eli," and she kissed him and laughed and twirled about in absolute ecstasy.

"Sit down," Eli said, smiling falsely now, as he had done from the beginning of his expedition against this human fiend, and he reached into his pants pocket and withdrew a small, black velvet box and slowly pulled back the top to reveal an engagement ring studded with many large, sparkling diamonds of the greatest carat, cut, color and clarity; Vivian, her entire being, her heart and soul and mind, was swept immediately into that great clump of squeezed-together carbon atoms and at once lodged inside them and was now peering out and seeing an upside-down, inside-out, and ugly world. She was remade in the image of her luminous captor, and she felt the blood of the mercenary bore up in her, and she embraced it, and she acknowledged all of it, and vowed to swallow any obstacle in her way, no matter its foul taste and smell.

She leaped into his waiting arms and kissed him and looked to the ring and smiled largely. "Oh, Eli, I love you."

No, Eli thought, you love only those who can give you what you want. "Sit down, Dolores," he said, and sat down with her. "I want to marry you, but..." He saw her quizzical look and his stolid face betrayed nothing of his internal loom that even now spun a judicious and cunning web around her. "You're about sixty pounds overweight."

"What," she cried, looking at her svelte figure, "sixty pounds overweight?"

"Your kids."

The glare of the ill humor faded from her face and she shook her head. "But you know I won't leave them, ever," she said, with great certitude.

"Then we can't be together."

"But there must be some other way..."

"No, there isn't; I have plans for us, and it doesn't involve custody battles with an ex-husband and being weighed down with two children; I want us to travel, and to move about the country with our business; that is correct, you heard me, I want you to help me run our business once we are married; I want to make you a full partner; I have seen the way you…"

"Stop," she shouted, waving her hands about angrily, "you will only marry me if I abandon my own children, my own babies?"

"You can visit them when we are in town." But he said it with such a skeleton of warmth that it cut out a chunk of ice right in front of her.

"You're cruel, you are," she said, shaking as if she felt a sudden chill, and her eyes took on the outline of piety in the form of a faint mist, but it did not proceed past this.

"You know, I have never seen you cry."

She stood up. "And you never will." She handed him back the velvet black box with the diamond ring in it, and he accepted it without argument, and then watched her walk away and leave through the front door.

"She'll be back," he whispered, nodding his head. "She'll be back, Abraham and Oscine, she will because she cannot deny her own idea of herself, and it is that she has no reason to live other than to take those treasures upon herself that we deem destructive; she can no more deny her own sinful heritage than a rattlesnake its need to strike and kill its prey; I don't know what she is or who she is or why she is, I only know that she needs to die, and the sooner the better."

For the next three weeks, Vivian made no mention of the engagement ring or the marriage proposal to Eli, and during this time, she came early to work and left on time and her relationship with Martha improved and her skills as a secretary proved exceedingly capable and efficient; she did not stay with Eli late or call him or make mention of their past as lovers. There was something claiming to be noble inside Eli that chipped away at his intransigent image of her so she might be deemed good, but he would not relent, it swung at his hardened heart and felt itself smash into particles of dust and mayhem, but Eli bore them up into his nostrils and exhaled them with great ease; no, he would have none of it, there would be no meekness in him as he marched against this tide of swelling darkness; he must not let sentiment and a yearning for all people to be good impede his quest to destroy her for her past transgressions.

It was a on a chilly and windy and rainy Friday of the fourth week that Vivian was at home tending to her twins after a long day at work, and she was in the kitchen fixing dinner for Heath and his three sons when her in-laws swept into the house and installed themselves on the white sofa in the living room, and like a dent in the time-space continuum, their imposing personalities slid any close bodies down toward their giant girths; thus, Heath and his boys and their grandparents began their ritualistic family fun night of board games on the white plush carpet and thus commenced their laughing and snorting and shouting and occasional wrestling about. Vivian loathed it all, loathed the idea of adults engaged in trivia, especially while she cooked in the kitchen as if she were the hired help. Dinner came and the entire brood sat around the glass table in the dining room and she endured the obnoxious commentaries by Bill on anything political or philosophical. "He preaches to imbeciles, who worship him as a god," she often thought when she heard his long-winded, grinding oratories. Tonight, he was preaching on the necessity of building fences on the borders to keep out illegal aliens and the necessity of the war on illegal drugs and the necessity of legalizing prostitution; he was always proselytizing on these issues and other issues of great import because he knew that his words were just as meaty and saucy and spicy as the food and just as likely to be ingested and digested and circulated to all parts of his hearers' brains and accepted as fuel as the warm cuisine; indeed, his son and his grandsons and his wife were an echo-chamber for his very thoughts on every topic he lathered with his rhetorical bread and butter; they were the bait upon which he expertly placed his pungent scent, the steel trap upon which he placed his bloody, fresh meat. Yea, they took it in and absorbed it and expounded on it and in so doing crowned him king with their every melting praise of his intellect.

Vivian was normally reticent on his overblown rants, but stung once too often, one can develop a strong reaction to the same stinger, and so she looked at him with all good humor drained from her beauteous face. "So, if prostitution were legal, would you use their services?"

Heath dropped his food from his mouth and the boys' ears pricked up and the drooping face of the mother-in-law blanched white: he dashed a quick discharge full of explicit profanities at her, and then said, "You don't talk like that around my father," he cried.

"Oh, no? Are we going to pretend now, are we?" and she looked to Bill, whom she never addressed by his first name. "You're just like any other man who can't be faithful to one woman, that's why you use your computer so much and why you are sometimes gone for so long..."

Heath reached out and slapped her, but she merely laughed as she looked him. "Do you think I am like your last wife, who could be cowed by that?" She looked to her mother-in-law. "Does it bother you when your husband does those things?" And she let loose a pompous verbal missive as her face radiated delight. "And don't pretend he doesn't." She received another slap of rebuke upon her red cheeks and then smiled as she looked at her attacker. Heath stood up and pulled her hair, but then she reached out and slapped him and he let go and she sat down again and looked once more to her mother-in-law, breathing heavily, her face flush with fever, just as if she were a combatant in a rousing fight, and cried, "And you're the most pathetic of them all…pretending…the faithful wife," and she spat on the pristine carpet, and then said, amiably, looking at the dinner table, "Now, shall we eat all this fine food?" and she took a mouthful of the sweet cabbage and tender sirloin and steaming hot mashed potatoes and thick gravy.

Bill was a king on a throne attacked by the court jester. "You little whore," he finally said, nodding his head, "you came into this family a whore and you can leave a whore—back to the streets."

"Pot calling the kettle black," she smiled, and then laughed, uproariously, as if her mind were suddenly unhinged.

"I don't have to defend myself against you or any other lowlife off the street," he shouted, and he took the hand of his shaking wife, "my wife knows I have been faithful to her all forty-one years of marriage."

Vivian looked at him with an enmity that had taken time to blossom and grow deep within her. "You," she laughed, with merriment, "you can't be faithful a week past your last retirement check."

"That's enough," Heath shouted.

"You're right, that is enough," she said, firmly, and she arose and went to her bedroom and slammed the door. She was glad she had finally exposed the hypocrisy of her father-in-law and she felt as if she no longer belonged in this house, with these unremarkable people; she had no feelings for the three boys and no love for her husband but abounding love for her twins; she wondered why tonight she had burst forth with revelation about Bill, and so she lay down and thought and thought and a light slumber descended upon her that blocked out the noise of the stupid voices downstairs, which she could no longer tolerate.

She dreamed that she was a creature that was standing on the earth and could see the naked world of people below her hustling and bustling about like blind ants tending to the anthill; she saw them all as faceless workers who could not see above or beyond their class, and she heard them say how happy they were and how necessary it was to keep what they had and not venture too far out from their precious homes; she scoffed at this and looked to those people who were building the mounds with their great machines and she saw them laughing and smiling and pouring honey upon the hapless drones; and then she saw the tall buildings and people in there who controlled the builders and she could see now the finely woven threads of silk streaming from the buildings to the machines down to the workers and she nodded and sighed, "There, shall I make my abode," and she felt herself going into the buildings and lying with these princes and lords, and lo, she saw herself attaching to them, her feet digging into their sides, and her hands digging into their backs, and her head burrowing into their minds, and she sunk herself deep into them and began to drink their blood and feel their power, and she was well pleased.

And then she awoke.

As she lay there, she thought of the gross receipts she had seen at work, the vast monies that were coming into the business and the paths to gain such wealth; but she was not versed in the ways of business, but versed in the ways of seduction, so she would gain this wealth through the conquering of the flesh; and so she resolved to be with Eli and leave her husband, but she was still perplexed about her twins, as she could never leave them. She crept to the door and listened to Heath and Bill speak about the necessity of ridding the house of her, and her wrath increased against her father-in-law. When all of her family had gone to bed, she walked downstairs and poured herself a glass of rich red wine and propped her feet up on the white bamboo chair and anticipated revenge against her enemies.

The next day the entire family went on a trip to visit their cousins, but Vivian stayed home, and immediately, she went to Eli and lay with him and told him of her plans to leave Patrick and her deep and increasing loathing of Bill.

Eli was sitting on his maroon leather chair as she listened to her story. "I don't know what you want from me," he began; "you know I want you, but not your twins. You're better off with your husband."

"How can you say that?" she screamed. "You say you love me but you won't take my babies! You're cruel!" and she grabbed her head on both sides. "I can't think, I can't think with that idiot father-in-law talking against me in my own house. You have to do something, Eli, you have to take care of him, you have to do it, you're the man, do it, Eli, do whatever you have to do so I can think."

He stared at her and raised his head on high and stood up erect. "You're amazing, you really are; I still haven't seen you cry, not once, over anything; I cannot trust you, Dolores, you don't talk to me for one month and now you're ready to leave your husband but you want his father out of the way, first; but this is what you desire today—and what about tomorrow? No, I cannot trust you because," and he screamed at her, "you are always scheming, even against me, scheming for something because it is your corrupt nature; no, I cannot trust you because everything you do is for yourself."

"I have risked everything for you," she shouted, "I could lose my husband and my babies and you, and what are you risking? You'll just find another whore!"

He stared at her, his countenance sober, as he stated, matter-of-factly, "And what does that mean? It is just more talk from a woman who wants what she doesn't have. If I could just trust you, you could have it all," and when he turned away, he smiled, and as he walked away, he knew his spiked words would latch onto her and drag her with him.

She sat up and followed him to the dining room, where he poured both of them a glass of sparkling white wine.

Her cell phone rang and she answered it in a sensuous voice full of devotion and love. "Hi, baby, how is the trip?" She talked for about a minute, and then said, "Love you," after he had said the same, and she folded up her black, razor-thin phone and plopped it into her black leather purse.

He raised his glass. "To the chameleon," he said.

She raised her glass and touched it to his. "I will do whatever I have to, to survive, until we are together, and then I will just love you," she whispered, and leaned over and kissed him passionately.

"If I could only be certain," he whispered, "if you would just listen to me and follow my instructions, everything would be all right," and stroking her dark beauty with his sonorous, masculine tone, and they fell into each other's arms and soon their bodies were enjoined in physical pleasures once more.

Two hours hence, she was marveling at his great endurance. "You must tell me how you can work so hard and long and then be with so many women all the time and never get tired," she said, lying next to him.

"It is time I show you my secret." He led her to a tiny refrigerator that was hidden under the sink and once it was opened showed her a large, plastic oblong container that had a dozen syringes filled with a dark liquid. "B-12 shots," he said, "I have one a week, and they give me all the energy I need."

"Lately I have been so tired, with housework and work," she said, staring at the container; "show me."

He reached in and took out a syringe and held it up for her to inspect. "In fact, I need a shot today." He took out an alcoholic pad and swabbed his thigh and was about to inject himself, when she grabbed the syringe and plunged into her own bare thigh. He cursed. "What is wrong with you?" he cried.

But she just laid back her head and smiled. "I don't trust you."

He violently took the syringe away from her and ordered her out of his house.

"No," she said, "you can't do this to me, I just couldn't help myself; I'm sorry."

His anger drained out of his face and he smiled at her, in the same fashion the master smiles when his unruly bulldog finally heels. "You have never said that before—that you were sorry."

She embraced him. "I was never ready to say it, before," and she kissed him, "help me, now, help me get rid of his father so I can make a decision."

"I will help you, but you must do exactly as I say, or you will lose everything, just like the dog with a bone in its mouth, when he sees its reflection in a pond, loses its bone when he attempts to snatch the other bone away."

She shook her head in disbelief and smiled a gentle smile. "Now, I am a dog."

"We're all animals, I just know it."

And so he devised a plan to rid her household of William, the would-be Conqueror.

He installed secret video cameras in her house that sent images to his desktop, laptop computer, and cell phone. He gave her shots from the syringes every week for one month, and for that same month he abstained from all sexual contact with her and instructed her to increase mating with her husband; and at the end of the month, during the height of her ovulation period, he advised her on how to entrap Bill.

It happened when Heath was outside with his boys and his father was inside and his wife was fast asleep on the white sofa and snoring loudly; Vivian had spent the last month shooting home movies and feigning reconciliation with her father-in-law by baking him pies and smiling at him and offering him and his son every comfort as they worked on their cherished cars. Eli had been very precise in his instructions to her regarding her attitude with Bill, that she must alter his brain chemistry about her through a series of too-long, come-hither smiles and too-long brushes of her curvaceous body against his, and too-long erotic looks with her pouting lips and yearning body language. The pattern had been set and the moment was upon them, and it was a hot, sultry day when she stepped in for a cool shower at noon to remove excess sweat, then stepped from behind the glass door's shields, and walked past the open bedroom door and allowed herself to be seen by her father-in-law, where she paused, dripping with a glistening wet sensuality, her black, thick hair pulled back, her comely face burning with desire, her chest heaving and her breath quickening as she stared at him and beckoned him into her lair with her come-hither countenance. He was captured now by an insatiable lust for scintillating, creamy flesh he could only purchase on the boulevard of guilt and shame, where he was reminded he would never be desirable to young women again; and so he went in, his mind, body and soul led in by his desire for mating with beauty and youth.

He was not gone long, and when he returned he stood for a brief time at the doorway, and he reimagined himself as father and husband and grandfather, where he would retake his role in this house as lord and master; but then he thought of her betrayal and his need to lie, and his cunning mind laid out a plan that would refute her story and drive her out for good, and once this was established, he rejoined his son and grandsons outside, walking past his still-snoring, fat and lazy wife of forty-one years. He grimaced, but was secretly glad of what he had just accomplished, and felt the vitality of his youth resurge, and those glorious mating days when he could easily conquer any woman with a confident smile and smooth talk.

Vivian did not alter her attitude toward Bill for the next week, nor attempt to seduce him again. Then, one Friday night, when the family was eagerly at play during their sacred game night, she announced that she was going to show home movies she had recorded the last month. She placed the DVD into the black plastic holder and touched the play button, but no one seemed interested in watching events that she had captured only recently.

And then the images changed for the worse.

They heard Bill saying very filthy things and they heard Vivian saying very filthy things and the entire family looked up and beheld the big screen television aglow with the old man seducing her the afternoon she had stepped out of the fateful shower. No one moved.

"Oh, this one is my favorite," she said, "this is the one about the moral father-in-law who cheats on his wife with prostitutes and then," and she used the most obscene terms possible to describe what the family had just seen; and then she turned to look at Heath, whose face was blanched white, "that would make two in a row," and she shook her head, "you just can't trust your own father, these days." She stood up and removed the disk and walked out of the house, got into her car and drove away.

She was with Eli now and she wanted to mate with him but he reminded her that the plan was not yet over. "But my father-in-law is through," she protested, "you beat him for me!"

"We have to be careful for a while; we can't give Heath any reason to think you did this except to rid the house of Bill; you wanted time to think, and I have given it to you."

"And you're sure he won't use this against me to get my babies?"

"And risk having the entire community knowing his father visits prostitutes and has relations with his own son's wife? No, this is his community, and his sons; and besides, you have the evidence." He took the DVD and placed it in a safe place.

The Unexpected

V ivian and Heath argued three nights, two souls poisoned by each other and by themselves, two hearts ripped apart by deeds done and deeds undone; the man and woman neither slept nor ate, neither attended work nor to household chores, but became a disturbing force of violence, disrupting everything and anyone in their path wherever they went; they argued and screamed upstairs and they hollered and shouted downstairs, they slammed doors in the garage,

they threw objects in the family room; they were an insep-
arable force, each trying to drain the power from the other,
each seeking to crush the other to tears and acceptance, each
determined to break the other into servitude for a final victory;
but neither would retreat, neither would admit remorse, neither
would capitulate or cry contrition. The rest of the household
hid in the safe shadows and listened as the two tenacious forces
feasted on the intense hatred of the other, and when the end
came, there was a still in the place that was like the calm of
the sea after a monster storm has destroyed every ship and
island and abode.

Heath, wounded unto shame and humiliation that he could
not cow his wife, sped away with his sons, in the black pitch
of night, to the faraway campgrounds to retrieve his manhood
and his sanity. Vivian reigned supreme.

Eli had watched, with great amusement, the verbal spar-
ring and physical combat through the video cameras; he would
watch a few minutes of it on his home computer while sipping
an icy tea, and then he would drive to work and watch an hour
of it on his office computer; on the third day he was lounging
by the pool and gazing at the computer screen, mocking the
two combatants, sipping his sugary drink, when he saw the
husband bolt out of the door with his three sons in tow. "A
victory declared," he said, amused, "now, after the bell sounds,
the final act." He was smiling and he was laughing when he
stood up and dove into the pool and then came out of it and
walked by the monitor. He was chuckling when he went inside
his house to shower quickly so he would be prepared when she
came to him; he was smiling like the hunter who has finally
found his prey after years of searching, but when he walked
by the monitor, his smile fell away. He sat down and stared
at the screen and his head was shaking as he watched the

woman carrying the two infants in her arms and glancing up at the hidden cameras with a knowing nod; he felt a chill in his heart and he instinctively reached toward his cell phone and tried to call her. She would not answer.

He was in his car and his heart was racing faster than the Ferrari engine when he tore down the long rock driveway; he was moving at great speeds along the avenue, darting in and out of traffic, running stop signs and traffic lights and narrowly missing other cars, but it did not matter, as he merely stepped harder on the accelerator. He would not call the authorities, he reasoned, he had to do this thing himself, as he watched the small screen on his cell phone and saw her putting the infants into the water-filled bathtub.

He nearly crashed his car as it slammed down on the driveway. He jumped out and ran to the door and opened it and ran swiftly up the steps and entered the master bedroom and then turned the corner and ran into the bathroom. There was no movement from the bathtub and Vivian was kneeling over the infants, humming.

His breath was heavy and his heart was pounding and his face was shock and fear when he said, "What have you done!"

She turned and looked at him, and said, rather stoic, "I did it for us, honey."

He was afraid to walk up to her but he forced himself; he walked up to her and then stood there so he could see what he did not want to see, and then he saw them, the two infants, and his face cried horror and his body froze in terror.

The twins were upside down and motionless in the tub of soapy, warm water.

Yet it was a curious sight to see him so genuinely shocked and shaken by this tragic event, as he had hoped for this and planned it from the beginning.

Beyond the Pale

"**W**hat is wrong with you!" he cried, as he burst past her and seized the two children and fed them to the waiting ground; neither of them was breathing but he applied the breath of life to the girl, while delicately pressing down on the chest of the male; and when the signs of life came to her, he moved to the male and breathed in life to him while continuing to press gently upon his small chest; and lo, soon the infants were crying and coughing up water, and Eli stood up with them in his arms. "What were you thinking!" he shouted at her still form.

Her mind had grazed on madness, and her face was like a candle blown out in the smoky darkness. "I did it for us," her voice, like words spoken through a sieve, was in a tone reeking with bewilderment, "I couldn't let him take them." Her eyes, once a luminous sclera and a chocolate brown iris and ebony-filled pupil, were blood red and dilated with grief. "I would murder my own for our happiness."

He was quickly recovering his sensibilities and his mission to destroy as he stared at her; and once he set the children down on her bed, he carefully removed the video cameras and then came back to the door and observed her drooping form and lost expression. To his great relief the rescue of the twins had preserved his unsheathing of the final sword of words against her.

"Vivian."

She looked at him as if he had just stabbed her heart.

"Vivian, you harlot," he cried, his tongue aflame with final judgment, "did you think your sins would go unpunished, did you?" He could see the swollen shock on her visage slowly melt. "That's right, Vivian, the victims of your past bear witness to the judgment I heap upon your head now, for what you did to untold victims, I tell you these things," and he moved closer to her and watched her now-feeble confusion recede as animal instincts bored up in her. "I will tell you what you are now—your future; do you want to know your future, Vivian, your future and Heath's future, too? I will tell you." He was directly in front of her and he stood proudly and boldly without doubt or grief or trepidation. "I have condemned you, condemned you as you wear the blood of those murdered on your hands; the injections I gave you, yes," he saw the drifting light return from the coffin she had imagined into her blinking eyes and dress them in a frenzied sort of terror, "the first was filled with B-12, yes, but the next three with the AIDS virus, the last two with the virus and gonorrhea and syphilis; yes," he shouted, nodding, "you have surely passed along your wicked heritage to Heath and his father and mother, you mother-harlot of all women; and I did it all for them, for those two you murdered long ago but have forgotten because they were merely in your way." He was about to weep but he restrained himself as righteousness bored up in him. "I did it for Oscine and Abraham, for those whom you and Heath murdered, I did it for them, I murdered you as you murdered them." His face was so close to her face that he could feel her hot breath upon him. "And the tragedy is that you thought you had it all, but you didn't know that you can't have it all if you take it by shedding innocent blood; did you think, Vivian, did you think you could spill innocent blood and live?" He stood up fully erect and his face was flushed with pride and honor and love as his heart and soul and mind spilled its creed against her, "Don't you know, harlot, don't you know that a dog returns to its own vomit?"

and he turned and walked down the stairs and out to the car and then drove away.

He felt as if he had been protected by supernatural forces or providence, something omnipotent, something beyond the reach of Man, watching over him, for if the twins had died, he would have been morally culpable, and he would have been just like Vivian. He felt light and unburdened as he parked his car in his driveway and entered his house and took a long, hot shower and then began to fall toward sleep on his plush silk sheets. He had won the battle and the war and now he could live again; life was good and life was kind and he had avenged the lives of two Innocents; life, he thought as he drifted closer to a delicious sleep, it is full of joy and pain and love and hate, a world where men turn away from bringing succor to those who have fallen before them and around them and in front of them; but he, he reasoned, had not stepped aside against the swelling tide of wickedness, but had stepped up and anchored himself to the good Earth with the golden feet of Virtue. And he had won, yes, he thought, nearly asleep now, remembering the golden images of those fallen before him; he had stopped the advance of evil.

"I am man," he thought, "defined by my actions," and then he fell into a deep and satisfying sleep.

The next day he awoke, refreshed and reanimated toward life. "Yes," he sang, "today I begin, for today I realize my place in the world; a man of honor." He ate a hearty breakfast and showered and then drove off to tend to his last remaining mistress, his company.

He walked through the front glass doors and saw the faces of his employees; he was still whistling and he frowned through his happiness and cocked his head as he stopped and stared at them. He wondered if Vivian had come by and caused havoc here; he hadn't thought of her reaching out beyond her gutted silence and into his private workplace, he hadn't dared to think she would come here and smear her bloody wounds on these pristine surfaces.

"What is it?" he said, his fear beginning to rise.

The television was on and his employees were looking at him with ashen faces, their eyes dilated with horror; he attempted to step on his exploding dread but it pushed him upward and he nearly slipped back. "What, what happened here? Did someone break in?"

"No," Martha said, her voice shattered by terror, "not here."

He nodded and expelled a long breath and a cursory smile appeared and so he wound behind the group of men and women and gazed, calmly, at the screen; it was then the words of the announcer came streaming in shaded bits and pieces into his now-unclogged ear ports.

"…Interviewing now a neighbor who knew the deceased." The reporter held his microphone toward the obese woman, who proceeded to speak in a curiously disconnected manner.

"I mean, they was always arguing, it weren't like it were a big secret round the neighborhood."

"Do you have any idea why this tragedy might have occurred?"

"Well, you know, the rumor was the first wife died a few years back in another neighborhood, and then this here new one come in and she just made herself at home, ya know, and she weren't too neighborly, neither, maybe it t'was drugs, dunno—and say, what's up with a woman using a gun on herself and her family, anyway; geez, ain't women supposed to use pills for themselves, and well, I don't know about…"

The female reporter, keenly aware that her first neighbor to be interviewed had a brain fog, quickly thanked the woman and smartly walked toward the house so that the camera could capture the front of the two-story home. "Police, so far, have no real clues as to why," and she looked down at her notes, "Dolores Thompson would have taken a shotgun and killed her husband, Patrick, her three stepsons, her father- and mother-in-law during the night, but not the twin boy and girl she had with her husband..."

Eli was gone, his mind was blown to smithereens; all words to him now were foreign bits of chatter, distorted and bleached sterile, their exact meanings stuck in the electrified air as his life-force drained out of him and melted through the concrete floor and clear to the fiery molten core far below him. "I am dead," he heard himself reciting in his paralyzed mind, "I am dead, I am dead, they are coming for me, they will find out; I am dead, what have I done; why, why didn't I think what she might do next—and I left the babies there, too—what, what was I thinking of; I went too far; I am dead, dead, dead, the police are coming for me; what should I do, where should I go; they'll find out about us and I'll go to prison and I went too far and I messed up and what have I done I am dead, dead, dead," his breath was fast and furious and his chest was heaving and his breath was shallow and quick; "what should I do, they will be coming for me, should I run and hide, do I wait here or go? Do I lie or tell the truth; but I did it, I did for Abraham and Oscine, doesn't that count for something?" And then everything around him vanished and he saw himself standing in chains before the hanging judge and he was pleading his case with passion, and pleading loyalty, "But I did it to avenge my friends, how was I to know?" And he heard the judge condemn him and sentence him to death as his limp form was dragged away to his awaiting cell—dead man walking.

But then this arcane vision evaporated and he was back at his company again and his employees were asking him myriad questions and he was giving them no clear reception, for his mind was now a blank slate and he was a baby again and the first words written upon it were, "Guilty."

He mumbled something resembling nothing coherent and then went back to his office and closed the door and sat down at his red-stained oak desk and stared through the white walls into a fast-approaching portent of doom. He was shaking like a frightened child who is waiting for his father to come home and administer a powerful beating to him for naughty deeds done. He sat and sat and sat and waited and waited and waited, voiceless and motionless, shivering from a piercing cold, numbed into a trance; a living mannequin of hard wax and frozen features.

And then a knock came to the door and he nearly snapped his neck when he looked up and saw through the cracks in the white blinds a dark blue uniform outside his door. His breath was coming in quick and jumpy spasms and he tried to collect his thoughts but when he stood up his hands were shaking wildly, and so he stuck them into his pants pockets and came to the door and opened it.

It was the deliveryman.

He gulped and suppressed a gasp and his face flushed relief and he flashed a genuine smile and heartily shook the hand of the man and gladly signed the proper form for the packages; he walked with the deliveryman through the back door and into the front office where the employees' attention was still stuck to the massacre; he shut his mind off as he moved past them and then out to the big brown delivery truck, and then he sent the deliveryman on his way; he stood there for a good while, simply observing the fine autumn day and wondering if it would ever seem so fine again. Everything seemed so tranquil and quiet; he could not imagine chaos springing from this simple offering of a gentle peace. "Somewhere, there is someone who is living this exact moment and they are not in trouble," and he sighed deeply; "that was me just yesterday, just yesterday it seemed as if I would live forever having whatever I wanted," and he took in the enormity and beauty of the golden dawn and the fresh aroma of fertile life, "it is as if I have never seen this before." He looked up and saw a black-and-white police car coming down the street, and he tried not to stare at it, but he did, and then he watched it pull into his driveway and park in his parking spaces, and then watched as two big men in black uniforms got out with all of their authority and power surrounding them like a halo from nuclear fusion.

He nearly fainted.

The Investigation

For one microsecond, he tried to avert his vision to anything other than the two hulking men, but he could not command his eyes to look elsewhere or his body to even move; the two men approached him and asked him if he knew where Eli Malone was. He told them who he was, and the two officers and Eli went inside and past the employees who had just turned off the television for fear that the officers would heap scorn upon them for leering at a human catastrophe. The three men disappeared through the back door and into the office.

"You know what has happened," the first officer said, still standing, and looking at Eli as if he were guilty of something, and when he saw an affirmative nod of the head, he continued on in his omnipotent voice. "This Dolores Thompson, or Vivian Younger, worked for you. Is that correct?" He offered another affirmative response. "What else can you tell us about her—her work habits, her dealing with other employees—any kind of odd behavior that might suggest that she was emotionally unstable?"

"I am being questioned for this now," Eli thought, "it is too soon, I need time to think; do I tell them the truth when they ask me now, or do I get a lawyer? Should I be truthful now or tell them a half-truth?" He heard the police officer's questions and nodded his head, and then uttered a cursory "yes" to a few more. He was thinking about other famous legal cases where the accused had lied in the beginning and had lied in the middle but was found out in the end. "They are always found out in the end," he mused, staring at the wide girth of these two linebacker-sized officers, "but is that only on big cases? This case will close quickly because there will be no trial, and I haven't done anything…" But now the questions were dissecting his internal reverie and he couldn't properly juggle the two entities as they launched queries against him simultaneously, so he ceased his own thoughts and concentrated on the probing words of the man in black before him.

"What was your relationship with the deceased?"

He knew the question was coming, had to come, as much as he had wanted it not to come, and he still wasn't ready; he was thinking again inside his seizing mind about all the lies he practiced against his paramours and his business associates and how that lifestyle had led him to the here and now where he sat in the floating waste of the slowly draining sewage that had been his miserable life. This epiphany struck him so hard he nearly blanked out on hearing the officer. "My miserable life," he thought, stunned, for he had never imagined his life as anything except exceptional and inciting jealousy in the hearts of common men.

But he had to respond, now. "She," he began, circumspectly, as if his mind was searching down alternate paths with alternate beginnings and endings to this question, as if he was seeing the results of many different answers; and finally, he said with a weighty resolve, "was my lover."

And just like that, it seemed as if the extra poundage of deceit he had used to hustle and win women and win over clients was now pouring like smoke from a cremation into the acrid air.

The officer wrote it down. "When did you see her last?"

"Last night, at her house; her family was away."

"What was her behavior like?"

"We broke up." He wanted to tell the officer about the injections right now, right now he wanted to inject the awful truth about the syringes into the conversation and not worry about waking up to hear men in dark uniforms crashing through his door and arresting him, so he could sleep at night—be it in prison or in his own cherished bed; he just couldn't have this awful banging of the Truth boring holes in his fragile mind. He opened his mouth to say it but the officer received a message on his shoulder microphone. He listened in agony and recited what he would say and he was about to say it again when the officer spoke.

"We talked to neighbors who saw a Ferrari there last night. Do you own a tan Ferrari?"

"Yes." He was very glad now that he had told the simple, elegant, purifying and naturally satisfying Truth, the unadulterated, set-yourself-free, never-to-be-contradicted, plain old-fashioned Truth.

"We need you to come down to the station with us."

"Yes." As he arose, he prayed that Honor and Truth stood up with him.

When he walked past his employees, he was not commander-in-chief, but a little, frightened boy found out by his mommy and daddy that he had been too long dipping into the liquor cabinet; he saw himself dimmed in their eyes, and his role as manipulator and survivor of all things bad directed at his company diminished; he walked out and got in his car and called his lawyer and told him all about it but to merely stand by, and then drove behind the black-and-white police car to the police station, his mind racing ahead to the room he would be in as he settled there and awaited his interrogators.

"I must tell them everything, tell them about the injections; but if I tell them about that, I must tell them why, about Abraham and Oscine, and the tapes," he thought, and now he was sweating so much that his clothes were soaked and his hair was wet. "A lawyer, I need a lawyer, but that means I have something to hide, but no, it just means I am being cautious, and smart." He had used lawyers to defend himself against lawsuits and to sue companies many times, and he knew their inherent value in the legal system, but he wanted this personal issue separated from his business life. "It is just me, now, myself and my past." And there, he was already pulling into the police station and parking his car and getting out and following the hulking men through the giant glass double doors and into a small office; and there, he was reduced to a micron of his social status as conqueror lover and business titan and man of luxury, for in this austere and lonely place of gnashing teeth and weeping hearts, all were as tiny children begging to be let go and hide underneath their big, fluffy beds.

He sat alone for too long in the small room while his mind began to stab at his plan to free himself of this burgeoning guilt. "But I must tell the truth or I will fall," he thought; "if I lie I will not remember the lie, and when I lie again and again, I will be driving down a dark road I will not recognize when I am asked about it later." He knew the dilemma of deception with past girlfriends, how his lies to one and his lies to another about the other, and his lies to more of them about some others—O, his lies, his lies, his infernal lies—lies about how he felt about them and what he would do with them and how he would take care of them had woven a false tapestry, increasing in the day and always unraveling at night; he had grown tired of perpetuating these lies but it had always netted him the best and finest women; he had used it to ensnare Vivian, but now he sought to wash his tongue of every area of these malicious lies.

The two detectives came in and he could feel the power of their authority dwarfing him, squashing him, their very cold stares cutting him into tiny pieces and reassembling later in a tiny cell of concrete and steel. They turned on a tape recorder and began asking him questions, and he served them the Truth, be it bitter tasting or sugary sweet, but he responded only to their direct questions, never veering into the perilous territory where he had built his house of vengeance.

He was answering their questions and weaving that false tapestry because they had, in their timeline, taken him up to the night before the murders; but he had left out the syringe and left out the hidden cameras and left out the names of Oscine and Abraham in his answers; he did not know if the police had his name in connection with the death of his friend, but if he told them, he reasoned, then all was lost; and so, here he was, answering truthfully but lying, lying but answering truthfully, he told himself, and with every word and aversion he was digging a deeper rut from which he might not ever escape. He tried to imagine what he was saying and sought to remember it so that when again they interviewed him he would remember the lie. "I must live it now, or I will live it in prison," he desperately thought.

He no longer wanted to be noble; he merely wanted to be free and never again be inside the menacing sweatbox of this grim place; he realized now that he wanted a lawyer and realized how foolish it was for a man with his business expertise to have acquiesced to sit alone with two men who were trained to gain the truth from suspects and witnesses. He wanted to tell these men how contrite he was about it all and that he would never again meddle in the life of a married woman, but somehow it seemed false.

And then one of the big detectives spoke, his face auguring a coming plague.

"We think she took the shotgun first to her husband and then to her mother-in-law, and then to her father-in-law, and finally to the three boys; all of them were sleeping when she killed them, except the father-in-law, who we determined had been crawling on his knees when he was killed." The man with the black face stared at Eli as he announced this revelation. "We know that she then went to look at her twins and then sat down in their rooms and took her own life." He turned off the tape recorder. His voice became cold and hard, like an unrelenting, pounding rain. "I know men like you, they are no better than pimps; they make prostitutes out of house-wives because they can; men like you have money and looks and so you cruise the neighborhoods looking for desperate housewives and you catch them up and take them to your mansion and show them a life they will never have, and you ruin their lives and the lives of their families, and you don't even care, do you; and sometimes, like this time, it all goes bad and the guilt of it all and the shame of it all causes the woman to murder her entire family."

Eli no longer wanted to boast of contrition but now of revelation, that Vivian and Heath were monsters and that he, Eli, was the avenging angel; but he knew how these men looked down upon him, and so he said, his countenance laid bare of guile, "Is there anything I could say right now that would make you believe how sorry I am and that I would never do it again?" Silence was their condemnation.

He was released after some four hours of questioning and then he went home and called his lawyer and then waited for the officers to come to his home and take him away for trial. The first day he looked at the phone a hundred times and a hundred times he thought it was about to ring but it never rang; the second day he waited for the knock at the door and a hundred times he looked at the door but the knock never came; then the third day and the fourth day passed, and when a full week came and left, he began to speculate that all was over.

And the entire time he was awaiting this verdict he masterfully blocked out the notion that he was responsible for the deaths of Innocents; yes, he blocked it out by concentrating all of his thoughts on the idea of prison; it was prison that he chiefly loathed, and so he thought about one verdict from a trial and no prison, and another verdict, and prison, and what he would do if one verdict came, and what he would do if another came; so, with this battle raging in his mind he was able to suppress the idea of guilt.

On the seventh day the phone rang and it was the police detective and he wanted Eli down at the station immediately.

Once there Eli sat in the same dread he had sat in a week previous; the lone detective came in and sat down and proceeded to talk.

"The coroner's report came back," he began, gazing directly into the face of Eli; "it seems that Vivian had quite a few diseases in her system." He held out his big black hands and lifted each finger up for every disease announced. "Syphilis, gonorrhea, AIDS; she also had cocaine and heroin in her bloodstream, and needle marks on her arms." His black eyes ran over the face of his listener as if he were looking for the abrupt surfacing of mental anguish. "It seems that her husband and father-in-law and mother-in-law also had syphilis and gonorrhea and AIDS, but they had had the AIDS virus for a year, according to County health records; it seems that the husband and father-in-law were busy cruising the streets for hookers, unlike you, who cruises for housewives." The stark conviction in his bold and black eyes was still searching for pain on the face of his antagonist. "But isn't this the way it goes when everyone involved is sleazy?" He wrapped his mind around a particularly searing, contemplative thought and his face produced a vulgar expression. "And now you have to live with this awful thing you caused, and with the awful disease I am sure you have and deserve." He stood up and stared at Eli. "Oh, you are free to go." He expelled a quick breath and nodded his head. "Free to be in an invisible prison." He watched as Eli stood up. "And who will go out with you now, you lousy, no-good home wrecker? Once word gets out that you have these diseases, what woman will risk her life to be with the likes of you, even with all your money and looks?" He shook his big lion's head and scorn pushed through unto his face like a righteous proclamation. "No, I don't think so." And he turned and left, leaving Eli alone, Eli, who only a few weeks ago was living the life of a royal prince.

Eli stood for a few seconds and then walked out of the door and drove home and then sat down on his plush, purple bed and cried.

The Search Begins

There is an infinite stream of decay left by the shattered minds of people from eons past; residence in this common club of broken-down hearts and suffering minds may be attained through diverse ways, chiefly amongst them by regret and self-guilt, through self-loathing and shame, by obsession and fear; now, this is not to say there are no other categories to qualify one to slip into this luminous trail of smoldering stardust and swirling gases. Herein lie writhing souls who have abandoned all hope; herein lie tormented beings who churn and crawl in self-flagellation and self-immolation; herein is the final refuge for some who seek escape from existence, from reality, from responsibility as they await the sweeper of bludgeoned souls, Death; herein, they enter this desert purgatory freely, having rejected all succor in the known world.

Eli fell into this hot and humid phantom zone and lay curled up next to an innumerable amount of babbling whiners and thumb-suckers; and in their moans and groans and loud wailing and crying, he took the shape of their soft and demure mistress, self-pity; O, how beautiful and full of sympathy was

She, O, how wondrous this soothing—like a narcotic punc-
tured into bulging veins—was She; like a soothing balm to
their boils and throbbing pain was She; and no blushing brides-
maid, either, but a saucy vixen licking their agony with her
addictive spit and entombing them in their own willingness
for self-destruction; here, in this living grave, the inhabitants roiled and retched and boiled and searched, searched
and searched for reasons why they had failed and why they
had been separated from humanity. It was here that they rose
and fell and dug and curled up and fell in between cracks and
crevices and atop the charred remains of self-murderers and
self-martyrs; it was here that they found cheap solace from the
world and its uncertainty; it was here that they either purged
their malady or yielded up their spirit.

But Eli was not one of them, for too many of those resi-
dents in this hollow house of pity were returning self-victims,
willing victims, desirous to be declared pitiful, and so he was
able to raise his head above this self-poisoning of his spirit
and lift it so high that he could just see over the black smoke
that sat above the mass of soft heads and soft wills.

And then a knock came to his door and he actually went
to answer it.

He had been ensconced in this chafing dimension for three
weeks when he opened the door, his slumping body adorned
in a dirty navy-blue robe and black shorts and bare feet and
messy thick, black hair and a fierce stink from an absence of
good hygiene.

It was the lead detective on the case and he was standing
motionless with a slender manila folder in his big black hands.
He was looking at Eli with repugnance.

"Come in, detective," Eli said, motioning inward with
his right hand.

The detective was simply staring at Eli with eyes afflicted by its own history, eyes sometimes dead from the abuse they had beheld, angry eyes from the injustice they had beheld, eyes full of sadness from the human suffering he had seen, eyes that had seen too much for one man and yearned to see only the Love and Beauty and Goodness in the world. "We found a tape that Heath and Vivian had of Heath's first wife, Oscine." He searched the eyes of Eli and he saw the faintest spark of anger splash into a pool of subterfuge. "Yes, you know what it was, what that tape was; yes, but you did not see that tape until after you and Abraham found Oscine. That's right, I found the police report about the death of your friend and Oscine." His black eyes were still boring into the soul of Eli and his voice was passing judgment on him. "Yes, you wanted vengeance on their deaths so you carefully built up a relationship with Vivian to destroy her and Heath; I know that as well as I know that I am standing here talking to you; yes, you made a plan to ruin them both, and that part I have not figured out; were you simply trying to ruin their marriage or was it something else?" He stepped closer to Eli, who was petrified with dread and unable to speak or move. "You planned something beyond this and my guess is it has something to do with the needle marks on her arm; Vivian, from our investigation, had not used drugs for years, but had definitely used them the night of the murders, we know that from the dealer we arrested, but that doesn't explain the other needle marks." He shook his great lion's head. "But that doesn't matter now, anymore; that doesn't matter because it's all over for them and it's all over for you because you have your own death sentence." He paused and stared at the silent figure before him. "Did you think that when there is an injustice, you merely put on your righteous armor and right the wrong, and being noble, it will protect you? Is this what a privileged life teaches you—that in war, bullets only hit the guilty?" and then he turned and gesticulated down toward the smoggy horizon, and his face grew weary and his voice grew in despair, as if right now he were living the torment of what he was saying, "and it is a war zone: a rotten, stinking, dirty war every day," and he turned round, "and you just cannot sit here and pick off only the bad people," and then his face became stern and his voice became mean, "things are never that simple, it just isn't reality—that is a fool's way of dealing with life." There, he had said what he wanted to say, said what his twenty-five years on the force had directed him to say based on all of the cases and all of the horror and pain he had seen.

But Eli could not speak because in his benighted mind he was waiting for the black-and-white cars to come rolling up his long driveway to take him in, but as much as he looked he did not see them, and this fact loosened his frozen tongue. "So, what now?"

"'What now' is up to you, Eli."

The man had said Eli's name, and he felt as if this meant something good.

The man held out his hand with the manila envelope. "It would do the taxpayers no good to prosecute your case, because there is no good evidence to show that a crime was committed—here are the police reports." Eli took the envelope. "It is your legacy, now; what you did you have to live with," he said, with finality, and he turned to leave and walked a few steps down the stone steps, but then hesitated and turned round. "What you did was wrong and you should suffer for it; we have laws in this country against vigilantes." He looked around at the sprawling place and then back to Eli. "If it had been my best friend, I would have done something, too; but you have paid a price too steep for vengeance that belongs only to God and Justice." He turned round and walked down the steps and out to his detective's unmarked white car and drove away.

Eli stood there weeping.

Wandering

The newspapers and television were full of the salacious details contained in the videotape of Oscine that Eli had planned on giving to the police to complete his revenge; neighbors who were clearly shown as the rapists or who were in collusion to cover up the rapes or who had engendered the acts were arrested, involving men and women from every social class, hiding their faces from neighbors as they were marched to the black-and-white squad car. The television news, the newspapers, the Internet websites, being the vampires and vultures and parasites they had become, and slaves to every event bearing the most obscene headline, clung to this story and sucked it dry and increased their coffers and increased their audience and satiated the desires of the weaker human vessels in Nature until, alas, the story lost its might and it was cannibalized by the next salacious spectacular.

Eli watched it all. He sat in the dead air of an unnatural blackness, enclosed in the rooms at his mansion, the blinds shut tight as he coerced himself to gorge on the ripening story; he wept during the day and wept during the night and he slept very little and ate very little, and he heard a stabbing poem form in his head, an ode to murder, and he heard its song, and it chanted his history and his name and his complicity in the sins of Vivian and its weighty refrain was, "Murderer, murderer, murder hides in your veins and runs to your black heart; murderer, murderer, murder buries your old self and rebuilds your name." And he could feel it, he could feel his old self being purged and this alien creature absorbing his thoughts and identity, and he would not fight it. "Let it come, let me die, I murdered those boys, I put my hand on her hand and we squeezed the trigger together." And he closed his eyes and imagined himself standing with her and then both of them aiming the gun at the three boys and pulling the trigger once, twice, thrice, and he could plainly hear the loud reports and see the faces of the boys implore for mercy and the bodies of the boys blown to bloody bits and pieces.

He would weep as he watched the news and he would weep as he read the newspapers and sometimes he would weep when he was walking around the house in his bare feet and bare soul; when the story lost its fame and the ghouls of the news media turned to another horror, he just sat in the thriving silence and wept, and as he wept, he felt his body being drained of its life-force and spinning down the filthy drain; yes, he felt himself dissolving with every tear into the filthy sewers, and he was not unhappy.

He would not return phone calls to lovers or friends or business associates, and he only communicated once with Martha, instructing her to keep the business functioning. He secretly wanted to die but he secretly did not want to lose his money; he secretly wanted to lose his business and move away and become a wandering spirit lost in the world, but this meant he would live; he secretly wanted to live, then, he secretly wanted to live and find God and find a good woman and find the meaning of life and then be happy, but this was betrayal for his bad deeds, and so he wanted secretly to die again.

To die seemed the easiest resolve to his torment, but to hasten his own death would require him to surrender his lustful youth and shrivel it to bits of flotsam and jetsam, and this he could not do; his life had been one of too much uncontrolled excess, and to abruptly change directions and smother his great passions was, to him, inconceivable; so, he would live, but he vowed not to live well.

His body was following the natural path into a harvest of grief, but once this pasture was dry and barren, he was forced to look elsewhere to bury his sorrows; so, one month hence, he left his stony mansion and left on a quest to find a Truth greater than those contained in flesh and mammon.

He averted his eyes wherever he drove so he would not see Woman, so he would not behold Her sensuous Beauty; and when he walked by Woman, he held his breath, so he would not smell Her sensuous perfume; and when he stood near Woman, he closed his ears so he would not hear Her sensuous tones; he drove around looking for something that would bring him solace, and on the second day he stopped at a Church and went inside and listened to the Pastor speak; it was the Church of the Jehovah's Witnesses, and he lingered there for hours; and when he was done, he later visited a Mormon Church, and lingered there for hours; and when he was done, he later visited a Christian Church, and lingered there for hours; and went he was done, he later visited a Buddhist Temple and a Hindu Temple and a Muslim Mosque, and lingered at each one for hours. He read their literature and heard their message and talked to their Ministers and much of it made sense to him; he went back for weeks and asked more questions and the messages began to blur in his head, and so he came back to his stony mansion and sat in his big black leather chair and found he could weep no more.

"But this must not be," he thought, "I must not simply live past what has happened, I must learn from it, I must." And he felt his weighty resolve weakening, and he could feel his old self beginning to stake its claim within him, and he knew that soon he would be back on the streets and in the nightclubs and in his business and all would be well and years from now he would have successfully lived past it all. "I won't let that happen!" he yelled, smashing a statue of antiquity across his room.

He was sitting in the gulf of a sable veil that assuages human guilt and he was wearing the fresh wounds of mental collapse when he abruptly jumped up and ran to his car and sped to his office and announced to Martha that she was temporarily in charge of the business, and then he jumped into his car and sped to the airport and ran to the ticket counter and bought a ticket to anywhere that was as far away from here as possible.

He boarded the plane and fell asleep as if he were in his mother's comforting arms.

He awoke in Australia.

When he saw the splendor and vitality and wonder of the place, he cursed himself for not demanding a remote country, and so he bought another ticket and boarded the plane and once again fell into a peaceful slumber. He awoke some time later, and realizing he had not eaten for several days, ordered a salad, and while he ate it, he looked out the window and the territory he beheld froze his jaws, and his mouth was agape; he set down the food and stared at the increasingly disturbing scenery of the barren and scorched land below.

The plane landed and he departed it and stood on the runway and his mind was captured by the raw scent of this new world. "Here, I shall stay," he whispered, "here, I shall find something that is not me," and he ventured away, entranced by the enveloping culture around him, traveling by car into the beating and savage heart of the untamed wild wherein both man and beast reigned.

Lorraine

He let his mind drain itself of everything he had become; everything that had built him from the inside out, he let fall into the heart of the African continent; all of his notions of what life was supposed to be and why it was rose up out of him and evaporated in the torrid heat. He was lost here as much as an elephant would be lost if it were to be liberated to the corner of Sixth and Broadway in New York City. Here, Eli looked to his environment to see who he was and he found nothing, for here he was nothing, nothing but an intruder, lost and confused, possessing an identity that counted for nothing in this bleeding continent; here, his money and his looks and his physical prowess with women and his legacy as entrepreneur were mere particles in a hot and dry desert wind; here, his golden crown and jeweled scepter as man and conqueror in the world of finance and love were lead, best buried in the ground and replaced with practical things.

He drove into small villages and big cities and he wandered amongst the indigenous people like a lost soul. No one noticed him, no one seemed to care who he was or why he was there or what he had to offer; no woman cast him a knowing glance, no man looked upon him with envy or admiration, as he had stepped into a world of pain and sorrow that had no room for his life of frivolity and carnality.

He was walking along a dirty sidewalk in a small town and he came upon two small children who were huddled together underneath a small piece of brown, water-stained and stinking cardboard. It was night and it was cold outside as people were walking around and over the tiny, shivering bodies.

"Where am I in the whole wide world," he wondered, first looking up into the black canopy of creation that spanned billions of light years beyond him, and then down to the most precious of creation's creatures, "that would create this?" He bent down and attempted to rouse them from their light slumber.

He attempted to communicate to the children, but failed; he attempted to enlist the aid of passersby to translate his words into the native language, but no one obliged him; he attempted to get them up and to walk away with him, but they merely sat together against the harsh red brick building, their small black faces fraught with fear.

"You are frightening those children," he heard a voice say, and upon turning round, Eli beheld a policeman standing behind him.

"I am glad you're here," Eli began, "these kids need help."

The police officer looked Eli up and down and his staid face never wavered. "You are an American." He received an affirmative response. His voice took on more resolve. "You aren't in America, now." He checked Eli's passport.

Eli stared at the man in his accustomed American indignation and incredulity. "Yes, I know," he said, nodding, "but that is off the topic, isn't it? These kids need a shelter to go to."

"You are giving me orders, American," the officer said in a tone that accented authority and defiance. "You are no one here; you are less than no one, here."

"You're still off the topic; where is the nearest shelter for the homeless?"

"In fact, American," the officer persisted, "you are not only less than no one, you are perceived as worse than that, a foreign meddler in our domestic affairs."

He was remembering how important he was back in the States and how he would normally deal with such an aberration, and his American philosophy of the way of things betrayed him. "Are you going to help me or not?" When he received nothing but rude silence, his mind caught fire with indignation. "Look, I don't know who you are or what your problem is, but I just asked a simple question and you refused to answer it; I will find the shelter myself."

"Arrogant American," the officer began, a brazen clump of scorn rising upon his black face, "who sees the world through his own eyes. I know about your country; you look at poor Africa and get so sad," and here he mocked a sad face, "and then you want to send us a big, big Band-Aid to help us to put over our troubles your European allies created, so you can feel so good inside, and go back to wasting your corrupt lives away."

Eli was ignoring the man and still asking passersby for help, but without success, and the officer continued to talk to him in this manner, and Eli was ignoring the man. Then, he turned round and shouted, "Look, go somewhere else if you won't help me!"

The stoic officer smiled. "I will go with you to the jailhouse."

When Eli was about to curse the man, another voice interrupted him and sent the first officer away.

"I have to apologize for my officer," said another policeman, who extended his hand to Eli, who cautiously shook it. "I am Captain Karani."

"All I want to do is help these poor kids," Eli said, "that is all; if I have committed a crime, then arrest me."

The officer nodded his head as he bent down and talked in a gentle manner to the children, and then turned to Eli and said, "You don't understand our country." He stood up and stood face to face with him. "I know America, I have been there; you have more than enough, and you waste it, because it doesn't matter; this is an alien idea here, for here, we do not have more than enough, we do not have plenty, and our leaders still waste it. It is a very frustrating model of government, but it is all we have." He looked to the children, whom the officer had each given a small chocolate bar. "Here, we do not have resources such as you have in America; there are few shelters, few agencies to take care of the homeless." His voice became thick with sorrow. "Here, there is more than enough pain and suffering, more than we can service," and he looked to the children, "so, the children simply lie on the street at night like any other beggar. It is the way it is because we have no other choice. That is why men and women walk by them, because our men and women do not have enough, either." He stared at Eli for a moment. "I can tell you do not understand our concept of life here, but it is the way it is, now; maybe tomorrow it will be different; every day I wake up and wonder if tomorrow things will change and we will have more than we had yesterday, and the little children will not have to raise themselves on the streets; but every day that I wake up, it is still the same, and so I do the best I can. It is all we can do, to do the best we can and try to think of a better tomorrow." He bent down and whispered again to the children, and looked up at Eli. "I do not expect you to understand, but it is the way of things, our world, and we do not know what else to do until change comes."

"Why can't you make change happen?" Eli asked, though his tone was one of bitterness and defeat, as if he had accepted the fatalism of the captain's words.

"This is not America," the captain said, "this is not Democracy, this is anarchy." He helped the children up. "But I know of a Christian Mission for them tonight."

Eli felt pride swell within his breast, and he stood up more erect and held his head up higher. "I am an American," he celebrated the idea of it in his thoughts, "an ambassador of Democracy wherever I go. It is important that I act accordingly." These words cut to his core and throttled him, for he had never thought of himself as a citizen of great merit in America, but apart from his homeland, he felt important and enlightened.

He followed the captain to a small dwelling that had the name "World Mission" written over its humble doorway. There were twenty beds inside and three food stations, and a slender woman with thick hair the color of burnt sienna who was tending to a sick child. The police captain introduced Eli and the children to her and he promptly left. Eli was standing and smiling and displaying his satisfaction at what he had done as the woman took the children by the hand and escorted them to the small, white cot.

After some time, she turned round and noticed that he was still present. "Yes, is there anything else?"

"Well," he said, still boasting of his good deeds in his very tone and manners, "I just wanted to make sure they were all right," and he turned round and departed.

He found a motel and went to sleep and slept with righteous judgment beside him. He awoke the next day and decided to tour the city and see what else he could see, but on his way out he found a pretty girl standing outside the motel, smiling at him, and for a moment, he was back in America.

He was back up in his room with her and after he had lain with her, she kindly asked him for a dollar. He frowned. "A dollar, for what?"

"You had your way with me; or maybe, fifty cents?" Her English was good.

He cocked his head and looked at her and his face blanched white. "You're not a prostitute?" He saw the nod of her head and he felt nausea rushing past his brain. "Not in the daytime? I have never been with a prostitute, not ever; I mean, you just seemed like a nice girl..." but he felt his scruples leaving him and the mockery of manhood buckling his legs, and so he stood in silence.

"I will take even a breakfast."

His breath was quick now and he was shaking his head. "How old are you?"

"Fourteen." She did not say it with a hint of tragedy, but said it plainly and simply just as if her schoolteacher had asked her age the first day of school.

He covered his mouth and sat hard upon the soft bed, looking at the girl before him. She was adorned in heavy paint and heavy perfume and colorful clothes but she was not yet fully grown; yes, underneath this adult veneer there was a young girl, he decided. "But I can't pay you, I can't be with a prost...I mean, you're not a prostitute, you're a young girl who should be in school."

"I do not attend school; this is my job."

His cheeks were hot red and his eyes were blurring, his breath quickening. "You ought to be in school, you should; and I did not sleep with you that way, I did not know what you were or how old you were, I am sorry..."

She hunched her shoulders. "It does not matter to me." She turned to go but halted. "Do you ask prostitutes in America their age before you have relations with them?"

He tried to wash this idea out of her head with a vigorous shake of his head. "No, no, you don't understand, I don't know women like that." He could see the shame in her sad green eyes. "I don't mean you, I don't; you're not one, you can't be, you're too young."

"So, I can be one when I am older?"

He was taken aback by the directness and savage odor of her questions. "No, you shouldn't be—and what a ridiculous question to be asked by such a young girl—now, just wait a minute, I forgot what I was going to say; yes, you need to be in school, you shouldn't be here at all." The intense frown upon his face reflected his miserable attempt to justify his actions, so he changed the subject to alleviate his guilt and find some joy in this girl's misbegotten life. "So, where is your family?"

"They are all dead. I am my family."

"What about your pimp?"

She nearly smiled. "There is no pimp, there is only me, and I need to eat."

"Where is your family?"

"They are all dead; my mother died from AIDS, my father died in the war, my brother and sister were kidnapped by rebel soldiers."

He felt a shudder travel on cold waves throughout his limp body, and when he spoke, his heart pounded. "Do you have AIDS?"

"I do not know, but this much I do know, that I need to eat, and if you do not pay me, I need to go and find someone who will." She looked him up and down. "Do you have AIDS?"

He lost his breath. "No." He recovered his senses. "Where did you get your education? You certainly don't talk like a typical girl."

She smiled. "The Missionaries taught me; they taught me about America, too, and about the things you speak of." She grew anxious.

She turned to leave once more, but he stopped her and escorted her out and down to the local restaurant and bought her a large breakfast. The woman from the Mission, having spent the morning negotiating with the owner of the restaurant to donate surplus food to the needy, walked by Eli and the young girl, and upon recognizing them, a black veil of disgust draped over her face.

Eli had seen her coming and was about to speak when he saw the dark shadow of condemnation descend over her visage. "No," he instinctively said aloud, but the woman continued on with an injured look that throttled him. "No, that isn't it," he protested now, looking at the girl, who was eagerly consuming her meal. He frowned. "Does everyone know you around here? I mean, do they know what you do?"

She hunched her shoulders. "Sure, it isn't like anybody cares."

"How about the woman who just walked by?"

The girl stopped eating and her eyes misted over with love. "She is one of a few who cares." She dropped her food and began to sob. He wanted to stroke her fine black hair and take her small, trembling hand, but his membership in the exclusive men's club whose residency is in America dictated that he refrain from such activities now, now that he had repented of his sin with her; so, in its stead, he persuaded her to come to the Mission and talk to the woman, to which she easily assented.

Eli and the girl walked through the doors of the Mission and stood before the plainly dressed woman like two shamed children seeking forgiveness; their heads were bowed, their bodies slumped, their mouths silent.

The woman stood before them and quietly and gently took the girl by the hand and led her to another woman, who then took the girl to a back room. The woman turned her gaze to Eli. "And what about you?"

"I," he stammered, "I just wanted to help."

"And how have you helped her?" she said, pointing accusingly to the back room.

Now, he was indignant, just as his American genealogy had taught him to be in such situations. "You're pretty fast to condemn a man."

She folded her arms. "Go ahead, then, tell me why you were with her."

He stood up now, erect now, as if his better posture were a barrier now against her righteous judgment. "I didn't know she was fourteen."

There wasn't even a change in her facial expression, just a subtle shake of her head.

"…The excuse of every man who is with an underage girl…"

"Is it a crime to be with her in this country?" He hadn't meant to say it, hadn't meant to make it seem as if he was not disgusted by his own actions, but he would not take it back now.

"Get out," she said, scorn written in triple verse across her comely visage, and she turned to walk away.

He wanted to walk away but he could not. "You are quick to judge."

She turned round. "And why are you here? Go back to America and do what you do there."

"I came here because I wanted to see what the rest of the world lived like, I wanted to help people…"

She nearly laughed. "Oh, no, another American on a pity crusade, just marvelous; we get about three of you a month; they come here looking for solace because of the sins of omission they have committed back in the States." She murmured something unintelligible under her breath, and then said, "Go back home, American, go back to the land of plenty and look at the pictures of the poor Africans dying of disease and starvation," and she reached up and mocked a stream of tears coming down her smooth cheeks with her dancing fingers, "and be real sad, and maybe, just maybe, throw a few spare coins at the picture so you will feel real good inside, so you can continue to consume to gross excess and stuff yourselves with every kind of greed and pleasure." She expelled a long, hot breath and walked to the back room and vanished through its cracked, peeling, pale doors.

He stood there unable to resuscitate his will to remove the carnal blemish she had heaped upon him. "It was not so long ago that I would have laughed at such a woman," he thought; "it was not so long ago that the idea of woman as anything other than a purveyor of physical pleasure was absurd; but now," he shook his head, "I don't know." He truly wanted to go, to go back to his hotel and back to America and back to live his rich life that was secluded from pain and suffering and resume his relations with beautiful women and forget about Vivian and Heath and mourn Abraham and Oscine; yes, he deserved to live again, he reasoned, after mourning the loss of his friend and taking vengeance against the murderers; yes, he knew, he had erred in his actions against Vivian, but Justice had been meted out. "But this is war," he decided, "and when men fight, Innocents will die." He wanted to just turn round and go back to the hotel and book a flight and fly away home and never return again and live happily ever after.

But he just couldn't move his feet. He cursed. He sat down on an old, sagging, splintered brown wooden chair and picked up a magazine that spoke of the philosophy of this gentle place.

Twenty minutes later she came back from the back room and walked past him as if he were not even there, retrieved some clothes from a table, and walked past him once more, ignoring him just as if he had no justifiable purpose for being there.

Smoky dusk availed itself over the land and by then she had gone past him many times, and each time she had availed herself to pour utter anonymity over his steadfast will to wait her out; and when it was time for her to leave, she was forced to address his still-sitting form. "Well, you just can't sit here all night."

He had her now and he was wont to punish her. "You certainly are quick to judge, certainly a most unchristian act." He stood up and flexed his muscular body and he spoke, his words steeped in a bitter gall, "I wanted to explain things to you but suddenly you don't seem worth it." He walked past her and refused to look at her and he exited through the wooden black frames of the door.

"You're right," she said, in a tone that was muffled and barely echoed down the dusty, dirty sidewalk.

He turned round and stopped. "Well," he began, and then said, bitterly, "you deign to talk to someone like me, how gracious of you; well, I don't care now."

"Well, I do, I should not have treated you this way; you are right, it is not my place to act in such a rude manner," she began, in a tone that was conciliatory and so earnest that he could not disbelieve her. "You have done good deeds, too, and it is not my right to judge you; I do sincerely apologize." She held her hand. "My name is Lorraine."

"Eli," he said, his anger evaporating quickly, and easily took her hand and shook it.

The harsh outer shell he had developed against her was now slain, he had no refuge now, and he expressed his sincerest contrition for his acts once more, and offered to buy her dinner, to which she graciously accepted.

They sat down at the small round table in the small square restaurant and ordered food.

"I want you to know I am usually not so angry," she said, nearly smiling, "I just have had a bad week," and she held her up slender, small hands, "which is not to make an excuse, really." He asked her how she had come to be in this country, and she complied.

She had been a top lawyer in a top law firm in the States making a top salary; she had been living a life of spectacular excess and hedonism, and she had never considered an alternate way of life because her entire life had been devoted to reaching the highest echelon upon which she then dwelled. She had it all, as she saw it.

As he listened to her confession, he observed her physical form. She wore neither makeup nor expensive clothes, and her long, auburn hair was pulled back in a ponytail; there was no paint on her fingernails, no perfume on her slender body, no jewelry adorning her fingers or ears or ankles nor any other part of her body women chose to pierce or encircle or surround. She presented herself simply as herself and no man or woman could honestly say she was just another hollow vessel filled with the extravagances of vanity.

She had had it all and she could not see what she did not have because her illicit treasures had blinded her to the real treasures in life, and then something happened that tore away the corruption of her youth and exposed her ignorance.

"My sister and her husband and two kids were killed by a drunk driver," she said, and he could see the pain breaking out on her quiet countenance. "The man that did it was a client of my law firm, and naturally I thought that my people would not take the case, but I was wrong." He heard, no, he felt the cloud of horror and pain permeate her every word, he felt the pain and sorrow of her heart rain upon him, he saw her beauteous face consumed with the indignation; he saw it all and felt it all and heard it all because in her he saw himself, and he was entranced to hear her sorrow.

"But this client was wealthy—beyond wealthy; he was devious and powerful and he was owed favors by my bosses and other bosses and when it came time for counsel, we gave it to him despite my most vehement protestations; my bosses," she nearly wept, "they told me to take a vacation." She lost her breath and held her head high and choked back her tears. "They told me to stand down for a murderer, and I did; I did stand down, and I took off time and I followed the trial for three months, and during those three months I was able to think for the first time in my misbegotten life, and I realized that I was no different from my bosses, and this hurt me the most, to realize that I had defended similar clients for money." She halted her narration and took his handkerchief and wiped away her pious tears. "Anyway, the swine got off, but of course he did, I knew he would, and when I was supposed to come back to work—well, I didn't, because by then I had doubts, and doubts to a lawyer are like holes in a ship, and what I didn't already know was that I had been sinking for years." She drank water from the glass and looked down at her empty plate. "I had many ideas at that point—to begin a small, private law firm, kill the man who murdered my sister—but none of them seemed practical." He scrutinized her face and saw only genuine expressions and patterns of honesty and fidelity. "One day I visited the Pastor where my sister had gone to work—don't ask me why—and I sat down with him and he told me that there is a reason for everything, that God would not allow my sister to die for no good thing; and so I went home and I thought about that for the longest time, attempting to comfort myself with lies, that she had died so that some other greater Truth might be discovered, but I did not believe it."

She put her hands together, elbows on table, and placed them against her chin. "And then one day I received a letter about World Mission—a letter I would have tossed had I still been working—and how they were dedicated to helping the poor around the world, and I called up the charity and asked them many questions, and I was impressed with their organization; I investigated them and found them to be reliable and honest; they had a small local chapter in my city and I visited it, and I was so impressed by the sincere affection of the workers for the people they tended to that I volunteered to help out, and so I did, for many months. But I was still troubled by the death of my sister, and I decided to go back to work, this time for a smaller firm, and so I worked there for about a year, still volunteering for World Mission on the weekends, and going to my sister's Church. And then one day, I just quit going to the Mission and to the Church, and I started putting more hours into my job again, and the injustice against the verdict in my sister's murder began to fade; I started going out more, and drinking more, and smoking more, and slipping into the fast life of a privileged woman. But I was fooling myself, and I knew it, but I did not want to believe it, until one day a boss of mine came to me and told me he wanted me to defend and help acquit a friend of his who he knew was guilty of molesting a child, and I just stood there and stared at the man, and then walked right past him and out the door and got into my car and drove home." Her tone grew melancholy. "It was just a typical case, like a hundred others I had taken and quite often defended successfully, but this time I saw it differently, and I just couldn't do it anymore; and then," she shook her head and smiled, "and then I went home and I put my house on the market and sold it quickly and sold my cars and gave away all of my clothes and fine things, and then I flew to the headquarters of World Mission and met with the President and I sat there in front of him and gave him a check that was the sum total of all my monetary worth, and I told him to give it to those in need, and that I wanted him to send me to the poorest nations on Earth so I might bring succor to the poor and sickly." She smiled again and nodded. "He is a good man; he smiled and took me by the hand and walked me over to a map, and told me that normally they hire local workers in foreign lands, but he would make an exception for me." She drank some more water and folded her hands together and placed them on the table. "And do you know that he still sends me personal e-mails once a week that are full of spiritual wisdom and hope? And that he and his wife have flown down here to visit me three times in the past year? He is a good man; he is, a very, very good man, one I will measure against all other men."

Her story was completed, and both of them sat there for several minutes, silent, until she said, "And what about you, why are down here?"

He shook his head. "Oh, no reason, really."

Tour

The next morning he met her at the Mission and helped her load her small, white sedan with food, and then they promptly drove away. They visited tiny shacks and tiny hovels, tiny holes and tiny burrows, all of which contained citizens who had been ejected from the safe harvest that sustains the world; yes, these poor people had been chased out of the plentiful harvest, booted out, dragged out, and either by poverty or subterfuge or illness or war or disease, but there they were, on the periphery of the steady flow of goods and services and proper hygiene and proper medical care and clean food and water and a proper place to sleep; there they were, gnawing on the last bits of desperation, stumbling about in the boiling sun, falling down in the inky darkness, alone, unloved, forgotten, sacrificed by their own to an early and shallow grave.

And the abandoned citizens were everywhere, too, residing on the top of latrines and inside latrines, dug into hillsides and under the hillsides, residing in disabled cars and under bridges, residing in filthy alleys and deserted buildings. They were like homeless animals, looking for a place to sleep and a morsel of food to eat. Anywhere there was an overhang, anywhere there was a protected space, anywhere there was a safe rooftop or structure or wall, there they were. Eli saw it all, and his heart felt a vast emptiness.

When Eli came upon the town dump later that day, the tiny, insular scales of vast wealth and arrogance that had been so carefully laid in all along the geographical map of his mind, his eastern front and his western front, and atop his northern peak and below his southern bottom, began to drop off in force; for here, he was viewing only the outer shell of the disenfranchised, a journey that would take him past fragile layers and finally into the very heart and horror of unfettered and lonely poverty, a loathsome, private poverty only possible in the long shadow of cowardly and egregious leaders and an apathetic world.

When he stepped out of the car and onto the hard dirt, he stepped from civilization and into a vast horizon unseen and unheard by industrialized countries, for here were citizens sheared off from the steady flow of good, clean food and water and proper medicine, citizens who had sunk to the first layer of destitution wherein food and water and shelter were still available, but in an unclean form.

The first thing he experienced was the drastic revulsion of stench plunging into his nostrils and capturing his senses, but this quickly subsided as he beheld the inhabitants of this waste mill. "Children," he murmured.

"We have children who are here every day looking for scraps of food to eat, looking for bits of metal or electronic parts to sell in town," Lorraine said. She came upon a child who was holding a rotting piece of orange in her hand and picking at the pulp, and she gently took the girl's hand and, speaking her language, gave her a fresh, healthy, bright red apple. The girl smiled and took the fruit and began to gnaw eagerly at it. Lorraine turned to Eli and said, sadly, "I run out of food every day," and she watched him walk over to two small children who were foraging through a heap of waste that was disfigured by a mass of black flies; he smiled and looked at them and held up his hand to show them the fresh fruit he held. The children laughed as they followed him to the perimeter of the dump, where he placed them on the trunk of the white sedan and gave them the luscious treats, and where he watched them, with great pleasure, devour the sweet meats. He felt a surge of fidelity and pride in his breast, and he turned to watch Lorraine wade fearlessly through the awful sloping mounds of rancidity and rot, and he felt a longing to be Good. "But I am too wretched," he reasoned, turning again to look at the smiling children, "and these poor creatures are better than I will ever be." It was the first time he had ever considered any other human being superior to himself—other than Abraham and Oscine—and then he looked to Lorraine, and thought, "I shall never be as Good as she, if I were to devote my whole life to serving the poor." He felt a sickness bore up in him, one that had been dug up in the presence of Virtue, and he felt as if anyone of a noble nature could now easily unmask him and see him for what he had been his entire life, to wit: that he had been devoted to himself, and himself alone, and that what he had done for Abraham and Oscine had been merely a speck on the grand tapestry of Love that people like Lorraine weave every day with their good and selfless deeds.

He felt a great impulse to flee this place, as if the unseen forces of humility and meekness these poor souls exhibited were pushing against him, condemning him, moving him toward his palace of hedonism back home. Here, he was profligate Man, scoffing Man, boasting Man, unable to care for those who were born into the ancient and arcane and seemingly Earth-eternal paradigm of the caste system, and he felt helpless and unwanted and unready to bleed proper empathy for the dying and the dead.

So, he merely turned round and walked away, his mind injured by this stark revelation; he walked clear out of the dump zone and onto the streets and found a taxi and hopped in and begged the man to race to the airport, where he soon jumped out and found a flight and boarded the plane and promptly went to sleep. He awoke when the plane was landing in the States and when he exited, jumped to the black concrete and kissed the ground, and then smiled and laughed. "I'm home," he whispered.

That night, he was in his own bed, in his own country, in his own familiar surroundings, and he felt reborn.

He certainly was home again and he sought to celebrate his return through the commingling of his flesh and the tender, spicy flesh of his many female acquaintances. He checked his messages and he found, to his intense delight, that two of his usual on-the-ready luscious female companions had called and were anxious for a good time. He went about the house smiling and laughing as he prepared himself for the grand flesh feast.

Two of these fantasy party girls, their sensuous forms awash in perfume and short skirts and heavy paint upon their youthful faces, rang the bell of his mansion at seven in the p.m., and then fairly leaped through the open maple door, ready and willing to do whatever was demanded of them so that they might keep their ranking in the exclusive club of rich and powerful men. But then, as he stepped toward them, he felt as if he were falling into quicksand, for his feet were like leaden weights; fear swept over him and he looked again to the eager harlots, but their erotic images began to wash out and fade. "Ugh," he thought, "what has happened to them?" Indeed, the appearance of the two giggling strumpets began to shift before him, and he recoiled in horror as their tasty, glistening and colorful flesh began to turn inward and their souls turn outward, so that in a moment's time he could see their loathsome souls. "Heaven protect me from these fiends," he cried, and he attempted to move but he could not, even as the still-giggling ghouls were converging upon him. He could recount all of their past sins that lay like warts and sores upon their tarred immortal spirit, he could see all that they were and aspired to be, there, on that gruesome, boiling tar pit, all of their future plans and past deeds, rotting and roiling there upon that oozing blob of eternity. His breath was fast and his heart loud as he listened to the cacophony of sounds the two sisters of debauchery emitted as they enveloped him in their cold shadow.

"You created us, you created us and our kind, with your money and your time, you created us and brought us fame," they sang, "you gave us life and we give you blame."

"No," he cried, "you vile creatures! You are no slaves of mine, I am no master of yours!"

"You," they cried, leaning upon him now with their hot, rancid breath, "tempted us, and therein lies sin."

"No," he shouted, attempting to flee, but still sinking into the mire.

"Yes," they sang into his ears as they lay upon him and forced him further into the bubbling muck, "Man is his own destruction and salvation, free to live or die."

"No," he protested, "there must be something greater than that, a way back."

A soft, gentle voice pierced the crackling air. "There is a way out," a woman said, and she held out her hand.

"Lorraine," Eli said, in awe, "but you are so plain, so common, I could never want you."

She held out her hand. "There is a way out," she said again, "you only have to come to me."

But he began to feel the pleasures of his two flesh fiends as they became one with him and he sank deeper into the blood-red mud, and he did put out his right hand, and he felt a strange and powerful sensation pulling on him; but as he felt it, the ecstasy of the carnal bond with these women began to wane, and he hesitated, so potent was its force; but Lorraine reached out both of her hands, and he reached out both of his hands and he felt himself lifted upwards and out of the embrace of the women, and as he walked toward Lorraine, he saw all his wealth disappear around him, and the ground beneath him turn to dry dust and hard, sunbaked desert land; but lo, he did not stop, and soon reached her and embraced her.

It was then that he woke up in a start, and looking about, professed great joy at seeing his stately room, and he laughed as he remembered his dream; but he did later check his messages and found many women from his party clan imploring him for a good time, and so he did call for them, and they did come over bouncing through the doors, like tarts through a prince's drawbridge; but, alas, as they came nearer to them, he recoiled from them, for he saw the visage of the young girl from Africa upon their heavily painted and perfumed faces. Now, he thought of all that he had done there and what he had done with Vivian, and he suddenly felt as if he were infected with disease, and he waved the women away, but they did not understand, so he escorted them out and went back to his room and sat upon his bed and contemplated his Life.

He looked around at this master bedroom that had been built with the finest materials and by the finest master craftsman; he had designed everything, from the grand closet to the grand entertainment center to the skylight, and then he looked to the luxurious king-sized bed and the luxurious bearskin rugs and the luxurious fine-oak dresser drawer and the rare antiques and the rare statues, and he felt as if he belonged here, too, as if he were a luxury item, a rare item, a fine item that he had built by his own master hands. "Why, this is who I am, I am simply part of my surroundings, just as poor people are part of their surroundings; I began poor and attained wealth, so can they; yes," he nodded, looking about, "this is as much me as a dilapidated shack is for a poor person; it is the way of the world; all of us can neither be poor or rich," and he held out his hands level to each other, "some are poor and some are rich, and they balance each other; yes, there must be a balance, and sometimes," and he moved the hands up and down, "some come and some go, but in the end, there will always be those who are rich and those who are poor; it is not up to me to decide, and I should not feel guilty because I have made good; I deserve this," and he stood up, his voice forceful now. "I made this, I did this, all of it, I worked hard for this, let others work hard for it, too."

He showered and ate a hearty breakfast and drove to his business and was able to step right back into the flow of things; within a week, it was as if none of it had ever happened to him: not the tragedy of Vivian, not the adventure to Africa—for work, his lover, his only lover, his loyal friend, his only friend, now righted and aligned him with reality again, and gave him purpose, again.

And he had a blood test that came back negative for all known diseases.

But he found he could not sleep much, and his appetite was wanting, and his enthusiasm for partying was waning. "What is wrong with me," he would lament, "that I cannot regain what I once had?" He found that he could not tolerate the women he knew, nor could he accept the waste of money he had once practiced. "Before," he mused, "I would spend a thousand dollars on a whim, to please myself, and now, I cannot spend a dollar without thinking about it; what is to become of me?" At his palace, he moved about as if he were ashamed. "Who would build such a place? It could hold three

families, and I live here alone." He would sit in the entertainment room and stare at the billiards table and the giant
screen television and the electronic games, and he thought of
all the times he had brought friends here, and it numbered
fewer than four a year. "Waste, waste," he murmured, and he
toured the mansion daily, looking at the fabulous statues and
paintings and fine parlors and bedrooms for his women who
stayed for only a few days, and he thought of his life and what
he had accomplished, and he saw only the vast accumulation
of material things. "What have I done but decorated my life
with fine things, and what have I done for anyone else?"

He slowly descended into a profound funk, sometimes
missing work, sometimes not leaving his home for days, sometimes not answering the phone or the door; he had not dated
his painted women since his return from Africa. And then
one night, as he lay on his plush bed, he thought of Oscine,
and what Abraham had often told him about her.

"She," Abraham had often boasted to Eli, "puts everyone
else before herself, and I often asked her about this, and she
would say, 'Abraham, if everyone did this, would not the world
be a better place? Are we not here to help each other? And
how would the world be if everyone helped only themselves?'"

Abraham had later said to Eli, "And do you know that
people always want to help Oscine because she is always helping
others? They want to help her because they see her goodness,
and it makes them feel good to help her; if only I could be thus."

Eli thought about this and thought of himself. "No one
ever has volunteered to help me, people always want to use
me; I am here for their convenience."

He began to visit churches again and talk to Ministers
again and read books again on philosophy and religion. There
were times when he wanted to just leave all of it and never

come back, but he secretly wanted to take his wealth with him. "I am too much a part of this place," he would say, walking about his mansion, "it is too late to undo that which made me."

He would lie in bed at night and think of all the things he had done to make the world a better place, but all he could think of was the lie he had oft told himself, that he had provided a stimulus to the economy and jobs to people; he knew that he had never done anything good for anybody unless it benefited himself. "How could I miss this, how could I not see that I am so selfish? Is it because I thought that since I have done no wrong to others, I need not do right to them?" And then he thought of Vivian and her family, and he felt laden with guilt; and he thought of Lorraine, who did more in one day to help others than he had done in a lifetime. "But all of us cannot be like her; where would this world be if all of us did that? Some of us are born to be businessmen, and that is my role; I am who I am and the money that comes with it is mine because I have earned it, and that is that." He would try and rouse himself with such speeches and then go to nightclubs and bars, but he would see the patrons as plastic, hedonistic, foolish vessels who lived for excess and self and frivolity. "Certainly, I am not like them." But he knew he was, and he was too old to deny that he had always been like them, people without direction or purpose, people who never questioned life beyond their cozy and lucrative borders. "How could I have been so blind not to see who I was?"

It seemed that it had been a long time since the death of Vivian. His business was thriving financially although the economy was somewhat faltering, and the money pouring into his hands was overwhelming and satisfying. He had everything to live for but nothing to die for. "And that is not right," he thought, "how can a man be happy if he has nothing to die for?" It was with this idea that he began to feel an irresistible pull from the East upon his person; he would wake up at night in a profuse sweat and he would feel this powerful force hovering over him and enticing him to come; whenever he happened to watch television and see shows on poverty, he would feel the force from the East sweep about him, singing its lyrical song of adventure to him; and whenever he drove about the city, and saw poverty, in the form of the homeless or those begging for food or those struggling to survive, he felt this sweetly scented aura envelop him and speak to him and caress him, and he began to only feel fully alive, fully human, fully aware of the world when these things happened.

And then one day he was at work and one of his employees was bemoaning the fact that his sister's family had lost their house and had nowhere to go, and that the young man would have accommodated her but his father and mother were living with him, and his brother, also; and Eli felt a surge of fidelity in his breast as he listened to this youth, for he wanted to help the sister; and then he heard two other employees talk of the problems of their relatives, and he wanted to help them, too. But he hesitated to speak, for he was afraid that his own employees would see him as weak and foolish and sentimental, a man wont to give away money, a man soon to be bothered for charity at every turn, and so he hesitated, and returned home. "I cannot cure all the problems of the world, I have helped people by giving them jobs," he reasoned.

He would go to work every day wanting to tell the young man that he would help the sister, but he could not bring himself to utter it; he wanted to tell the other employees he would help their relatives, but he felt an internal lock on such verbal debris, as if the desire to proffer such assistance was held hostage by his austere business sense. One day, he sat down with Martha in the front office when the other employees had gone home.

"Martha, do you think I am generous?"

Martha smiled, her old, wrinkled face kind and gentle. "No."

He lost his breath and looked about the place. "No?" he restated it as if he wanted it to mean something else, as if it were an answer to a different question. "What do you mean?"

She smiled again, and took his hand, as only an elderly woman could. "I mean that you are a good man, but you are tight with a buck."

He cursed inside himself, and cursed himself. "How can I not be generous? Don't I give bonuses to everyone at Christmas? Don't I give raises?"

She smiled warmly and touched his arm. "Do you want me to lie?" and when she saw the firm shake of his head, she carried on, "No, you are not generous, Eli; you make the appearances of generosity, but generosity comes from giving that which you need to others. Eli," she said, earnestly, "you make five million dollars a year, and how much do you pay your employees?" She saw his grave visage. "That's right, ten dollars an hour, barely enough for them to live on; and the bonuses you give are paltry compared with the bonuses you give yourself; no, Eli, you are not generous here, but maybe outside of here." She gazed into his eyes, which were misting with shame. "Do you give to charities?" She saw his still form. "Do you give your time to worthy causes?" She saw his still form and his growing shame. "Eli, you know what you do with your money and your time; I shouldn't be telling you about your life…"

"It's all about me, isn't it?" he said, his eyes downcast now. "The money, the women, the trips, the mansion, the business, all of it, every penny to line my coffers, and I rationalize it all away by saying I have done nothing wrong to anyone," and then he murmured, "everything to live for and nothing to die for."

She lifted up his chin with her hand. "How many men would realize who they really are when they are so young, when there is so much time left in the world? Eli, you are not an eighty-year-old man on his deathbed admitting regret; the great wonder about being young and realizing you have made mistakes is that you have plenty of time to be reborn again," and she looked to the clock, "right now, at five-thirty p.m." She sighed. "Many men die never knowing themselves; you just got lost for a while."

He nearly smiled. "How many men talk like this and just go back to what they think they are and must be?"

She hunched her shoulders. "It doesn't matter, Eli, for they are not you," and she pointed to him, "you are you, and I know you, and I know that you are ready."

"I am ready, aren't I?"

She nodded her head. "Every real man knows when his time comes."

He stood up. "I am ready, I am, I know I am, but I have been fighting it; I know I can't go like this anymore." He looked about the place. "It is time to move beyond self." He walked over to the back door and opened it and looked at the great expanse of warehouse that was the hub of his business. "I have some phone calls to make, arrangements to make," and he looked back to her, "will you help me?"

She smiled and nodded her head.

He sat down and took out the employee handbook and then picked up the phone and promptly put it back down; his breath was faster now and he picked up the phone again and looked at the numbers and began to dial but then dropped the receiver down on the phone. "I can't," he said, wringing his sweaty hands, "I can't do this, I can't be who I am not." He looked to Martha, who had been with him from the inception of his business. "You know me, this is my lifestyle, this is me; I can't be someone who just walks away."

She waited until she heard his appeal to her in his anxious voice. "You know who you are, Eli, you know what you were before; who you are now, your own creation, and you have been this way for so long you have forgotten what you were before."

"I can't do this," he said, as his head fell into his hands, and he began to weep; "I want to be noble and self-sacrificing, but it just won't work."

He looked up at her and told her about his adventure in Africa.

She sat there, listening to his emotional narrative, and when he was done, she knew what must be said. "It is Lorraine; she is the one you need to be with."

"But why can't I have all of this," he gestured about, "and find a girl like that here?"

She smiled. "Why did Lorraine leave?"

He stared at her. "She gave up the good life to help people who have nothing." He nodded his head. "I will never find her, here, no, not here, where there is too much opportunity and availability for everyone—for such a woman will go to those places where people have nothing and bring them solace; yes, I need to leave." He felt fidelity and virtue bore up in him, and then he smiled. "I know now what I need to do; I will leave, but I will do it my way."

And so the two set to work, laboring far into the night and into the first rays of a golden dawn, and they both stood there, outside the glass doors, and they hugged each other.

"You know what to do," he whispered to her, and he hopped in his car and drove away.

That day, Martha called for a meeting with the twenty employees, and told them that Eli would be gone indefinitely, and that he had left her in charge, for now, and that he had opened his house to be used by his employees and their families whenever poverty happened to strike them.

There was also a trust fund set up for Abraham and Darla's baby boy, and for the twins of Vivian.

By early next morning, Eli was on the continent of Africa.

Full Circle

E li exited the plane and ran to the airport terminal and out to the parking lot and waved down a taxi and told the driver where to take him. He sat nervously in the white cab, thinking of Lorraine, thinking that he had been gone for too long, thinking now that he was a fool for coming back, foolish for coming back to a woman he had known only for a day, foolish for coming back and leaving an empire he had built for fifteen years where he had toiled like a slave to keep it financially solvent. He had given jobs to many people and treated them right and he had paid his taxes and increased revenue for the city and now he was leaving it all on a caprice, and he suddenly wanted the man in the taxi to turn around and go back to the airport. "Stop," he said, almost in a whisper, and when the man did not, he yelled it, and the frightened man halted the taxi. Eli sat and brooded while the car was parked on the side of the road, but he decided that now he was here, he should at least visit Lorraine, so he encouraged the taxi driver to move on.

When the taxi pulled up to the dirty curb of the Mission, the shame and embarrassment and foolishness of it all was revealed to him. "I cannot believe I came here for her; what was I thinking of?" he thought. "I will stay for a day and then leave for home, for good, this time; but what will Martha think? Oh," he smiled, "she will understand, she will, she is a good woman," and he exited the taxi and casually walked through the Mission doors, feeling confident that he had, as usual, an "out."

"Hello," he said, into the empty chambers, and when a man came out, he asked, "I am looking for Lorraine."

The man shook his hand and introduced himself. "John Corcoran."

"I am looking for Lorraine; do you know where she is?"

"She isn't here anymore—she has moved out into the country to help with the villages."

"Villages? And where might those be?"

"The villages are about one hundred miles west."

"What are they like?"

"It is where the people live in the worst poverty, where there is no clean food or water, no medicine, where the people live in mud huts and despair."

Eli felt a healthy narrative of retreat bore up in him, and it began, thusly, "I tried, I came back but she wasn't here, so I have an excuse to go back now and stay in the States, where I will give to charities and the such; but what about the people I was going to let live in the house? Yes, I will find them an apartment to live in, and I will pay the rent for the first year, that will be good." And he felt Honor take seed inside him.

"Well, thank you," he said to the man, and turned to leave.

"Aren't you Eli?"

Eli turned round, incredulous. "Yes."

"Lorraine told me about you." He walked over to a letter that was still lying on a small, round table, picked it up and walked over to Eli. "She said to give this to you if you came back."

Eli was distraught, for his escape plans were beginning to crumble. He took the letter and read it. "Dear Eli," it began, "I am sorry you left without saying goodbye. But I want you know that if you do come back, you are welcome to stay. I would be proud to work with someone like you. Love, Lorraine."

He frowned. "Did you read this? I mean, not to imply that you read it without her permission, but did you?"

The big man with the grey hair smiled. "Yes, Eli, I know its contents; Lorraine read it to me after she told me about you."

"What does she mean when she says 'you are welcome to stay'? I never told her I was coming to stay, I was just visiting."

"You're here now, Eli." When the man said Eli's name, it was as if it was a father saying the name of his son. "She said that if you came back, you were coming back to stay."

"But that doesn't make sense, I was here for a day, just a day, and then I left, and that was months ago; why would she even write a letter; after all, she said other Americans sometimes come here…"

"Yes, they do, sometimes Americans do come out, but, she said, they were not like you, and they don't come back." He smiled, gently. "When people come here from other lands, where there is plenty, you see them in a different light; you can often tell what kind of person they are in a short time, whether or not their internal lamp is lit or dark."

Eli nodded as he recognized the inherent qualities of this analogy, and then he said, "Isn't it amazing that someone else knows if your lamp is dark, but you do not. Lorraine must have known this about me."

John persuaded Eli to sit, and so the both of them sat down, upon old, tattered brown wooden chairs. "Here I am, now, and here you are, now; but where will you be tomorrow?"

"Back in the States," he replied, without hesitation or reflection.

He nodded his head. "You came back for another one-day visit?"

He was about to answer in the affirmative, but the longer he gazed at the tall, slender man with the kind face, the more he found his world of subterfuge falling apart. "No, no, I did not; no," he hung his head low, "I don't know why I came back." He looked up and shook his head. "I don't know why I am here, I don't know; I thought I knew yesterday, but now I don't know; yesterday I was ready to commit to this life and help people, but today…"

The man stood up and poured the both of them a cup of herbal tea, and Eli took the white foam cup and slowly drank the warm, honey-flavored drink. "Tell me, Eli, why did you come to Africa the first time?"

"I don't know, I suppose I just wanted to see how poor people lived."

"But why did you choose Africa? Why not go and travel about in America; there are plenty of folks in need there."

Eli stared at the man. "Yes, I suppose so, but I wanted to get as far away from ease and prosperity as I could."

John looked at the youth for a moment. He smiled, and nodded, his head askew. "Do you think you are the only person to see the insidious consequences of the love of money? Most of us out here have left everything we owned, everything," he exclaimed, "many of us left great wealth," and he hunched his shoulders, and he put a little space between his index finger and thumb of his left hand, "some of us just a little, simply leaving a life of no consequence." His voice became gentler when he said, "So, whose wealth were you running from, Eli?"

Eli stared at the man, awestruck, and then he spoke, his voice strained by grief, "My own wealth, my own story, me, I was running away from what I had become, and I knew that being here I could not be what I was in the States."

The man nearly smiled. "Lorraine lives in a small hut of palm leaves and sticks and dry mud, tending to the needs of people who have never seen a cell phone, a computer, never felt air-conditioning, who don't even think that there is a world beyond a horizon of yellow sun and a harsh life; she lives there, now, because she knows that there she is the woman she knows she was meant to be."

"She is greater than I will ever be," he said, solemnly, "she is beyond me."

"No, Eli, only God is beyond all of us; people can always better themselves, striving for perfection; that is the greatness about being a human being, we can effect change for the good if we choose to." His face seemed lit by the eternal light of wisdom that all men share when they stop thinking only of themselves and ponder the world about them, when he said, "Animals and insects have an excuse for what they do; we do not."

The two men talked for hours, well into the day, and when the conversation was over, the two men were traveling on a road that led into the vast wilderness of the desert.

When Eli exited the beige sedan, the coolness of night had descended over the land, and he shook hands with John, then he turned round and began walking toward the small village that contained multitudinous small, thatched huts.

John watched him walk up to the woman and he saw the two embrace, and then he smiled and drove away.

"You came back," Lorraine said, smiling largely as she walked with him, her left arm around his waist; "a tourist visit?"

He stopped. "I have come back to stay." He felt the impulse to kiss her, but he refrained, and the two of them walked toward the humble community.

A year hence, after he had labored with her and eaten with her and admired her, and listened to her and conversed with her and come to understand her; and after he had toiled to bring succor to those in need and eaten with them and admired them, and breathed in the fumes of their disease and cried when they died and cheered when they lived; and after he had become one with the land and realized to go back to whence he had come would be a betrayal to his new self, his true self, his forever self, confessed to her about what had happened with Abraham and Oscine and Vivian and her family; he wept and she wept, and finally, he lay there, his head upon her lap, the two of them looking up through the small opening of the entrance and out into the clear, cool, black sky at the glittering white stars.

"It is the tragedy of women," she said, mournfully. "Woman, who is the bearer of so much pain in the world, if She does not know who She is and what She wants and where She is in society, She can destroy nations; yes, Man can destroy civilizations from without, but Woman, by looking for that which She cannot have, can destroy from within; She needs to know why She is here and what She must do and not do, and only then can She save civilizations; God shows us the Truth, but Truth understood only through Faith." She mused upon what she had said. "I would like to have known Oscine: she was a good woman who should have lived; and

Abraham, too, he was a good person, I would have liked to know him; he would have—both of them—would have been good for Mother Africa." And then she smiled, and looked down at Eli. "But I have you, now, and both of them will live through you."

He frowned and shook his head, and then looked up at her as he said, "But how, Lorraine? People are fond of saying such things, but how will they truly live through me?"

She stroked his black, curly hair. "All the time you knew Abraham, his goodness affected you, even though you did not see it; you wanted to be his friend because you recognized his goodness in him, and when he knew Oscine, her goodness lived through him, and therefore, it lived through you, and now you are here," and she touched his chest, "and they are here, with you, inspiring you. No man is an island, after all." She smiled.

"No man is an island," he repeated, and then he lay still for a good while, and thought about what she had said, and then said, with great sincerity, "My life is a living manuscript, turn my pages slowly."

She smiled at his wisdom, and said, with great passion, "I shall, my darling."

They did not talk for a long while, and then he said, lovingly, "And herein shall I make my abode, my good and beautiful bride, and Oscine and Abraham shall dwell with me."

She smiled. "Spoken like a prophet."

"Yes," he answered, looking up at her, "and looking into your joyous face, I know the future."

She smiled, and said, lovingly, "And with thee, I shall make my abode, my good and gallant husband."

-Finis-